Also by Kristopher Triana

Full Brutal
Toxic Love
Body Art
Shepherd of the Black Sheep
The Ruin Season
The Detained
Growing Dark

THE LONG SHADOWS *of*
OCTOBER

KRISTOPHER TRIANA

Grindhouse Press
PO BOX 521
Dayton, Ohio 45401

Grindhouse Press #054
ISBN-10: 1-941918-50-6
ISBN-13: 978-1-941918-50-0

For Tangie,
who bewitched me

... Ah, can it
Have been that the woodlandish ghouls—
The pitiful, the merciful ghouls—
To bar up our way and to ban it
From the secret that lies in these wolds—
From the thing that lies hidden in these wolds—
Had drawn up the spectre of a planet
From the limbo of lunary souls—
This sinfully scintillant planet
From the Hell of the planetary souls?

> — Edgar Allan Poe, *To----Ulalume*

Before I fade thin
Cast a shadow no more
Before the dark hour
I'll pass here once more.

> — Willard Grant Conspiracy

PROLOGUE

SHE STOOD AT THE WINDOW, watching the sun fall behind the tree line, the changing leaves bleeding, reminding her of what had to be done.

It was time.

All signs pointed to it, and as a wife and mother she had to do what was best for her daughter.

Gladys Snowden stepped away from the glass, letting the pale, orange light hit her shoulders. There was no warmth to the sunlight. The chill beyond the window was wintry, far surpassing the normal lows for October, and she wrapped her shawl around her skeletal frame to shield her aching bones. The house was old, drafty, and she rarely turned on the heat because the furnace made startling noises. She had enough startling things in her life. They'd been with her for decades, and now it was all coming full circle.

She swallowed hard.

In the kitchen she made herself some tea. When the whistle blew it reverberated off the high ceilings and traveled through the lonesome hallways to the upper landing, then on to the next story. The house creaked mournfully in reply. She poured the tea into one of the china cups she and Arthur had received from her aunt Prudence as a wedding gift. The warmth of the cup felt good against her arthritic hands. Thinking of the wedding, she realized this coming spring would mark their fortieth anniversary. It was a thought that came and went with ugly bitterness and then flaked away for more important thoughts involving the plan.

The first step would be to find some young boys, and that was where she was having the most trouble. They were mandatory. Nothing else would do. Not for her family, not for her little girl. But how was a woman in her seventies supposed to meet teenage boys? She supposed she would have to get more creative than she'd been in the past, as this was a much bigger deal than all of the plans that had come before it. There was more than one anniversary coming up, after all.

She would never forget that night.

Nor did she wish to.

With her cup in hand, she walked through the library and across the reading den, looking up at Arthur's book towers. There were classics, including many of the great Russian novels, and several collections of poetry. He had a plethora of works on history, physics and other intellectual odds and ends. There were whole volumes devoted to the minutia of individual life forces, such as shellfish, earthworms and ameba, and endless encyclopedias and atlases.

But the largest collection was comprised of books on different religions, which included the most popular faiths, such as Christianity and Judaism, as well as the novelty ones such as Satanism and Scientology, and even more volumes on dead religions—Nordic gods, druid rituals, voodoo. On all of these topics, Arthur was an unparalleled scholar. He was a renowned priest and professor of theology, with an uncanny memory that gave him a knack for reciting quotations, always philosophizing with anyone who cared to start a dialogue on any religious topic they could name.

Gladys had not indulged him in some time.

She opened the glass door that lead to the swimming pool. The sunset made golden slivers on the surface of the crystalline water. They writhed like snakes, giving her a girlish thrill. A smirk came across her thin lips but faded quickly as she reached the shallow end and stared out at the ripples. Even though the sun had not gone all the way down, there was already an eerie blue glow coming from beneath the surface, though the light of the pool wasn't on.

She had no need for it. She never dared to go in.

Gladys watched the water for a moment, knowing the source of that azure shine beneath the surface. She could hear it too. Not coming from the pool, but rolling through the mountain that ran across the valley beyond, sounding like the softest rumbles of distant thunder, only churning beneath the earth like giant, hungry worms.

She finished her cup of tea and felt the bite of the breeze on her neck. It nipped at her hands and ruffled the bell of her housedress. And as the sunlight deepened to the same color as the changing leaves, Gladys stared at the black silhouette that fell across the water, knowing the shadow was not her own.

PART I

A TOUCH OF EVIL

CHAPTER ONE

"COME ON," JOE SAID. "THAT'S pretty steep."

Linda smacked her gum, a slight Elvis sneer on her candy-red lips. She had one knee bent with her foot bracing her against the brick wall, hands in the pockets of her leather jacket. Her dark eyes flashed, dominating.

"Look," she said. "If you want cheap get him one of those hood-rat bitches."

"But three hundred? I mean, seriously, it won't take but a few minutes."

"You got my price."

Joe shook his head and looked to Danny, who was standing there like a boulder wrapped in a letterman jacket, his eyes scanning the legs that jutted out of Linda's tight skirt. Black stockings hugged them like a second skin. Joe tapped his friend's arm to wake him up.

"Whaddaya think, man?" he asked.

"Shit," Danny said. "I mean, three ain't too bad, I guess. We don't want The Cherry messing with no hood-rats or crack heads, right?"

Joe grimaced. "He's my brother, dude. I wouldn't throw him to no poison pussy, especially not for his first time. It'd give him a complex or something."

Linda smacked her gum again, eyebrows raised in impatience.

Joe smiled. "How about half up front and half at the . . ."

"Fuck you," she said. "All of it up front. I'm not stupid."

Joe wondered about that. Linda may not have been the biggest slut at Central High School, but she was definitely in the top five. That didn't necessarily make her a bimbo, but it did lead one to believe that the AGS program wouldn't be enlisting her anytime soon. Still, she was an entrepreneur, and since junior high she'd evolved from flashing her tits for five bucks to giving handjobs for twenty. Joe and Danny had both hired her services and been pleased with the results. That's when they'd started thinking about Joe's little brother Robbie, the virgin. His sixteenth birthday was coming up and Joe wanted to get him laid and rid him of the moniker of The Cherry, which he had gained by foolishly telling total bullshit stories about his sexual escapades, ones so obviously made up that the other boys had seen through him, and then cut through him. Joe had never so much as seen Robbie kiss a girl, let alone bang one. Being almost two years older than the runt, he felt he had a responsibility to guide him into manhood, especially since they didn't have a father around.

"Two thirds up front," Joe said. "The rest as soon as it's over."

Linda blew a bubble and seemed to mull it over. The bubble popped and Joe watched the blue goop twirl on her expert tongue.

"Y'all are lucky I wanna buy that car," she said. "That's the only reason I'm doing this. Stroke jobs ain't no big thing but I ain't ever fucked nobody for money before."

Joe didn't give a shit. "Is it a deal or what?"

"Fuck it." She shrugged. "He'll probably pop like a champagne cork before he gets all the way in anyhow."

"As long as he gets in."

"Yeah," Danny agreed. "We're not paying three hundred for no handjob."

Linda squinted. "He's gotta wear a rubber. And once he's done, he's done. I ain't hourly. I've got better shit to do."

Like other people, Joe thought.

Despite her crass attitude and the almost scary fact that she was turning tricks at seventeen, Joe knew Linda Lelane was worth the money. She had a hard but pretty face and her body had blossomed beyond her years, imbuing her with large, yielding breasts she never imprisoned behind a bra, thighs that were thick and pale as skim milk, and a slim waist that gave way to an ass that turned any boy walking behind her into a foaming zombie. Robbie had talked about her several times, but was always too nervous to pay her to pull his pud.

"When ya wanna do this?" she asked.

"We don't have all the money yet," Danny blurted out, making Joe wince.

"But we'll get it," Joe said, giving his buddy a nudge.

"Whatever," she said. "You know how to get a hold of me. You get me two thirds and we'll make it a date." She smacked her gum once more and stepped away from the wall, flipping her russet hair out from under her collar. The ends of it danced on the autumn wind. "I'm guessing you won't be forking over twenties for handy Js for a while, huh?"

"Guess not."

"Then piss off."

"How much is two thirds of three hundred bucks, anyway?" Danny asked.

They were sitting on the hood of his rusted '88 Oldsmobile. The huge clunker belched exhaust, had no air conditioning, and an oil leak that made Danny carry a few quarts with him at all times, but at least it was a car.

Joe blinked. "Two hundred, Danny. Jesus Christ." Sometimes his buddy had a head as clear and organized as New Year's morning.

"Hey man, you know I ain't no good at math."

"Or English, apparently . . . "

"Kiss my hairy ass. You skip as much as I do."

Joe couldn't argue with that. Actually, he skipped school more than Danny did because Danny risked getting booted off the football team if his grades slipped too deep. Not that Danny was that interested in playing. It was the only thing he felt made his dad love him, and it was definitely the only reason the old man had given him the Olds. Danny wasn't that good at the sport, but he was naturally stocky and made for a great defensive wall being twice as wide as most of his teammates.

Joe, on the other hand, was lean and wiry, with no athletic ambitions whatsoever. His interests were heavy metal, weed, and pussy. He looked upon everything else with either indifference or disdain, and his spiky black hair and general delinquency made him just popular enough to get laid, but he was also seen as enough of a waste to cause his teachers to abandon him. They believed he was destined for a life of manual labor at best, and Joe didn't exactly disagree with them.

"I've got maybe sixty bucks stashed away," Joe said.

"That's all you've got left after a whole summer of mowing yards?"

"Where did you think all the dope and gas money came from? You think it was my allowance, you dumb shit?"

"Still thought you would've saved a few bucks."

"Well, between smokes, movies, and Linda jacking me off so I don't have to wear out my wrist, I'm amazed I have anything left. How about you?"

Danny shook his head and looked at the dirt beneath them. "Shit, man, you know I want this for The Cherry too but—"

"Call him Robbie for Christ's sakes."

"Sorry . . . I mean Robbie. But anyways, I ain't got shit for cash."

"But your old man had you doing chores all over the neighborhood all fucking summer. You painted fences, cut grass . . . Hell, you even tarred a roof on a hundred-degree day."

"Yeah, man, that *sucked.*"

"So where'd your fucking money go, man?"

"The old man keeps most of it."

"What?" Joe said, his brow tightening, jaw slack. "Are you serious? He keeps it?"

"He gives me a few bucks to keep the car running."

"But he keeps the rest for himself? What a shitbird!"

"Come on, man," Danny said, his head sinking toward his chest. "You know how tough things have been."

All Joe knew was Danny's old man was a deadbeat who kept his nose in booze instead of work. He'd had three jobs in the past two years, all of them menial ones in the food service industry. Danny's mom worked as a customer service rep for a company, and Joe figured it was her hard work that kept the lights on and the toilets flushing. He couldn't understand why she put up with it, especially considering how good-looking she was.

"So how much you think you have, then?" Joe asked.

"Maybe forty bucks—more if I roll my shoebox full of change."

"Well, that gives us a hundred to start with, at least."

"Yeah." Danny burped and crushed his can of PBR.

"There's not a lot of grass to cut anymore but people still need their leaves picked up. I usually only work for Mr. Herbert in the summer, but he says he always needs guys in the fall too. Maybe we could both get a few gigs from him."

"Shit yeah. Long as I don't miss practice."

"I know, I know."

"We might be able to scrape the money together in time."

"A hundred more bucks is no problem."

"Two hundred."

"But, two thirds is . . . "

"Two hundred, Danny. We'll still have to pay her the rest when it's over."

Kayla refreshed the page again, hoping a reply would appear, but from what the screen said the message still hadn't been read. Looking at it now she cringed at the two typos she'd missed and was filled with self-doubt over whether or not she should have sent it at all. Was it lame to flirt with a guy online because you were too nervous to do so in person? She really wasn't sure what was cool and what wasn't, especially when it came to dating. She thought it was up to the guy to ask out the girl, that the girl's job was to flirt, bat their eyes and smile to let the guy know they were interested, thereby encouraging him to ask for a date. It had worked out that way for her in the past, but she had never been as interested in those other wayfaring beaus the way she was with Joe Grant.

He was a wild child, always dressed in shredded black jeans and a metal band t-shirt (*Slayer, Carcass, Ghost*), hair like a wet skunk and the thin beginnings of a goatee. He strutted the halls like John Travolta in the opening of *Saturday Night Fever*, adjusting his nuts without shame, spitting, cursing, and whistling with menace like a rainforest insect. At times his vulgar behavior put her off, but more often than not his cocky attitude enticed her. She actually liked him because she knew how much dating him would piss off her mother, and his bad reputation with the teachers made her squirm excitedly whenever she thought about him, especially when she was alone in her room with the door locked.

Kayla put her phone down so she would lay off refreshing the page. She was "friends" with Joe on the social site, but while he had a page he rarely posted anything, which, in a way, made him all the more cool and mysterious. It was rare to find someone her age—even a boy—who wasn't self-obsessed and didn't smother social media with selfies and updates on the trivialities of their daily lives. His lack of interest in this norm gave him an even more rusty edge.

She was acquainted with him in person. They shared some of the same friends even though he was from the wrong side of the tracks whereas she grew up in a gated community. Her parents weren't exactly rich, but they were upper middle class (to put it mildly), and Kayla had never wanted for anything.

Well, anything other than Joe.

She got off the bed and pushed the canopy sheet aside. Going to her dresser, she briefly glanced at the photos of she and her best friend, Maxine, stuffed into the sides of the mirror before catching her reflection. She removed a spec from one blue eye and smiled shyly, trying to get her upper lip to cover her teeth. She had protruding incisors most of the boys found cute but made her incredibly self-conscious, even though she had a lovely, heart-shaped face framed by natural blond hair. It did make her feel better once she'd seen that old movie *True Romance* and how pretty the actress Patricia Arquette was even though she had the same teeth Kayla did. Guys *loved* Patricia Arquette in that movie, so maybe her teeth weren't so bad after all. Still, she felt self-conscious.

While somewhat awkward around boys, she easily attracted them, much to her mother's chagrin. Her father probably wouldn't have liked it either, but he was away on business more often than not, the important job of executive vice president of a small organic food chain being a great enough calling to sacrifice raising his daughters and maintaining a good marriage. The food he sold put a focus on health, but he made little effort to keep his family unit healthy. Kayla had a younger sister—named Patricia, funny enough—who was only five, and she took up most of her mother's time, leaving Kayla to fend for herself. At least she had the assistance of a hefty allowance and a new Dodge Charger.

Leaving her room, she walked across the landing of the second floor and trotted downstairs, landing on the bottom floor with a bounce. In the living room she went to her father's liquor cabinet and opened it up. Selecting the twelve-year-old scotch, she grabbed a tumbler, poured a hearty glassful and carried it out to the back porch. She looked out on the terracotta foliage that spread across the land and crawled up the juts of Black Rock Mountain, which today was cloaked in a thick, Scottish-moor mist. She sat down in her favorite wicker bowl seat, tucking her feet under her, and sipped the drink, savoring the bitterness as it hit the back of her throat. She was drinking more often these days, but she had lightened up on cutting her upper arms with the razors she pulled from her lady shaver. She'd become embarrassed by the scars that ranged from faint lines to gashes as ridged as an embroidered book. Because of them, she'd stopped wearing tank tops and baby dolls with high sleeves.

The scotch burned the thought of those scars away and dulled the urge to make fresh incisions. She was paying for these lost afternoons of numbness less and less, her body adjusting to the sweet poison of booze so hangovers were nothing a quick glass of the-dog-that-bit-her couldn't fix. She finished the rest of her drink with one big gulp, wanting the alcohol to hit her faster and soothe the anxiety she felt over sending that damned message to Joe.

She realized she'd left her phone upstairs so she got up, leaving the bowl chair swiveling. The churning mist slithered through the trees. It careened down the mountain, concealing the strange rolling of the land that cracked the large rocks and made the earth tremor before falling back into a silence that was merely temporary, considering what was to come.

As she watched them work from her front porch, Gladys laughed at herself for not thinking of them sooner. The grass sparkled like tinsel as the young men raked and used leaf blowers to rid it of the browning leaves, their lean, muscled bodies sprinkled with the sweat of their labor even in the slight chill of midday.

Gladys smiled.

The tallest one was the boss. He had blond hair and a bandana around his forehead. His tanned body hinted at frequent trips to the gym, the tight triceps enticing her. Gladys figured him to be somewhere in his early twenties. The other two boys were younger, teenagers, one of them a big-boned boy in a New York Giants jersey and the other a punk rocker with a cigarette dangling between his lips, gray tufts exiting his nostrils.

After the revelation hit her she went to the musical jewelry box with the dancing royal couple on top and twisted the lock. She had just under eight hundred dollars of petty cash stashed in the box. She took it out and cupped it in her hand. Her other hand fiddled nervously with the pearls that hung low around her neck, clacking them above her skeletal chest, which smelled of Joy Perfume by Jean Patou. She waited until the eldest boy started packing his equipment while the other two bagged up the neat piles they'd made. He glanced at her and gave her a nod. She smiled wide.

"Hello, Mrs. Snowden. Can I help you with anything?"

One of the things she liked about being an old woman was that everyone was more than willing to help her with anything. It was clear people thought of their own grandmothers when they saw her, and this urged them to be extra charitable and philanthropic. Though the boy likely wouldn't have asked for money even if she'd asked him to move the grand piano in her living room, she slipped him a twenty to get the conversation going.

"Oh, ma'am, you're too generous," he said, handing it back to her. "We're paid to do this job."

"You can't except tips?" she asked, her green eyes gleaming in the sun.

"Tips are always appreciated but never expected."

"Well then, take it. You always do a such a good job, mister . . . "

"Billy Herbert."

He shook her hand, cradling the fragile bones as gently as a wounded dove.

"Call me Gladys."

"All right, Gladys."

She handed him the bill again and this time he accepted it. "I'll split it evenly with the guys."

"No, no. That's yours. I'll gladly tip them too."

"Mrs. Snowden—"

"Gladys, remember?" She winked. "And don't argue with your elders, young man." This made him chuckle, and she went on. "I am looking to hire some people for a special job. I thought you and your team here might be able to help me, if you're interested."

"You need landscaping?"

"No, nothing like that."

"Well, that's what I do, forty hours a week and sometimes more. I don't have a lot of time for anything else. What is it you need?"

"Well," she said, looking at the many acres of the manor, "I will be out of town for a few weeks and will need the property looked after."

"We can take care of that. I can add you as a regularly scheduled client. We can come out as often as once a week if that suits your needs."

"It's not just the property, there's also the matter of the house." She tilted her chin in a dignified manner. "I could hire maids, of course, but I need more than that to make me feel comfortable while I'm away. I'd like someone to housesit."

Billy blinked and tilted his head like a dog. "Housesit?"

"Yes. I prefer to have someone stay in the house rather than merely visit it once a day to water the plants and check the mail. I have many antiques inside the manor that are irreplaceable. I have a state-of-the-art alarm system but being out here in the boonies I doubt the police could get here in time to save my thousand-dollar vases and original art pieces. I have a Mia Henry on the wall of my den that is worth nearly nine thousand dollars."

Billy whistled with surprise.

"What I need," she said, "is a young man—preferably two—to watch my estate, maintain the property, and take care of the house. Dust, clean the pool, all those kinds of thing. Other than these minor chores they merely need to stay here. They're welcome to enjoy the amenities. I have a heated pool and Jacuzzi, a rumpus room with a shuffleboard and a pool table, even a small gym. My refrigerator will be well stocked, and my wine cellar is filled with vintage . . . *spirits.*"

The last word came out of her like a cold wind.

"Sounds like a resort," Billy said.

"I welcome the caretakers to enjoy themselves. And they will be amply rewarded for their services. I'm prepared to offer five hundred dollars a week."

She unfurled the wad of bills in her hand to show him she was serious and ready to hire him, and hopefully his helpers, on the spot.

Billy eyed the cash. "How long did you say you'd be away?"

"Three weeks in Salem. I may extend my stay for a few days, but will pay for an additional full week if it comes to that."

Billy rubbed his chin. There was a look in his eyes she knew all too well. *Temptation.* But eventually he shook his head, making Gladys' heart fall into her stomach.

"Sorry," he said. "It'll be a great gig for somebody, but I'm really swamped this time of year with all of the leaves, and my boss won't take kindly to me taking the time off right now."

He nodded toward the two boys carrying stuffed garbage bags to the curb. "You could ask Joe and Danny there. They're both looking for more work but there's only so much the boss man can give 'em. They'd probably jump on it."

Her heart rose again, flushed with the possibility. While three would be ideal, two would suffice, and she knew these boys, being younger than Billy, would better suit her needs.

"Thank you."

She walked off with a wave and made her way toward the boys who were looking at her with silent anticipation. She wondered if they'd overheard. Either way, Gladys knew she had them before she even asked.

CHAPTER TWO

THE HALLWAY WAS LINED WITH white pillars, as if they were in an ancient library, and it opened into an immaculate room with expensive-looking porcelain statues protected in glass bookcases. Italian leather furniture was spread over Chinese rugs, accompanied by antique, solid oak tables, the bases of which had been carved to look like elephants, cheetahs and sharks.

Danny marveled at the craftsmanship.

His own home had tables from IKEA and a couch his mom had ordered online from a discount warehouse, which was now already stained by Doritos crumbs and spilt beer. The walls of his home were spotty from his father's bad patchwork on the holes that had been put in them over the years, and the shelves were always covered with a thin layer of dust from infrequent cleaning.

Mrs. Snowden's house was spotless. It possessed a debonair elegance that reminded him of museums, the artwork making him feel like he was in a gallery (though he had only seen galleries in movies). He had never been in such a huge and lovely home. As she led them through the stainless steel kitchen to a dining room nearly half as long as the school's football field, he realized he'd been walking around with his mouth open like a goon.

"You have a beautiful home," he told Mrs. Snowden.

She put a hand on his shoulder. "Aren't you sweet."

Out of the corner of his eye he saw Joe make a kissy face at him behind Snowden's back. He ignored him.

"This is some dining room," Danny said.

"When this house was built, dining rooms were more important. Nowadays it seems that families don't even eat together. Everyone's on their own schedules. Dining rooms have become an after-thought, tucked into the corner of the kitchen. When I was a little girl, a dining room was essential to family structure. It was a stand-ard of American etiquette, a tradition carried over from Europe." She ran one hand across the table as her heels clicked on the marble floor. "A proper dining room is the key to a happy home."

Her smile seemed off to Danny then and he looked away, unsure why he was uncomfortable.

"When was this house built anyway?" Joe asked. "So much of it looks new."

"Yes, the floors and walls have been redone and the kitchen has been updated several times over the years. We had central air con-ditioning installed decades ago and added the porch and pool. But this manor has been standing since 1918, built just before the end of the First World War. Its original owner built an empire out of oil. His wealth, like his profession, was similar to John D. Rockefeller, one of the wealthiest men of that era. His name was Henry Snow-den."

"Your grandfather?" Joe asked.

"My husband's grandfather."

"Three generations."

"That's right. I'm an old woman with old money. And while we've remodeled and added to the manor, it remains in its original form. At night you can sometimes hear the age in the walls and the sound of the wind whispering through the eaves."

Though Danny wasn't sure why, the old woman's phrasing spooked him. His skin pimpled like a plucked bird beneath his jer-sey. They followed her to the open doors leading into the study. The ceiling was high here, allowing the built-in shelves to climb the walls and hold nearly as many books as a Barnes and Noble.

"Whoa," Danny said. "You must really love reading."

"I do. But most of these volumes belong to Arthur."

"And where is he?" Joe asked.

She hesitated before answering. "Not with us at the moment."

Danny let his curiosity slide and followed her past an enormous globe and a full red suit of Japanese bugyo samurai armor that stood on a pedestal in the center of the room. Though very old, the suit gave off a blood-like sheen under the chandelier's glow.

Finally they exited the house and stepped out onto the patio. Danny was excited to see the pool and hot tub. The Jacuzzi was large enough to seat eight people, with jets, multi-colored lights, and stereo speakers that sprung up from each corner. Beyond it, a giant swimming pool stretched out in a long, blue river that extended to two larger ponds at each end. On one side there was a waterfall and a bubbling fountain near the shallow end. Exotic trees surrounded it in a makeshift lagoon, and Danny thought of his girlfriend Maxine, how he'd like to skinny dip with her here and have her ride him in the hot tub as they smoked joints and downed a twelve-pack of Pabst.

Mrs. Snowden saw the childlike joy on his face. "Almost like a payment of its own, am I right?" She touched his shoulder again. "I'm sure you boys will enjoy it. You may invite over a friend or two to enjoy it with you but please, no big parties, and make sure you keep guests away from my vases."

"Absolutely."

"So," Joe said, "you're willing to pay us five hundred a week to stay here?"

"To stay here and upkeep the manor. Basic things like skimming the pool of leaves, watering the garden, collecting the mail."

"That's fifteen hundred for us to split," Joe said, still mocking Danny for his poor math skills.

The old woman nodded. "If I stay an extra day or so, we will prorate it, but you'll be given two grand if I'm gone any more than two additional days."

Joe's eyes widened. "Then by all means take your time."

"We do have school," Danny admitted.

Joe gave him a mean side-eye, wordlessly telling him not to blow the deal. Joe only went to school for a few hours on the days he bothered to go at all, and that was merely to catch up with girls and handle drug transactions. There was no reason they couldn't keep a watchful eye on Snowden Manor, especially for the crazy amount of money the old bat was dishing out.

"I understand," she said. "As long as you're here in the mornings and overnight, I'll be a happy woman. And you can enjoy your weekends shooting pool, swimming, and watching movies in the home theater."

They hadn't even seen the home theater yet. More and more, Danny was spellbound by the opulent luxury of the house. He cracked his knuckles to ease his excitement.

"So, when do we start?" Joe asked.

"Oh, I'm just so happy you've accepted!" She patted them both on the shoulder and they smiled, unwittingly touched by the motherly gesture. "I'll be leaving this weekend. I realize it's short notice. Is that too soon?"

"Not at all," Joe said. "We can be here bright and early if you like."

Danny had football practice but decided not to bring it up.

"That won't be necessary," she said. "I leave at five o'clock Friday evening. As long as you arrive twenty minutes beforehand I'll be able to turn everything over to you."

"We'll be here at four forty-five on the dot."

Mrs. Snowden beamed.

Danny turned away again.

That night Joe went online so he could start inviting people to the party he planned to host at the manor house. He saw he had a message from Kayla Simmons, the blonde with the crooked smile and the hourglass figure. His eyes widened and he clicked on it.

Hey Joe. What's up? Didn't see you at school today. Was wondering what you were up to this weekend. Maybe we could catch a movie? Just an idea.

At the end of the message was a winking smiley face, followed by her phone number. He snickered and felt a slight stirring in his groin. Aside from Linda's handjobs he hadn't been laid since he'd dated Dana, and they'd broken up two months ago. The idea of sliding between Kayla's legs flushed him full of testosterone and he jumped off his bed and did a few high kicks in their air. He kicked on his stereo with Black Flag, cranking "TV Party" as he punched the air, making gentle gusts that fluttered the band posters and *Penthouse* centerfolds tacked to his walls.

Yeah, we can watch a movie, he thought. *In that fucking theater Snowden has in her house. Then we can get into that hot tub, girlie. That's where the real entertainment will be.*

He pulled a cigarette butt from his overflowing ashtray and flicked his Zippo, smelling the sweetness of the lighter fluid as he hit the flame. His head bobbed to the music.

What a great fucking mood he was in. He'd secured a really sweet deal. All he had to do was live in a mansion for three weeks—

something he would have done for free—and he'd have his hands on seven hundred and fifty bucks, more money than he'd ever come close to having at one time. He and Danny would have the money to get Linda to bang Robbie, with plenty to spare to blow on weed, Pabst, concert tickets, and whatever else he'd always wanted. He might even be able to get a car of his own. Snowden was going to pay them half up front and half at the end, so they would even have a good amount of cash to spend on throwing the most bitchin' party this town had ever seen.

He considered sending a return message to Kayla but decided that sort of thing was for pussies. Any dude with balls would call the chick, so he added her to his contact list and dialed her up. She answered on the second ring.

"Hello?" she asked, her voice breathy.

"Hey, babe. It's Joe."

There was a pause and then she said, "Hey! What's up?"

Her voice was higher now, excited. This one was practically a done deal.

"Got your message. I only wish I'd gotten it sooner."

"Oh, that's okay."

He rubbed his crotch a little. "Listen, I have something pretty cool going on."

"Oh yeah?"

"I'm house-sitting this place out past McLeary's farm. The place is huge—like a freakin' castle. It has everything."

"That's awesome."

"Yeah." He let a moment of silence hover on the line, enjoying the tease. "I was thinking about having a few people over for, like, a get-together ... to test it out before Danny and I throw a way live party. I wanna see you and talk more about our date. What're you doing tomorrow night?"

"That's great!" she said. Her voice had more cheer than a Christmas carol. "Wait, what's tomorrow, Friday?"

"Yeah."

"Aw, crap."

"Something wrong?"

"I have Odyssey of the Mind after school. It runs until eight."

So she was a brain. "That's no problem for me."

"Great!"

A small squeak came after her laugh and Joe pictured her bouncing on her toes with giddiness, those perfect breasts of hers jiggling like Jell-O molds.

"You've got wheels, right?" he asked.

"Yeah. I should be there before nine if it's just past the farm."

"Cool. I'll text you the address."

"Great!" she said again.

"Oh, and Kayla . . . "

"Yeah?"

He gripped his semi-hard cock through his jeans. "Bring your bathing suit."

On Friday afternoon Danny and Joe left early so they could meet up with Mrs. Snowden. Danny had practice at six that night. Coach would crucify him if he missed one this close to their game against Fillmore High, so he was planning on dropping Joe off to take care of the handing over of the house keys while he tried to make it back to school in time. Hopefully the five o'clock traffic wouldn't slow him down too much.

"Is Maxine on board?" Joe asked.

"Shit yeah, she's coming tonight. All she needed to hear was *heated pool*. She loves to swim so much you'd think she was a freakin' mermaid."

"Good."

Joe smiled. If Kayla had one of her friends there she'd be more relaxed, and that's what he wanted. As much as he would have liked for the two of them to have the place to themselves he knew it would put her on guard to be in a secluded house in the middle of the night with a boy she hardly knew, even if she was clearly very enamored by him. Having Danny, Maxine, and Robbie there would make the echoing mansion less creepy and Joe unthreatening. And once Kayla dropped her guard it would be much easier to lead her into one of the bedrooms.

"This is gonna be lit," Danny said. "That house is gonna wow them."

"I know, right? And listen, I was thinking—maybe we should go ahead and set up Robbie's little rendezvous with Linda too."

Danny shifted uncomfortably. "I dunno, dude. I think that whole thing will really weird out the girls, don't you?"

"Not if they don't know about it. We'll tell Linda to keep it hush-hush."

"I don't think Maxine likes Linda very much. A lot of girls don't like her because they think she's a slut."

Joe chortled. "She *is* a slut."

"Shit, man, I know it. All the more reason I don't want her around. If Maxine finds out I've been paying the bitch to jack me off I'll be dead meat."

Joe hadn't considered that. He certainly didn't want it to slip out around Kayla that he'd paid Linda for her special talents. "Okay, you've got a point. We'll set it up for Saturday then, and we'll get it done early so we can have people over again."

"We don't want to have too many people over though, dude. Mrs. Snowden won't like that. Remember what she said about no parties?"

Joe waved dismissively. "I don't give a rat's ass what that old bag said. She ain't never gonna know the difference."

"Naw, man, too many people means something's gonna get broken, and that means we won't get paid."

"Take it easy, big guy. We'll close off some of the rooms. They all have locks and we'll have the only keys. We can keep everybody to the kitchen and the den. We'll just take out all the pricey shit and put it in the dining room. Everything will be safe and fuckin' sound."

They drove past McLeary's farm where cattle grazed against the backdrop of a picturesque autumn day. To the east, Black Rock Mountain loomed like the lair of a super-villain in one of the comic books Robbie was so passionate about. Joe could not see the top. A layer of low clouds ensnared it in gray wisps. Odd. The rest of the sky was a clear, stunning blue. The clouds swallowed the mountain only, seeming to have no interest in releasing it.

When they reached the manor Mrs. Snowden was waiting for them on the front porch. She was dressed in an elegant, lime-colored pantsuit with white high heels and matching gloves. A Lincoln Town Car was idling in the circular driveway and a stout man was loading a suitcase into the trunk. Danny pulled around to the opposite side so as not to block them and they got out of the car.

"So punctual," she said. "I knew I chose the right men for the job."

"You look very nice today, Mrs. Snowden," Danny said. "Your husband is going to be happy to see you."

Joe saw a slight pinch in the center of her face, almost like a tic, then her smile washed it away.

"Why thank you, Daniel." She came closer with the keys. "Everything is in order. I had the refrigerator stocked with cold cuts, greens, and soda. There are some nice sirloins in there too. I suggest you try out the propane grill. I don't know why everyone always wants to grill in the summer and stand over an open flame when it's ninety degrees. Fall is the time for outdoor cooking."

"Sounds great," Joe said, taking the keys. "Thanks for the grub."

"Of course! This way you won't need to run out for groceries. You can keep focused on the house." She winked. "Now then, do you have any questions before I go?"

"No, I think we covered everything the other day."

"Good. There's a corkboard near the kitchen closet. I put the number of the hotel I'll be staying at in Salem. Please, only call in case of an emergency, unless it's something that requires 911. In that case, just call them. I don't want my house to burn down!" She laughed. "I won't be in my room often, so just leave a message at the desk. They'll get it to me."

"Don't worry," Danny said. "There won't be any problems. Everything's gonna go according to plan."

Her smile fell just slightly and her eyes drifted.

"That's what I'm counting on, Daniel."

Kayla was so happy when her after-school program let out she nearly leapt through the door before it was all the way open. She skipped along the sidewalk, humming a Taylor Swift song, and hit the unlock button on her keys as she approached her car. She slung her backpack onto the passenger seat and the tires gave off a screech as she went into reverse. One of the Odyssey of the Mind nerds she'd never bothered to learn the name of saw her peel out and he gave her a disapproving look from behind his thick glasses, his arms crossed over his argyle sweater. She ignored him and rolled down the windows. The electric rush of autumn wind danced across her flesh and whipped her hair like a hurricane. It didn't matter. She was going to do herself up at home before heading out to the manor.

She had to look *perfect* tonight.

Kayla debated between her short red skirt and the low cut sweater that let her cleavage wink or a pair of tight-fitting jeans with the blue blouse that made her eyes pop like fireworks on a summer night. No matter which outfit she chose, she knew exactly which bathing suit she was going to stuff into her purse—the sky-blue bikini with the bottom that was tied on each side. Once when she'd worn it down by the lake, two guys had stared at her so long-

ingly while walking that they smashed into each other and fell onto
a sandcastle, making its seven-year-old constructor cry. She figured
she might as well stick with a winner. She just hoped the darkness
of night would hide the scars for a while. She didn't want Joe to
think or *know* she was a freak. He was bound to see the cuts at
some point. She just hoped she could postpone it.

When she got home she showered, did her hair, and applied her
makeup, using just a little extra eye shadow tonight and opting for
the cherry-red lipstick. She decided on the blouse and jeans and
grabbed her fall coat on her way out. The day's chill had deepened
as the sun sank, and had she not taken so much time on her hair she
would have gone back in for a ski-cap. Kayla zipped up and when
she got into the car she took one of her scarves from the backseat
and wrapped it around her neck.

The sickly glow of the streetlights illuminated the roads, the lit
windows of houses muted by the rows of maple trees that lined the
sidewalks. The occasional dust devil of leaves spun before the car
and vanished into the darkness. She put on the radio, not really
paying attention to the music and chatter but glad for some white
noise to drown out the eerie silence of the empty streets.

Sitting at a red light, she glanced around at the lonesomeness of
the night. Hung from a wire, the traffic light swayed in the breeze
like a docked sailboat. When it changed, the green light washed
over her, making her hair look white in the rearview mirror. She
brushed her bangs out of her eyes and drove on, letting the GPS
guide her into the sticks on the edge of town. Out here the darkness
was thicker, like spilled ink. As a prelude to the forthcoming Halloween, she and Maxine had watched some horror movies last
weekend, and now she cursed herself for remembering their most
terrifying moments as she wound through the desolation. Visions of
masked men with machetes and young girls turned into ghouls
flashed through her mind, making her chew the inside of her cheek
as she passed by McLeary's, where the large shadows of animals
stood against the distant glow of the farmhouse.

She thought about calling Joe to let him know she was close. Her
GPS signal kept fading in and out; she might need him to give her
directions. But she would rather make a grand entrance. She looked
good tonight—*damned* good—and her desire to impress him outweighed the spookiness of the winding drive.

You're a big girl, she told herself. *Suck it up.*

She caught the sign just in time to make the turn and the car
wobbled as the pavement turned to a trail of pebbles. She slowed

down as she passed by horse fences, the towering trees shaking in the air like pompoms. Even in the darkness she could see the outline of Black Rock Mountain. It made her think of lost summers spent hiking, back when she'd had a family. Finally she saw the open wrought-iron gate and the sign beside it that read *Snowden Manor House.* It was perched there on the hill, lit up by lawn lights, seeming to hover in the blackness. It was larger than even the most impressive house in her gated community; a towering building of multiple stories, towers at each end with onions on the top and a widow's walk. Oval windows looked out at her like the eyes of a crouching giant.

She parked behind Danny's hunk of junk. The air was colder up here. Its gusts raked the grass at her feet and chewed her face. She hugged herself against it and trotted toward the front porch with her knees close together. Before she reached the front door it swung open and the teenage rebel she'd fantasized about in the bathtub last night came out of the warm glow of the house. He smiled like a million dollars.

"Come on in," Joe said. "The party's just gettin' started."

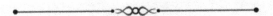

Robbie reclined in one of the lawn chairs, watching the others splash in the pool, the guys laughing and the girls shrieking with a joy alien to him. He had a hard time imagining what he was seeing was as fun as it looked, but somehow he knew it was even better. His brother was splashing Kayla in the shallow end and the cold air made her nipples stand out like almonds beneath a top that struggled to contain her breasts. In the deep end, Danny's hulking body was lifting Maxine over his head as he used her for shoulder presses. His muscles were hard and tight and Maxine's brown hair had been dyed black by the water, accentuating her mysterious eyes. She didn't have Kayla's curves, but she had a beautiful face and a petite frame that turned Robbie on. His attention turned from one girl to the other and then back again as he put another pretzel in his mouth. His brother swam forward.

"Would you stop being such a faggot and get in here?" Joe said.

Robbie shifted in his seat. "It's too cold."

"It's a heated pool, dingus. Now come on."

Robbie wasn't worried about the temperature. He was just uncomfortable being half naked around the girls. He had a scrawny body with a bird chest and hadn't developed any hair on it the way

Joe and Danny had. He also knew how swim trunks liked to cling to him when he got out of a pool, and how unkind cold water could be to the size of a penis.

"Come on, Robbie," Danny said. "Get your ass in here before we throw you in."

He looked at the water, once again getting a strange vibe from it. He couldn't put his finger on it, but there was something about the glow that seemed peculiar to him. It wasn't the normal blue-green color lights gave to swimming pools at night. There was something different, something spiraling in the deeper end. It seemed as if the others hadn't noticed it so he hadn't mentioned it either. Maybe they couldn't see it as he could from this angle. But it was there. It was a circular, azure glow entirely different from the color of the pool itself. It made a small pit in the deep end that looked somehow alive, but as soon as he thought he saw it move it went out of focus and it took him a few minutes to find it again.

Maxine was released from Danny's clutches. She draped her arms on the concrete ledge and gave Robbie a smile that could melt solid steel. She bit her bottom lip and raised her eyebrows.

"*Robbie* . . . " she said in a singsong manner. "You wanna little kiss?"

He felt himself blush and looked at Danny, expecting him to be furious. But the big guy was grinning.

"Come here," Maxine said, cooing.

"No way. You're gonna pull me in."

Joe and Kayla were watching. His brother had his arms around her waist and to Robbie it seemed like they were in a murky dream. Maxine pushed herself out of the pool. He knew she must have been freezing but she didn't show it, she just started walking toward him, her black one-piece dripping. Her hair was slicked back, making her look like a chic supermodel. When she bent over and put her hands on the armrests of his chair, she gave him a view down her suit.

"Just one kiss," she said.

His heart picked up speed and, despite her motives, her plump, parted lips lured him like the song of a siren, which he found rather befitting, as Maxine was an aquatic creature by nature. He sat up, defensive as well as excited. Her face came closer and her tongue darted out. It ran over his trembling lips, both of them keeping their eyes wide open. In the pool, he could hear the guys hooting like they were at a strip show. Her hand snaked around his wrist but he was too bewitched by her kiss to resist it, and just as he felt her begin to tug, a loud boom came from behind them, making them both jump. Everyone turned toward the sound, looking into a house that was supposed to be empty.

"What in the hell was that?" Danny said.

The sound was like something heavy falling onto a hardwood floor, a noise that shook the walls and echoed through the manor with menace. Joe was out of the pool in seconds. He wrapped a towel around his waist and motioned to Danny to get moving. He inched toward the doors and swung them open. Danny went to his side. They all listened for a moment, waiting for another thud, but the house had fallen silent and still, leaving only the ambience of the bubbling fountain. The boys hesitated and it made Robbie feel better to see they too were susceptible to fear.

Joe turned to his buddy. "We should check it out."

Maxine stood a few feet in front of the chair, the cold getting to her now, making her shake and hug herself. She turned to look at Kayla, who remained swimming as she watched the boys, her expression blank. Just as Joe was about to step across the threshold, he turned to his brother.

"Get off your ass."

Robbie looked to Maxine, as if she would help him somehow, but she didn't notice. He didn't want to investigate any noise that could rattle this massive house like the stomp of Godzilla. The sound had startled him and the shaking that followed made his blood sour, a childlike fear quivering through him. He worried that if he stood up the others would see he was trembling.

"Come on," his brother said, more forcefully this time. "We'll search the place faster with three." He turned to Maxine. "Get back in the pool, would ya? You're starting to look like a Smurf."

Maxine jumped back in before Joe could change his mind, obviously just as reluctant to go back in the house as Robbie was. The girls sat on the ledge by the waterfall, the flow keeping them warm as they watched the boys intently, waiting for them to say everything was going to be all right. The glow of the pool made them look like wet poltergeists.

Reluctantly, Robbie stood and joined the guys. Joe had always protected him against bullies and guided him in the absence of a father, so Robbie depended on him for advice on how to be a real man. Part of that advice was to always step up and face fear, especially in the company of ladies. Robbie fiddled with the zipper of his hoodie as the three of them walked back into the house, moving through the dimly lit den as they made their way toward the winding staircase.

"That definitely came from upstairs," Joe whispered.

"What do you think it was?" Robbie asked.

"No idea."

"Maybe it was just the house settling," Danny said. The Grant brothers turned to him with a disapproving glance. "Well, shit, I dunno. I mean the place is, like, ancient. Didn't the old bat say it was built after the Civil War?"

Joe shook his head. "World War I, moron."

Danny glowered but said nothing.

"Could be the pipes," Robbie said.

"Yeah," Joe said with a shrug. "Could be. But it sounded like a goddamned whale landed on the place."

The trio hesitated at the foot of the stairs, still listening, waiting for another bump in the night.

Joe sniffed and rolled his shoulders, cocky now, his chest puffed. "To hell with this, right? The sooner we check this out the sooner we get back to all that pussy waiting on us." He nudged Danny and winked. His friend smiled halfheartedly. "Let's go."

They passed by the electronic seat that carried Mrs. Snowden up and down the stairs, and as they began their ascent Robbie gripped the handrail harder than he needed to. The slick wood felt good in his fist, as if it was securing him in the real world. Joe stayed in the lead with Danny and Robbie tailing him on either side as they reached the second floor.

"All right," Joe said. "I'll check the old lady's room. Danny, why don't you check out the guest bedroom. Robbie, you check out the shitter. Anybody see anything give a holler. Otherwise we'll hit the reading room and whatnot."

Robbie nodded and Danny turned down the hall. Joe pointed out the bathroom door and Robbie watched as his big brother disappeared into the shadows of the master bedroom. He gulped, left on the landing alone. The light was muted here, making it friendly to the blackness that lurked in the corners and swallowed the hallway where the bathroom awaited him.

Man up, he told himself. *Don't let the guys see you standing here like a sissy.*

He pulled up his saggy jeans and made his way down the hall while he still had the nerve. He didn't breathe, but he reached the door without encountering the boogeyman.

Robbie had not been in the bathroom yet. It was at least twice as big as the living room, with ivory-colored tile and countertops where a row of golden sinks sparkled. The walls were mirrors, making the room look even bigger than it was as it bounced back images of the Jacuzzi tub, the long walk-in shower, and the toilet and bidet. Rounding the corner, he saw a door of frosted glass. The blur of it intimidated him, as did the memory of Norman Bates' famous attack in *Psycho.* He wished they'd all stopped in the garage for baseball bats and crowbars before heading upstairs, but it was too late for that. He slid the door open as fast as he could and jumped back. Behind it was a sauna complete with a stack of stones in the center.

Robbie exhaled and turned around to check the shower. It was the only one he'd ever seen that was so long it actually had a turn in it. Once he was finished he got out and looked around, checking the ceiling and then, not knowing what else to do, moving on to the cabinets. Everything was organized and sterile-looking. Closing the last cabinet, he saw himself in the mirror, as well as the dark shape of the nude woman who stood in the doorway behind him. Jolted, he gasped and spun around.

The doorway was empty.

Robbie gulped.

She *had* been there—a woman with a pin-up's body and long brown hair that concealed the nipples of her heavy breasts. Her face had been obscured, as had the dark triangle between her legs, but her amber limbs and torso had been clear to him. But now there was only the stale hallway and the layers of darkness that waited beyond. Robbie rubbed his eyes and let out a stress laugh. He'd been watching too much porn! Still, he had trouble believing it had only been a figment of his imagination. But what else was there? Had Joe and Danny been playing tricks on him? The woman clearly wasn't one of the girls downstairs. Though the glimpse was brief, he saw that she was an adult, shapely brunette. Besides, she had vanished in a flash, without a sound.

But now there was noise.

The ceiling began to creak just slightly, sounding like someone sitting on a noisy bed. The boards behind the drywall groaned and crackled like popcorn.

"What the hell is that?" Joe called out. "Robbie, where are you?"

He gladly left the bathroom and moved down the hallway toward the other boys. The ceiling continued to grind, reminding Robbie of the sound of old ships bobbing over choppy waters. He felt suddenly cold and hoped it was merely a draft coming through the open doors to the patio.

"Third floor," Joe said. "Somebody's up there."

Robbie and Danny looked at one another and Robbie saw how pale the big guy had grown.

"We should just call the cops, man," Danny said.

Robbie nodded. "I agree."

"No way," Joe said. "We do that and they'll call Snowden. She'll come running back here and we'll be out all that cash."

There was another creak. Robbie's spine straightened. He wanted to tell the guys about the woman he'd seen but didn't want to face the ridicule.

"It's probably a burglar." Joe cracked his knuckles. "We nab his ass and we could get a reward."

"Come on," Robbie said. "You're not making sense. Let's just call the police. Whoever it is could have a gun, and maybe there's more than one of them, huh?"

"Your brother's right, Joe." Danny put the towel around his shoulders now, also feeling the sudden chill. "No sense in getting ourselves hurt or killed."

A sudden thud shook the ceiling, making them start. There was a rolling sound then, like a bowling ball slowly spinning down a lane.

"Okay," Joe said. "This is getting pretty weird."

Danny stared above him. "My phone's out by the pool."

"Mine too."

"We should get out of here anyway. I want to get Maxine safe. Kayla too."

Robbie was impressed with Danny's chivalry. It was a side of him he hadn't seen before.

"Let's split," Robbie said, glad that he and Danny were in an alliance.

"All right," Joe agreed. "But I say we see what's going on first. We can get up to the third floor landing nice and quiet like."

Danny squinted. "What the fuck for?"

"'Cause I don't want to drag the cops out here just because that senile old lady forgot to tell us there was a machine on a timer up here or some shit."

"Come on, man . . ."

"No, *you* come on. We're supposed to be watching this place, right?"

"Yeah, but—"

"We don't want the police ruining our fun tonight just because of a noise, do we? It could be nothing. Maybe somebody's up there, but it could just be a squatter. We can chase them out."

"I don't like this."

"Don't be a faggot. There's three of us. Four if we count you twice, big boy."

The ceiling moaned again, softer this time. Robbie realized they hadn't heard anything that sounded like footsteps; he wasn't sure if that made him feel better or worse. He was devastated when Danny caved.

"Okay," the larger boy said. "We'll check it out. But we stick together this time, and at the first sign of trouble we haul ass."

"Can't argue with that." Joe's eyes stayed on the ceiling as he headed toward the coil of stairs. "We'll get the girls and run to your car without stopping."

Robbie wanted to do that already. Instead he followed them onto the stairwell. They climbed gingerly, not speaking, listening for the slightest noise. Whatever was upstairs had fallen silent and they could no longer sense any movement, which made him wonder how they were going to pinpoint the source of what they'd heard. Was it waiting on them, crouched in the dark, mouth foaming, eyes like fire? His mouth felt dry as they reached the third floor. Its one saving grace was the chandelier, which better lighted it than the second floor, lessening the creepiness.

"What now?" Danny whispered.

From the look on Joe's face he clearly didn't know. He glanced down each side of the hall. Gray, closed doors lined both sides like tombstones as the hall stretched back into the swallow of shadows. He put a finger to his lips to hush them and started down the hallway to the right. Robbie and Danny stuck close by him, but Danny kept looking over his shoulder, securing their backs.

They jumped in unison at the sound of a voice. "Hey."

Robbie couldn't tell where it was coming from, but it was clearly a woman's voice. It sounded mousy and frightened. It came again, louder and clearer.

"Joe? Danny?" it called.

It was coming from the ground floor.

"Are you guys okay up there?" Kayla asked.

Her voice carried and bounced off the walls, circling their heads. Robbie looked to the other guys and Joe put his finger to his lips again. It was clearly more important not to give away their position to whoever might be on this floor with them rather than assure the girls downstairs with an update.

"Knock it off," Maxine said, less concerned than her friend. "Quit trying to scare us!"

Joe shook his head. "Let's get this over with, before she wakes the dead."

Robbie grimaced at Joe's phrasing.

They moved down the hall, losing light with each step. Danny ran his hand along the wall, searching in vain for a light switch, and as the gray deepened there was a sudden creak. They stopped and waited. Robbie's mouth was chalk. He heard the creak again. It wasn't above or below them now. It was coming from *behind* the wall at the end of the vestibule, a wall they could barely see in the dimness. Whatever was making the noise was on the same level as they were.

Robbie swallowed hard. "Oh shit."

"Be cool," Joe said. The quiver in his voice failed to reassure Robbie.

The creaking gave way to quick snaps followed by a soft rumble, like someone belching with their mouth closed. Robbie's spine pushed against his skin. The sound rose and fell in a low growl.

"Jesus," Danny said. "What in *the fuck* is that?"

Joe whispered, "It sounds like a—"

Two round lights appeared at the end of the hallway. They seemed to sail in the darkness until they centered there, hovering two feet above the hardwood floor. The growling grew louder, giving way to wet snorts.

Those aren't lights, Robbie realized. *They're reflecting eyes.*

He had adjusted to the dark and could see the light switch to his right. He reached for it slowly so as not to startle the creature in the dark. He tapped his brother with his other hand to show him what he was doing. They had to be ready to run.

Click.

The light came on in a blinding flash.

No one breathed.

A Rottweiler stood before them, its hackles raised in a mohawk. Its teeth took up half its giant head as it snarled and drooled, its black body tight with flexed muscle. Above its eyes were two brown spots that bent down like angry eyebrows. It growled louder and the creaking intensified behind the wall as if cheering him on.

"Oh fuck me," Danny said.

The dog sneered but didn't move. Neither did they. Joe put his hands up in front of his chest as if he were under arrest. Robbie licked his lips and avoided the dog's gaze. Going with his gut, he went into a squat, moving slowly so as not to startle the agitated canine.

Joe tugged Robbie's collar. "What are you doing?"

Robbie didn't answer. Instead, he kept his palms out. He didn't get close to the dog. He just laid his hands open, hoping it would sniff instead of bite. The hair on the dog's back stayed up but the curl in his lip lowered and his eyes went to the hands, to Robbie's face, and back. After a moment it stepped forward with one paw, held it there a moment, and then withdrew.

"It's okay, boy," Robbie said.

The dog let out a gentle *harumph* and Robbie inched closer.

"You wanna lose a finger, idiot?" Joe said.

The dog stretched its neck and lowered its nose to Robbie's palm. It sniffed it a few times and then licked it for good measure. Robbie smiled. After a few more licks the dog's hackles went down and Robbie was able to pet him.

"Atta boy."

A moment later the dog was nuzzling into him.

Joe and Danny sighed with relief.

"What the hell is this?" Joe said. "Snowden didn't say nothin' about no goddamned pooch."

"Maybe he wandered in when the doors were open," Robbie said.

Danny put his hands on his hips. "A stray?"

"Could be a lost dog. He has no collar though." Robbie realized the grinding behind the wall had stopped. "That noise though, that creaking, it wasn't him."

"Dude," Joe said, "it *had* to be."

"No, it's true. It was something else. Something behind the wall, in the room behind it."

Joe shook his head. "There ain't no room behind it. That's the end of the house. Nothing's beyond that wall but the outside."

"But . . . we all heard it."

"It had to be the dog, man," Danny said. "I mean, shit, look how big the fucker is."

The Rottie snorted.

"But I heard something in the wall even when he was right in front of us."

Maxine's shrill voice rose from below, calling her boyfriend's name. It sounded like she was climbing the stairs.

"Let's go," Danny said, "before she has a conniption fit."

"What about the dog?" Robbie asked, still petting.

Joe looked down at it, shrugged. "Bring the beast downstairs, I guess."

CHAPTER THREE

SHE SWAM THROUGH THE WALLS.

The planks stretched as small cracks appeared on the inside of the plaster, sending dry snow through the black hollow. Pressing on, she extended her arms in a dive, her long, auburn hair cascading in the darkness. She didn't see through this darkness, she *felt* her way through it, sensing each nook and cranny just as a bat sees with its scooping ears. The stuffiness did not bother her, for she did not need to breathe, and the tendrils of webbing she broke did not deter her, nor did the riot of spiders that fell upon her naked back and skittered across her flesh like raindrops.

The sound of the youths on the bottom level of the house shuddered her in the most wonderful ways, and her icy body responded to their presence with palpable desire. Beneath her breasts her heart battered away and her nipples stiffened, her sex moistening, her tongue darting in and out of her mouth in rabid anticipation, tasting the boys' musk in the air. She scraped her long nails across the walls and dragged her toenails across the floor.

She was ready to join the party.

CHAPTER FOUR

KAYLA WASN'T AFRAID OF THE dog the way Maxine was. She dug into the rolls under his chin and he lapped at her face. She'd always wanted a dog of her own, but her mother insisted she had an allergy, though Kayla suspected this was yet another one of her mother's cries for attention. Mom didn't care what kind of attention she got and always had some new ailment to get it.

"So it was just a dog?" Maxine asked.

"Looks like." Joe had already lost interest in the whole ordeal. He popped open a can of Miller Lite. "No worries."

"There's no way that a dog made that big bang."

"He must have knocked over something. I don't wanna search the whole house right now to find out what. That would take all night."

Danny agreed. "Yeah, we can do that tomorrow. Let's not waste tonight on that. I say we get back in the pool." He laughed toward the dog. "Maybe poochie here will jump in."

Kayla tensed. "Don't push him."

"Yeah," Robbie added. "That's cruel."

Robbie seemed to believe this but clearly enjoyed siding with her. His shy smile and wide eyes told her so. Kayla saw no harm in his little crush; in a way it was flattering. And he did look a little like his older brother. In a few years he would be just as handsome. All he needed to do was grow a stronger backbone and a little bit of attitude, and he would have the girls hanging off him like ornaments.

"You think he belongs to Mrs. Snowden?" she asked.

"Doubt it," Danny said. "I mean, she would have mentioned it, right?"

Joe burped, licking beer foam off his upper lip. "She's old. Old folks are forgetful."

"She seemed pretty sharp to me."

"Well, if it's hers then where the hell is the dog food?"

"We have to find his owner," Kayla said.

The dog wagged his stub tail, his whole butt wiggling. He slobbered on her arms but she didn't mind. Maxine, however, made a sour face.

"Look, we'll handle all that in the morning," Joe said. "Now let's get back in the pool already. Unless you're ready for the hot tub."

He wiggled his eyebrows and she blushed a little and hid her face from them until it passed. Maxine, bored of this situation, seemed to like the idea. She skipped along the floor, butt wiggling just like the dog's, and passed through the doors and out to the Jacuzzi. Danny and Joe followed. Kayla looked up at Robbie who stood over her. She noticed his eyes dart away from her chest.

"It's so weird that he was just upstairs like that," she said, petting the dog.

"I thought so too."

"You sure there wasn't somebody up there with him?"

Robbie shook his head. "We didn't see anything . . ."

He trailed off.

"What?" she asked. "What is it?"

He was reluctant at first. "I thought I heard something else. Sort of scratching, behind the wall."

"Coming from one of the rooms?"

"No. I mean from *behind* the wall. Like, *inside of it.* Joe said on the other side there was no more house. It just led outside."

She mulled this over. "Maybe it was a bird or something? Like a woodpecker digging into the side of the house or a burrowing squirrel?"

"I dunno. Could've been, I guess."

The dog moved over to him, demanding more affection.

"We should name him," Kayla said.

"But he's not ours."

"I mean just for now. We have to call him something. What's a good name for a silly Rottie like him?"

Robbie crossed his arms and looked to the ceiling. "How about Horace?"

Kayla laughed and Robbie smiled down at her.

"Horace?" she said. "Where did that come from?"

He shrugged—goofy, gangly.

She looked at the dog. "I like it. He looks like a Horace."

Horace panted with a smile of his own, as if in total agreement.

As they soaked in the hot tub, Horace watched on eagerly. His true name was unpronounceable, but the master allowed visitors to give him new ones. It created a sentimental attachment the master could use to her advantage. There was an energy to these young people that was so different than what Horace was used to, both from the old woman and the younger one who came and went, who commanded him and pleased him by giving him a job to do.

She'd let him out of the wall and he'd thought she wanted him to get the newcomers out of their house, but then she'd soothed him, telling him there was no need to growl or attack. She wanted these young people here. He could feel her comfort with their presence, and though he did not understand why they were welcome, he did enjoy the playful ones and the way the young women smelled.

The youngest male interested him most. He was timid and would be easier to dominate than the strong smelling, older males. Horace did not wish to dominate him yet, but the option was reassuring, even though he knew the master would be the one to dominate them all, if she so wished.

And she would.

The warmth of the hot tub felt good, as did Kayla's smooth thigh under his hand. He glided his fingertips up and down the inside of it, itching to get closer to the sweet spot but taking it slow, monitoring her reactions to every touch and tease. Joe popped open two beers. Getting her drunk certainly wouldn't hurt his chances, unless she got *too* drunk and spent the night with her head in the toilet. He would have to monitor that too.

They had the hot tub to themselves now. Danny and Maxine had gone inside the house for some privacy. He wished Robbie would get the hint and take the damned dog for a walk or something. There was no way he was going to get Kayla's top off with his little brother sitting there. Robbie was always a cock-blocker like this, and Joe felt like any other brother would never let Robbie hang around because of it. The kid had a knack for dorking up whatever he was part of.

It bothered Joe to see his brother failing to launch. He still collected comic books, watched cartoons, and ate fruit snacks and licorice all the time. Joe tried to get him to drink beer and smoke a J, but Robbie was just too timid. Hell, he couldn't even get him in the pool tonight! At least Robbie showed an interest in girls (much to Joe's relief) but he never had the nerve to approach any of them. It was depressing. It caused Joe to decide on getting Linda to come over tomorrow night to give the kid a taste of what always grew boys right the fuck up.

He looked at his little brother. He was staring at the pool, the blue lights reflecting on his face in gentle ripples. Beside him, the dog sat watching Joe, his eyes glowing eerily as he stared, unblinking. Joe held the stare for a moment, annoyed, before deciding that having a staring contest with a dog was idiotic, especially when he had Kayla sitting next to him in a skimpy bikini. He'd known she had a nice figure but had not been prepared for the voluptuous body that came out of her clothes. Had it not been for the scars on her arms she would have been perfect. The cuts didn't detract much from her beauty, but they did reveal the deepness of her insecurity, her need to be loved. They were a clear cry for attention—and probably help—and from the amount of them it was obvious her pleas had gone unanswered. He was no psychology expert and couldn't fully explain her self-mutilation, but he knew signs of weakness and low self-esteem when he saw them and knew from experience that both these traits in a woman made her easier to get into bed. They wanted to be loved, held and caressed; most of all they wanted to be wanted. They searched for a place to be accepted, and if it had to be beneath a man's thrusting body, they would be glad to lie down. It gave their pursuers an added advantage, one Joe was not above taking.

As if she knew what he was thinking, she tilted her head back and rested it on his arm behind her neck. She looked at him, lips parted, the bubbles churning in her cleavage. She opened her mouth to kiss him. Soon enough she would open her legs for him just as easily, he thought, as long as he continued to play the game, do the stupid dance of courting as if it were a sacred ritual, and manipulate her based on her insecurities.

He tried to kiss her as passionately as he could.

Almost like he cared about her.

The king-sized bed of the guest bedroom yielded beneath Maxine as Danny climbed on top of her, planting sloppy, half-drunk kisses on her nipples. The room was spacious and decorated with ottomans and standing mirrors. She'd bit her lip with jealousy at the sight of the walk-in closet that was nearly as big as her bedroom at home.

It was so nice in this house.

The soft breath of the running heat serenaded them, the light low and pink from the delicate lampshades. Her boyfriend's fingers tugged under her bathing suit bottom and she arched her back so he could slide it off. His erection grazed across her leg, making her skin tingle. She brought her foot up to it and caressed it, making it pulse beneath the cold wet trunks, and Danny tugged faster and flung the bottom of her suit over his shoulder. It hit the wall behind him with a squish and Maxine giggled. He removed his suit and climbed onto her, tonguing her pussy and anus, making her squirm with ecstasy. Fully flushed, she pulled his hips toward her face and put his cock in her mouth, twirling her tongue along the bottom of his shaft as she gripped his waist. Nothing got her wetter than sucking a guy off. It made her feel irresistible—a teaser, a tempter. He turned to concrete in her throat and then shoved her onto the mattress and pushed into her insides, just slightly at first, but then fully, deeply, making her toes curl as she wrapped her legs around him.

Maxine closed her eyes and let a series of faces dance across her mind. Some were boys from school, others from movies. One of her Dad's younger friends returned to her, a regular fantasy. Danny turned her on, but she liked to imagine more than one man pleasuring her whenever she was in the throes of sex. There was something animalistic about the fantasy, like creatures instead of men were ravaging her—sexual werewolves and man-beasts overrun by a frantic desire to fuck her senseless. Thinking of the fantasy embarrassed her whenever the sex ended, but it was one she always fell into during the throes, helpless to think of anything else.

The bed creaked and squealed as Danny got a rhythm going. But as the noise increased there came another sound. She couldn't tell where it was coming from, but it was a deep thrum, like a machine whirring somewhere in the house. She opened her eyes and looked over his shoulder.

The ceiling was a cyclone of blood.

It spun like a whirlpool, a vortex of gore. Sailing within it were dozens of free-floating eyes that seemed to glow within the murk, cataracts milky, blood vessels burst. The eyes wandered, attached to nothing, drifting through the crimson pool like tiny asteroids. Each of them looked upon her with what she sensed was loathing. The rage and wrathfulness within them chilled her. In the center of this tornado was a blackish drain surrounded by a mouth full of chattering, piranha-like teeth that flickered slickly, gnashing and spraying spittle, a yonic nightmare vomiting the remains of a dozen mauled faces.

Maxine screamed.

Thinking it was a sexual cry, Danny shouted, "Oh yeah, baby!"

She screamed, louder and louder, swatting at his back so she could get free, get the hell out of the house entirely. Above them, stalactites of fizzing gore stretched down from the ceiling, bringing the bloodshot eyes closer as they dangled in greasy yellow pus. They stared at her as Danny fucked her harder, and the chattering teeth formed a giant, hungry grin of white razors.

At last Maxine's screaming got Danny's attention and he stopped thrusting to look down at her with confusion.

"What the fuck is wrong with you?"

Maxine didn't say a word. She couldn't. She pushed her boyfriend off, got to her feet, and headed for the door. She ran through the hallway naked and headed for the stairs, taking them two at a time as hot tears flashed across her cheeks. She heard Danny calling to her from the landing, but she did not dare turn around.

CHAPTER FIVE

AT FIRST ROBBIE WAS EXCITED to see Maxine running through the living room naked. He'd never seen a naked girl in person before. Heck, not even a topless one. The sight of her tender parts jiggling thrilled him, as did the sparkling-wet heart of her thinned pubes, but the excitement quickly faded.

She was screaming. Screaming like she'd just walked in on the Manson murders.

Kayla was the first to react. She climbed out of the hot tub and ran through the doorway toward her friend. Joe looked at Robbie. By the time they got inside Kayla had Maxine in her arms and Danny was bumbling downstairs with his swim trunks on backwards. Robbie saw Kayla's eyes burn toward Danny. In her grip, Maxine twisted and shrieked like a lunatic being dragged to the electric chair.

"What the hell did you do to her?" Kayla demanded.

"Nothing!" he said, and the look on his face made Robbie believe him. "She just flipped out all of a sudden."

Kayla tried to look Maxine in the eye as they made a circle around her without getting too close. In her grip, Maxine's writhing lessened.

"Max," Kayla said, "it's me. You're okay!"

Robbie took the throw blanket off the sofa and brought it over. Kayla took it with thankful eyes, wrapped it around her friend. It seemed to comfort Maxine despite her continued tears. She scanned the walls and ceiling, paranoid, waiting. She kept looking back at the stairs, as if a bull was going to come charging down at any moment.

"She just flipped out," Danny said again. "We were ... um ... you know, *fooling around*, and out of nowhere she screamed and ran outta the room."

"Well, did you scare her?" Kayla said, still angry. "Maybe you pushed her a little too hard, huh?"

Danny frowned. "Hey now, we weren't doing anything we haven't done plenty of times before."

Joe rubbed the back of his neck. "Well something tripped her out."

Danny's face changed. "Fuck."

"What?"

"The ecstasy."

"What are you talking about?"

"I had two caps of it. We popped them a few hours ago, before we went swimming. I figured they were duds, man, 'cause I haven't felt shit."

Kayla's face soured. "Jesus, Danny."

"X don't make you freak out like this," Joe said. "It's not like fucking acid."

"Well, something must've—"

"The eyes!" Maxine interrupted. "All that ... *blood*." She was shaking but no longer flailing. Her mania had cooled to a quiet shudder. "Blood was *everywhere*. On the fucking *ceiling!*"

The group looked to Danny and he threw up his hands, just as perplexed as anyone else.

"You're saying you saw blood?" Kayla asked. "Like, a stain on the ceiling?"

Maxine gritted her teeth. "Not a stain. It was still wet. It was ... *moving*."

Joe shook his head, his look of concern changing to one of near-mockery. "Man, she *is* tripping."

"There were so many eyes ..." Maxine muttered.

"Max," Kayla said, "did you take any other drugs tonight?"

"It wasn't drugs!" she said, pulling away from her friend. "I'm not fucking stoned. I know what I saw."

They fell silent.

Joe turned to Danny. "You see anything?"

He shook his head. "Nah, man."

"It was above him," Maxine said. "Behind him. It almost *got us.*"

"How can blood *get* you?" Robbie asked, not in a provoking way but out of general confusion.

"It was, like, *alive.* It was reaching out for us ... staring at us with all those eyes."

Robbie suddenly thought of the woman he'd glimpsed in the bathroom and the sounds that had come from somewhere behind the walls.

"Maybe it's all tied together," he said.

Joe looked at him. "Maybe what is?"

"Maybe it's related to the noises we heard. I heard something coming from behind the dog, through the walls. And you remember that first noise; it shook the whole house. There's no way Horace did that."

Joe leaned forward, eyebrows high. "Horace?"

"The dog," Robbie admitted, embarrassed.

"Maybe we should check the house again," Danny said. "You know, check out every single room this time."

"I'm not going back up there!" Maxine said. "I wanna go home!"

Joe groaned. "Come on, guys. Would you listen to yourselves? You sound like a bunch of kids afraid of the monster under their bed. I thought we were here to have a good time tonight, not sit around the fire and tell ghost stories."

Maxine clutched Kayla's arm. "Please, take me home."

"Sure."

Joe's face dropped. "Goddamnit."

Kayla looked at him but Robbie couldn't read her. Figuring out what girls were thinking was a difficult art no man ever truly mastered, and he was a novice.

"I'll take her home," Danny suggested.

"That's more like it," Joe said, obviously glad his piece of tail wasn't leaving. "Maxine can go home and we can keep the party going until Danny gets back. Everybody wins."

No one else seemed as happy as he did about the idea. From what Robbie could see, the party was over, but Joe kept trying to give it CPR anyway.

"It's getting kind of late, Joe," Kayla said.

As inexperienced as he was, Robbie knew these were the words of doom every Casanova loathed to hear. It was their kryptonite. He saw the twitch in his brother's lip, too subtle for anyone other than his own kin to recognize but there, a window to his simmering anger.

"Fine," he said, turning his back to them.

After the girls left, the three of them sat in the living room, Joe and Danny finishing off the twelve-pack while Robbie played with the dog. Danny felt the fury radiating off Joe.

Like it's my fault Maxine flipped out, Danny thought. *At least* you *don't have blue balls.*

They'd gone back to the room he'd been fucking her in and found no blood, eyes, or whatever else she'd hallucinated. Not even traces of blood. They hadn't heard any more noises either, and they'd gone to every single room now, uncovering nothing they could attribute to that first, house-shuddering bang. Now they sat around, listening to the grandfather clock ticking away toward midnight, getting drunker with every tick and tock.

"What a bullshit night," Danny said, hoping to warm Joe up by agreeing with his clear disappointment.

Joe frowned. "You got that shit right."

They sat in silence a few minutes, and then Joe's face lit up like Christmas morning. His eyes went wide and a shit-eating grin spread across his face. "Hey. I just thought of something that could spice the night back up."

"Oh yeah?"

"How about we call Linda?"

Danny snickered. Maybe after they got Robbie taken care of he could get a little something from her too, so he could finish off what he and Maxine had started. "Now *that* is a good idea."

"Linda?" Robbie asked. "Linda who?"

"Linda Lovelace," Joe joked.

Danny doubted Robbie knew who that was.

"Um, okay," the kid said.

Danny clapped his hands. "Think she's up this late?"

"Shit," said Joe, "we're talking about Linda here. It's Friday night. If she's at home in bed then I'm Justin Bieber."

Danny slapped his knees. "Then you suck cock!"

They cackled, more from the excitement over Linda than the joke.

Joe howled. "There's only one person who's gonna suck cock tonight!"

They laughed again, and this time Danny nearly fell out of his seat, which only made them laugh harder.

Linda had just left the concert when her phone rang.

The local punk band, Tears and Vomit, had been mediocre, and she was getting a little worn out on the company of her friend Dee and her dimwitted boyfriend, Street. She was thinking about calling it a night but knew her old man had been drinking and didn't want to come home to one of his late-night lectures. When her caller I.D. showed her who was calling she smirked and shook her head, laughing at the horn balls.

She liked Joe all right. He was a cocky bastard, but cool. Danny was okay sometimes, but she had a general dislike of jocks. She found them dense and self-centered, always more focused on their big games than treating their ladies right. They acted like they had everything coming to them just because they could catch a lousy ball. It pissed her off.

The phone rang a second time. There was no doubt what they were calling about.

She'd been reluctant to accept their proposal but needed money if she was ever going to get a car (she currently just borrowed her mother's now and then, as she did tonight), one that could take her out of this jerkwater burg for good. She would be eighteen in November, and she'd had enough of upstate New York. She'd been to Manhattan only once but was determined to live there. If that meant pulling some peckers and popping some nerd's cherry, then she was willing to do that. Dreams came at a high price sometimes. Now and then a girl just had to swallow her pride, amongst other things, if she expected to get anywhere in a man's world.

She answered the call.

Robbie's jaw dropped when she walked in the door.

The short, leather skirt and jacket, with a red baby doll t-shirt of *Blondie*. Hair in chestnut ribbons, legs ensnared by fishnet stockings.

This wasn't some Linda named Lovelace.

This was Linda-fucking-Lelane.

She was one of the hottest girls in school, a senior whose tough attitude and curvy body made her the prize of all the boys, though none of them had been able to possess her for very long. Robbie had heard dirty things about her in the halls and sometimes thought the other guys were just pulling his leg, but in a way he wanted to believe them because it added to her sleaziness and heightened his fantasies of her.

"Some party," she said, smirking at the three of them.

"That's why we called on you to save us," Joe said.

He handed her a beer and she popped it open, cocking her hip to one side as she took a pull. The wetness of her lips stirred something in Robbie. Linda looked at him and winked, and that made it even more intense. She'd never so much as glanced at him in school. He gulped in reply. Joe led her into the room and Danny waved a hello. She looked at the dog lying at Robbie's feet.

"Nice mutt," she said. "He yours?"

"Nah," Joe said. "Just a wanderer."

"Probably a rain dog," Robbie said, and then immediately wondered why he'd blurted it out. Even Horace looked at him.

"What in the hell is that?" Linda asked.

He gulped again. "Well, dogs find their way home by scent. Sometimes they wander off and then it rains. It covers up the scent and then they're lost."

Linda rolled her eyes. "We ain't had no rain lately, kid." She turned back to Joe. "So we good to go?"

"Yeah, yeah."

He took her by the arm and walked her through the kitchen. Danny just sat there, smiling and burping.

"What's going on?" Robbie asked him.

"Don't be scared."

"Scared of what?"

"You're gonna like this."

Now Robbie *was* a little scared. Mostly he was nervous. He heard Linda's heels clacking as she came back into the room and he tried to control his trembling. Joe put a hand on his brother's shoulder and nodded him toward the kitchen. Once there, Joe spoke in hushed tones.

"Danny and I got you a little birthday present."

Robbie blinked. "My birthday's on Sunday."

"Dude, shut up. We're gonna get you laid."

What little control he had over his trembling was suddenly gone.

"W-wha-what?"

"You heard me. Linda is gonna fuck you blind." Joe's smile stank of cheap beer and cheaper cigarettes, his eyes half-closed and bloodshot. "How do ya like that, little brother?"

Robbie couldn't think. "Um . . . um . . ."

"Come on. Don't be a fucking fag."

"I'm not! And you shouldn't call people fags."

"Said the fag."

"Why does she want to have sex with me? I don't understand."

Joe snickered. "We convinced her it was a good idea."

"How?"

"Don't worry about it. Just thank me for the gift and get her sweet ass upstairs. Then thank me again on your wedding night."

Robbie scratched his head. "Wedding? I don't want to marry her."

His brother groaned. "That's not what I meant, for Christ's sakes."

"I don't understand–"

"You don't fucking have to! This is just part of being a man. Trust me, you're gonna *love* this. I see you shaking, and that's all right. Everybody's nervous during their first time."

"It's not my first," he said, pathetically trying to cover up his shame.

"Don't bullshit a bullshitter, bro. It's up to me to help show you the ropes. Dad doesn't give a shit about us, and Mom ain't never gonna talk to you about screwing, and thank God for that, am I right? You know I wouldn't steer you wrong, now would I?"

Robbie was silent for a moment. "No, you wouldn't."

"Fuckin' A. Now get your pimply ass up there and crush that pussy."

CHAPTER SIX

THE ROOM HELD A FAINT perfume smell that accentuated the soft lighting, but Linda turned the lamp off after opening the curtains, letting pale moonlight set the mood.

"You're shaking, baby," she said. She had her arms around his waist and was pressing her body close against his. "Just relax. Linda's gonna fix you up real nice."

She took off her coat and let it drop to the floor, then took his hand and placed it onto her breast. She wasn't wearing a bra. For a moment Robbie couldn't move, but then he began to grab it, feeling its yield, and his erection jutted beneath his jeans like a flagpole the day of the parade. Linda leaned in and ran her tongue along his bottom lip. It was nothing like the few sloppy kisses he'd shared with Wendy Parks in the sixth grade, the bookworm with the shiny braces and *Star Wars* backpack. This was far more sensual, womanly, and he didn't know how to kiss back. Linda sniggered at his nervousness and took his other hand. She glided it along her thigh as she pulled one leg up, letting the lip of the skirt ride higher. He brushed the stockings and she guided him up her bare thigh.

"Touch me," she said into his ear.

He wasn't sure what she meant at first, but she pulled her skirt higher, bunching it around her waist. He saw her black panties as she pulled them to one side, revealing the thin tuft of hair over her sex. She placed his hand at her warm opening. His hard-on raged, a manic monster. Linda let him play with her clumsily for a moment, and then pushed his finger up inside her. The moist flesh made him shudder. She popped open the button of his jeans, unzipped him, and put her hand into his underwear. She pulled him out and squeezed hard. He twitched twice, moaned, and abruptly flooded her hand with semen. It spattered across their clothes, all his passions already spent.

"What're you doing down here?" Joe asked.

Linda didn't look at him. "I'm done."

"Whadda ya mean *done*? You've been up there for like five fucking minutes."

Her hands went to her generous hips. "Don't blame me! It's not my fault he's Johnny Two-Stroke. All I did was touch him and I struck oil."

She pointed to the milk crust on her skirt. It looked like his little brother had had a real storm brewing. Still, if all she did was touch him, that wasn't exactly what she'd been paid to do.

"Get back up there."

Linda's mouth opened. "Excuse me?"

"We paid you to fuck him. Sounds like all we got was an overpriced handy J. We talked about that before and you said he'd tap it."

"I don't remember that."

"Like hell. Don't welsh."

"I ain't welshing shit. I was gonna fuck him and then he blew his load before I could. Done deal."

Joe felt a bad heat brewing in his chest. There was only one way to handle her. "You either give him another chance, or we're gonna let everyone know what you're willing to do for a lousy three hundred bucks."

Linda's face turned to slate. "You wouldn't dare."

"Hold up your end of the bargain and you won't have to find out."

Danny butted in. "We just want what's fair, Linda. You did say he wouldn't just get a hand job. You said he'd tap it."

Linda stewed. She looked like a sexy gargoyle. "Well, he still got a hand job. I'll go back up there and try and screw him, but now you're paying for a hand job too."

"No fuckin way!" Joe said, the anger getting the better of him, encouraged by his beer buzz.

"Take it easy," Danny told him. "I'll give it to her. Let's just settle this. Remember, we're doing this for The Cherry."

The three of them looked at one another for a moment as if they were in a spaghetti western standoff, and then Joe resigned.

"Fine."

"Fine," Linda agreed. "He's still up there. Probably still has his pants around his ankles, the poor, little fuck. I'll give him a sec to get himself back together. In the meantime I want to throw these clothes in the wash and clean his spunk off me."

Horace didn't know what all the yelling was about, but it didn't concern him. The master was speaking and she didn't like what was going on. That meant she had work for him to do. He sat up excitedly but remained in a sit, eager to obey, remembering the deep satisfaction it always gave him when his master commanded him.

The boys and the new female did not hear the master upstairs, behind the walls, expanding the frame of the old house and putting miniscule cracks in the tiles. But he knew the sound of her slithering and could smell the rich scent of rot that came off her body.

Something was happening, something big.

He went upstairs to find the female.

The shower was luxurious. She'd never seen anything like it. There were jets and massage settings and a bench if she wanted to relax. The hot water hit her and she lathered up her thighs, clearing off the dried cum.

She liked Joe a little less than before she'd come over, but his runt of a brother seemed like an okay kid. He was virginal and she'd almost felt embarrassed for him back there when he'd come all over the place before they could really get started. She hoped now that he'd let loose that easy one he'd be able to go all the way, even for a little while, so she could go home and stash the hundreds into the cigar box she used as a bank. She was a night owl, but it was past one in the morning now and she'd had enough of the lackluster night.

She'd only meant to rinse off her thighs but the shower was so beautiful and welcoming she decided to go all the way in and let it wash through her hair. The jets made her scalp feel alive and she ran her hands down her body, lathering herself entirely. There was a sensual touch to the shower she'd never felt before while bathing. She thought maybe it was because she'd been about to have sex, however pathetic, and the letdown had made her flesh extra sensitive. She suddenly found herself running her hands over her breasts, the gaps in her fingers flicking over her nipples. She considered taking the showerhead down to use the massager on herself.

Maybe I'll have the kid take me in here, she thought. *At least then I might get some pleasure out of it.*

She heard the creaking of the bathroom door and turned her head toward the sound, wondering if he'd had the same idea.

"Robbie?" she said. "You in here?"

She heard feet scuffling on the tile.

"Who is that?"

She wasn't ready to provide a peep show, at least not for free, but the idea she wasn't alone sort of excited her. Perhaps she should have been more cautious being in a house alone with three boys, but she had a hard edge and didn't take crap from guys. These three weren't the type to attack her. Danny and Robbie didn't have it in them, and for all his huffing and puffing neither did Joe. It would take someone with a stronger constitution to dominate her, someone powerful not just physically but spiritually.

"You want a titty show it's gonna cost extra," she said.

But the water felt so good and her body felt so wonderfully acute. She wasn't so sure she would be able to resist a man at this moment, even if all three of them tried to pile inside the shower with her. The notion was so foreign it made her step back against the shower wall. Arousal like she had never felt before coursed through her like an electrical current. It fueled her blood with lust and made her most sensitive parts vibrate. She was no longer in control of her own desires, even though she was consciously aware of the absurdity of them.

"Come to me," she whispered to whomever—or whatever—was out there.

Through the frosted glass a black shape appeared. It was short and stocky, clearly not one of the boys. A paw print appeared on the glass. She fell out of her trance and snickered.

"Oh, brother."

Linda wasn't a dog person. Even if she were, she wouldn't like one as large and mean-looking as a Rottweiler. She would probably go for one that would fit in her purse, one of those pea-brained Paris Hilton dogs that were always shaking for no reason. Better still, she would just stick to cats, which she preferred because they shared her independent, bitchy attitude.

The paw rattled the door.

"Get out of here, Air Bud."

The paw came up again, pushing the door harder. There was a low growl and suddenly the water wasn't quite as warm. The dog's claws dragged down the glass, screeching. He started barking.

"Joe!" she yelled. "Joe, Danny, get this stupid mutt outta here!"

They were all the way downstairs. Would they even hear her? Maybe the kid was still on this floor.

"Robbie! Come help me out, will ya?"

The dog jumped up on his hind legs and hit the door with both front paws. It shook and clamored in a riot. Linda shrieked and nearly slipped in the suds.

"Somebody get this fuckin' dog outta here!"

There was movement in the corner of her eye and Linda froze up. Something was behind her. There was a strange noise. It sounded like grinding inside of the walls, like pipes bending on their own. Something splashed, sounding like footsteps in rain, and suddenly hands were on her, slithering up her legs to her buttocks. She screamed and the dog pounded and pounded, and as she spun around she saw no hands on her but she could see her flesh yielding and indenting as she was groped, as if she was being molested by an invisible man.

Linda ran to the door, preferring to face the dog than deal with whatever was in the shower with her. But as she tried to open it the dog jumped against it, closing it back on her. She tried again and he did the same. Panic seized her. She tried to force past him but he was too strong, too fast. The door kept slamming in her face.

Linda was trapped.

She tried to scream but something slithered over her mouth. It felt like lips. Water fell into her eyes and she squinted against it, feeling a long tongue dart down her throat like a fat, burrowing earthworm. She gagged and flung her arms and the tongue backed away, and as she batted her eyes open she saw a woman standing in the shower with her.

Linda's body locked in place.

The woman was tanned and beautiful, with feline features and dazzling, amber eyes. Her breasts were large on her slim frame, hips prime for child bearing, legs fit and defined. Her beauty was stunning, almost otherworldly in its perfection. She was under the showerhead with Linda, and yet her hair wasn't wet. It was a flowing lion's mane, the same uncanny color of her eyes, and it hung down past her navel, covering her like she was Lady Godiva.

"Who the fuck are you?" Linda said.

The woman smiled and drew her arm backward, punching Linda in the stomach. The fist went through her like a machete—shredding, tearing, nails twisting her intestines, spilling bile as the fingers twirled in her insides like a ceiling fan. Linda groaned one last time before the blood filled her throat.

"They're *mine*," the woman said. "You can't have them! They're *mine,* you little whore!"

Linda's eyes fluttered closed and when she opened them again the woman's face was skinned. There was only a glimmering, crimson skull. Putrid muscle and sinew twitched as two angry eyes swam in her face, swarming like angry flies as they watched Linda die.

CHAPTER SEVEN

HIS BROTHER WAS SURPRISED TO see him come into the living room.

"Christ, what're you doing down here now?" Joe asked. "You're supposed to be up there fuckin' her." Embarrassment flushed Robbie's face. "I know you blew your load but she was supposed to clean herself up and come back to you for another round."

Robbie looked away. "Well, she didn't."

"Maybe she's still showering," Danny said.

Joe glowered. "I don't hear the water running in the pipes anymore."

"She's not in the bathroom," Robbie said. "I just took a piss in there. The shower was wet but turned off." The three of them looked at each other. "Maybe she left."

Danny shook his head. "We didn't see her come down."

"Her clothes are still in the wash," Joe said, going to the window. "She wouldn't have left naked. Her mom's car is still out there too."

"Then she's somewhere."

They heard a rumble on the stairs and turned to see Horace trotting down, panting happily. He went right to Robbie's side to get a head scratch.

"He sure was barking earlier," Robbie said. "I tried to find where he was but sound really carries in this place. It makes it hard to know where noises are coming from."

"Forget about the damned dog." Joe threw up his hands. "That bitch is somewhere in here. She might be stealin' shit or something. We've gotta find her ass."

They searched for almost an hour, covering every floor, every room. The only sign of Linda they found were her panties crumpled up on the bathroom sink. Robbie was convinced she'd left because she was disgusted with him, but it didn't make sense that she would leave butt-naked and without her car. It was barely 45 degrees out there and the manor was at least a quarter mile off the main road.

"This is ridiculous," Joe said. "What's with all these girls? It's like *God* is cock-blocking us."

"It's really weird," Danny said.

Robbie was glad to hear he was not alone in being spooked by everything that had happened tonight. It made him feel like less of a wuss. That Linda could vanish after Maxine had screamed about seeing blood upstairs was enough to make him want to get out of the house.

"So what do we do?"

Joe grabbed Linda's purse off the counter. "We've got this and her keys are in it. Her clothes are in the dryer. If she wants to tease us with this naked hide-and-go-seek horseshit then fine. When she's through fuckin' around she can throw you a bang and then she can have her stuff back. Until then, to hell with her." He turned around, calling out in the wide-open space. "You hear me, Linda? You ain't going nowhere until you screw my fuckin' brother! You can't hide forever!"

"To hell with this, man," Danny said. "I'm gonna crash upstairs. Maxine and I already tainted the old lady's bed, if you know what I mean. I'll take that one."

"Go ahead. There's like eighty goddamned beds in this place."

Danny shuffled away.

"We're gonna stay *here*?" Robbie asked. The thought made him gulp again.

"That's the whole job."

"But, you and Danny are doing the job, not me. I'd rather go home, man."

"Look, it's late and I'm drunk. You're gonna have to crash here tonight."

"But I don't want to!"

He was surprised at the volume of his own voice. The house had spooked him even more than he'd initially realized. He tried to tell himself haunted houses were just for movies and stupid ghost hunter reality shows, but there was something foreboding about all that had happened, and he a bad feeling it was just a preview of what the house might have in store.

"Would you man up for once?" Joe said. "Pick a bed and get some sleep. I'll get you home in the morning."

"Something's going on here, man. It's creeping me out."

"It's just broads being broads, brother. Get used to it."

"What about all the noises?"

"I'm tired, Robbie, let's just—"

"I saw someone upstairs." He couldn't help it. It just blurted out. "A woman."

"What?"

"In the bathroom."

"Linda?"

"No, it was before she came over, while we were searching the house and the girls were downstairs. She was a grown woman, maybe thirty or so. I'm not sure. I didn't see her face, only her body."

Joe gave him a suspicious look. "Did you take any of that ecstasy?"

"Come on, man. You know me better than that. I wasn't tripping. I saw a woman up there, I swear."

"You talk to her?"

"Well, no. She took off before I could."

"So why didn't you tell me about her before?"

"I didn't think you'd believe me."

His brother laughed. "Well, you got that part right at least." He started toward the living room. "If she's good looking, send her to the third guest bedroom. I'll be waiting."

"Joe! I'm not making this up. Why would I?"

But Joe didn't care. "Take the dog with you when you go to bed. Maybe he'll protect you from the boogeywoman."

Danny lay flat on the mattress and stared at the ceiling, again looking for any sign of the carnage Maxine had sworn to. It wasn't like her to freak out or make up crazy stories. He'd been seeing her on and off for seven months and she'd never had a meltdown like the one he saw tonight. There was nothing wrong with the ceiling. There weren't even spots or stains. It was clear and white—no bumps even. He turned over and switched off the light, moonlight filling the room, giving it the color of gunmetal. Outside a tree branch was swaying. Its skeletal shadow climbed the walls like a big spider. He closed his eyes and pulled the sheet over his shoulders.

As he entered the doorway between consciousness and sleep, images began to dance through his mind like wisps of smoke. They were not quite thoughts and not quite dreams, but they were incredibly vivid.

A teenage girl was in a large bedroom. She was about his age, but he had never seen her before. She was a stranger, and an exceptionally beautiful one. She was sitting cross-legged on the hardwood floor in front of an arrangement of candles. Her eyes were closed, a wide smile on her face. Danny could hear her whispering although her lips barely moved. The words came quick, as if she had memorized them, and she repeated them over and over in an ominous chant. When she was finished, she got up on her knees and Danny saw there was a five-pointed star painted on the floor in front of her, half moons hovering over each point. The girl inched closer and hitched up her nightdress, and blood trickled down from between her legs and speckled the star. Danny felt something cold come over him. The vision was so strong he could smell the rich copper and salt odor of the blood. The girl turned around and faced him. Her eyes snapped opened. They were a lovely, autumnal shade, and as he gazed into them he saw the color shift, changing from brown to orange to blood red. She rose up and he felt a profound sense of fear and tried to back away, but his feet seemed to be stepping through quicksand and the more he struggled against it the deeper he sank.

"I've been a bad girl, Daddy," she said.

He awoke in such a panic he fell out of bed. He looked around for the girl with the crazy eyes but she and her candles were gone. There was only the blue darkness now, but he could feel a presence in the room with him. The cold from his dream state had seemed to carry over into reality.

Breath clouds appeared in the shadows across the room.

Danny went rigid. "Who's there?"

He got no answer, but a pair of feet appeared in the corner, the rest of the body lost in blackness. They were women's feet, with red nail polish and a ring on the pinky toe.

"Who is that?" he asked, his words fast, breathless.

The feet moved closer, revealing smooth legs and velvet vulva. The nude body came into view, followed by a pale face.

"Linda?"

She stood with her head cocked, her eyes black holes in the low light. She licked her lips.

"Where've you been?" he asked. "We looked all over for you."

Linda's shoulders twitched. "I waited in here. For you."

There was something strange about her voice. It sounded raspy, like she was coming down with a cold.

"You waited . . . for me?"

"Yes, Danny. I want you."

She stepped forward and Danny stood at the side of the bed. Her arms wrapped around his neck like white serpents and her large breasts grazed his bare chest, one of her legs riding up his. He touched her, winced. When Danny was a child he had gone to his great aunt's wake, and when his parents forced him to kiss her goodbye, he'd been terrified by how cold she was. Linda was even colder.

"Jesus, you're like ice."

She pushed into him so he sat down on the bed. Straddling him, she took his erection in her frozen hand and stroked. "Then warm me up. You want me, don't you?" It was more of a statement than a question.

"Oh yeah."

"You want to give yourself to me."

"Oh, I'll give it to you, baby."

This was incredible. Linda had wacked him off before but they'd never come close to sex. She wasn't even asking him for any money!

"I am all that you desire," she said. "And because of that, you will surrender yourself to me."

Danny chortled. "Okay. Sure, baby."

He slapped her ass and she hissed like a lioness and put her face in his. It startled him until he felt her hand slip him inside of her. Her sex clenched him like a fist. Even her insides were cold, as if she were a corpse, as if she were his shriveled, dead great aunt.

"Jesus!"

He tired to slip out from under her but she took his wrists and pinned him down, nails digging into his skin. He tried to struggle against her but she was freakishly strong. The blackness of her eyes widened and as they became all pupil her tongue filled his mouth, curling around his own in several loops, tying it up so he couldn't scream. She continued to ride him, viciously, and despite the cold of her body the walls of her vagina flexed and crushed, and his erection grew harder. While there was fear and confusion, a dizzying wave of eroticism had come over him, blocking out all other thoughts. He watched Linda's heavy breasts sway hypnotically above him as her hips rocked. She arched her back and her face fell under a blanket of shadows, and when it came back into the moonlight it was no longer Linda's.

The girl from his vision was on top of him.

The one who rained blood from her pussy onto the pentagram.

CHAPTER EIGHT

KAYLA WISHED SHE'D GONE BACK to the manor after dropping Maxine off, but she'd been too rattled at the time and hadn't felt like partying anymore. Now she worried she may have blown her chance with Joe. She was so disappointed with herself she pulled out her secret shoebox containing her blades, her father's old straight razor, the safety pins, and the matches she sometimes used on the soles of her feet. But she slid it away when she thought of having fresh wounds when she was back in her bathing suit, if she was lucky enough to have Joe ask her back to the manor.

She turned her phone in her hands, wondering if it was too early to call him, wondering if it would seem weird or desperate if she did.

Well, you are desperate, girl.

Maybe she was, but she didn't want to *seem* like it. She wasn't desperate for just anybody. She wanted Joe, and the way he'd touched her leg in the hot tub last night had solidified her infatuation. His bad boy demeanor simply electrified her. Even when he was being a jerk it lured her in. She felt hypnotized by him sometimes and could only hope she didn't seem like a gushing schoolgirl whenever he looked at her too long.

But is he the one you want to give yourself to?

She wasn't sure about that. She felt like it was time for her to lose her virginity. All her friends had, and many of them had been to bed with more than one guy. Hell, Maxine had been screwing around since they were in junior high. Whenever Kayla saw her flirting with boys she was so alluring Kayla found herself thinking of the girl in *The Sound of Music* singing about how she was sixteen going on seventeen. Kayla was certainly old enough for sexual intercourse, but while she'd messed around a little with other boys she had never taken off her bra or panties. And as she'd gotten older the boys were getting less and less satisfied with just making out. They wanted more now, and in a way she did too. But she was nervous. She didn't want anyone to laugh at her for being inexperienced, especially not Joe.

She knew he'd been with other girls. It was in the way he moved and spoke with carefree charisma, the way he didn't have to try to impress girls, how they were just naturally drawn to him. His sexuality was unrelenting, unlike the quivering doubt and bumbling hands of some other boys. And his fingers moved with purpose, as if they were tailor-made to caress her.

She didn't want to disappoint him.

She didn't want to look stupid.

She'd waited so long now. Being a virgin was rather scary.

The morning light was cruel. Joe's only defense against it was a wake-up beer. Nothing better for a hangover. He stood in the kitchen and chugged it down, bitterly recalling all of last night's nonsense.

He blinked at the empty counter. He had forgotten to take Linda's purse upstairs, but when he looked for it, it was gone.

Shit.

He went to the window and his suspicions were confirmed. Her car was gone. And she'd already taken their money.

She is so dead.

He crushed his beer can and slung it across the counter like a live grenade. Robbie appeared with the stupid dog beside him, his hair a California tumbleweed, puffy rings under his eyes.

"You look like how I feel," Joe said. "Sleep okay?"

"Not really. Laid there for a while before finally passing out. Had weird dreams too. Really vivid ones."

He didn't elaborate and Joe was grateful. Nothing was more boring than listening to someone else describe a dream. Joe had had some rather bizarre ones last night as well, equally vivid, but he didn't bring them up.

"I slept like a rock," he said. "You happen to see Linda before she left?"

"No. She's gone?"

"Yeah, the bitch bolted."

The dog made a deep whine.

"What's his problem?"

"Horace is just hungry," Robbie said. "I am too."

"Why do you keep calling him Horace?"

Robbie shrugged and gave him a shy smile.

"Aw, jeez." Sometimes it seemed the kid was never going to grow up. "Well look, don't get too attached. He doesn't belong to us. Right now someone's out there searching for their little Bo-Bo or Rex here."

Robbie made himself a bowl of cereal and gave one to Horace as well. Joe skipped breakfast and went out onto the patio for a smoke. A cloud had drowned out the sun and he was able to open his eyes to the copper valley and mist-cloaked mountain beyond it. It was almost ten. He could call Kayla soon, play the good guy by telling her what a good time he'd had and fake concern for Maxine. Maybe he could get her back to the house tonight so they could get back into that hot tub. He thought the odds were good. Danny would want to get Maxine over too, but hopefully that crazy bitch would still want nothing to do with the place. He didn't need her blowing another opportunity to get Kayla upstairs.

He thought about the party he wanted to throw. Not a little one like last night but a real rager. With Halloween approaching, it would be cool to make it a costume party. That kind of shindig got people more excited to come, and better yet it encouraged the girls to dress up in the hooker outfits that passed for costumes these days. Next weekend would be ideal. They would just have to get the word out at school.

It suddenly occurred to him that Danny had practice at noon, so he went back inside to wake him up. When he reached his bedroom, he found it empty. He called out to him in the hall as he made his way toward the bathroom. He wasn't in there either.

I'm getting sick of this crap, he thought.

"You're gonna be late for practice, fat shit!"

He hopped down the stairs in frustration. When he looked outside, Danny's car was still parked in the driveway.

I'm getting really *sick of this crap.*

Robbie was still in the kitchen, giving Horace a second helping of Cheerios.

"You see Danny around?"

"No. He's not upstairs?"

There was a twinge of fear at the corner of Robbie's eyes.

"Son of a bitch," Joe said.

"He's missing, isn't he?"

From her suite, she looked out upon the city skyline and thought about her husband. Gladys had only picked at the room service breakfast. She was too nervous. It had only been one night but that was all it took, unless her daughter was playing games. Lord, how she did love to play her little games.

If only her father could control her.

But as strict as Arthur was, he'd never been able to. Not even back then, before the terrible night when Gladys had walked into her daughter's bedroom and her slippers had filled with blood.

So much blood. Oh, Hazel, what have you done?

She shook the memory from her mind and picked up her cup of tea, enjoying the warmth of the cup in her hands. Her eyes left the window and she looked at the plain beige walls of the suite.

They're so still. So quiet.

She turned back to the window and tried not to think about anything at all.

Joe was just explaining to him that Danny must have run off with Linda when the door came open and the football player walked in. Horace left his bowl of cereal to go sniff at him, which surprised Robbie. From Horace's voracious appetite he would have never expected anything would pull the dog away from food.

"Where the hell have you been?" Joe asked.

"Just out walking." Danny's face was ashen. He seemed smaller somehow, thinner. He looked as if he hadn't slept at all. "I wanted some fresh air."

"You look like a bucket of shit, man."

"Not feeling so good."

He shuffled into the kitchen and went into the fridge, and when

Joe told him he'd taken the last beer he shut it and leaned against the counter. Robbie thought he looked like an extra in a zombie movie. It was almost comical.

Joe shook his head. "You know you've got practice, right?"

"To hell with it."

"What? Dude, you guys are playing Polk next Friday."

"I'm not going."

"Coach is gonna cream you."

"Coach can suck a fart outta my ass."

Robbie snorted a laugh.

"Hey," Joe said to Danny, patting his shoulder. "It's your funeral." He went to the dish with the keys in it and tossed them to Danny. "If you're gonna ditch we should at least make the most of it. You think your sister will buy us more beer?"

"Probably."

"Cool."

Robbie turned to Danny. "Did you happen to see Linda?"

His brow furrowed as if in deep thought. "No. I didn't. But, I think I dreamed about her though."

"Oh, really?"

"Yeah. I dreamed she came into my room and wanted to bang me."

"Well, if she went though with it, it *must* have been a dream," Joe said.

Danny looked distant. "It was weird though."

"How so?" Robbie asked.

"Because it was her, but it *wasn't* her. And it seemed so real, like it couldn't be a dream. I mean ... I could *feel* her body. I could smell her skin and taste her lips."

There was a silent moment and Robbie sat there with his fists clenched. He didn't know why he was so anxious.

"It wasn't like any dream I've ever had," Danny said. "It was like something totally ... *different.*"

"Man," Joe said. "The two of you are giving me a headache."

"So you didn't see her leave?" Robbie asked. "'Cause it looks like she did. Her car and stuff are gone."

Danny's brow furrowed deeper. He seemed lost within some invisible world, his mouth hanging open as if to speak but no words coming out. Horace sat in front of Danny then, looking up into his face. The dog stared and gave a soft bark, followed by grumbling. Danny shuddered.

"No," Danny said suddenly. "I didn't see nothin'."

CHAPTER NINE

HE WENT TO PRACTICE AFTER all, though late.

Coach was more than a little peeved with him, and in front of the rest of the team he gave him a lecture about the importance of the upcoming game, telling him to get his head out of his ass before his sphincter cut off all the oxygen to his brain. Then they resumed practice, and Danny went into human barricade mode, slamming back the offensive line and charging the football chutes.

He was extra aggressive today, determined to let no one pass, and he smashed into the pads with the force of a battering ram. He felt like a bull charging a matador who had taken a fatal misstep. Despite how shitty he'd felt earlier, there was a strength to him beyond what he was used to; he was powerful, agile and hyper-alert, correctly guessing the offense's moves with each play. He sacked their quarterback three times and made an interception he took all the way home.

Coach Brown gave him a smack on the ass. "Looks like you paid attention to what I was saying after all."

When practice was over he skipped a locker room shower and headed for his car. His mind was clearer than it had been that morning. He'd been in a sleepy funk earlier, but now his brain seemed to be operating again, and as he reached his car he had a sudden flashback of driving someone else's. Had it been in his dream? It must have. And yet the memory seemed so real. But why would he have forgotten it until now? He flashed on being behind the wheel of a Pontiac, driving through the violet light that welcomed dawn. He searched his mind for more details but it all seemed fragmented, a nebulous, receding memory.

A hand fell onto his shoulder, startling him.

"Easy, big boy," Maxine said. "It's just your lil' ol' girlfriend. I was watching you play from the bleachers. I guess you didn't see me."

"Guess not."

They kissed. He wasn't sure why he'd been so jumpy.

"Ugh, you're sweaty."

"You would be too."

It was a crisp day and the wind felt good as it sent a pack of dead leaves scratching across the pavement. Maxine was wearing a tight sweater that accentuated her breasts and he couldn't help but think about finishing what they'd started the night before. The thought of sex brought his dream of Linda to mind, and when he thought of how her face had changed he went cold.

"Sorry about last night," she said. "I don't know what was wrong with me. I think maybe the molly and booze mixed together might've been a lousy idea."

"No big deal. We all have bad trips sometimes."

"It just seemed so real, you know?"

He did. All too well.

She wrapped her arms around his neck. "Anyway, I was thinking I could make it up to you." She winked and licked her lips. "It's not always unsportsmanlike to go below the belt."

He liked the sound of that.

"I'm still watching the house."

"I wanted out last night, but I'm okay with going back. It's a really nice place, and besides, we can do things there without worrying about either of our parents hearing us."

"It's no big deal," Maxine told her.

But it was to Kayla.

She'd never spent the night with boys. She didn't think she was ready for that, even if there was no sex involved and she got her own room. The house certainly had enough of them. Still, she felt uneasy about it, despite Maxine's master plan of telling one another's parents they'd be staying at the other's house. Neither of their folks were likely to check on that. They were latchkey girls. She wasn't really worried about getting away with it, but the concept made her nervous. Agreeing to it seemed to *imply* sex, and things were too new with Joe. She certainly didn't want to give him the wrong impression.

"I don't know, Max. Maybe we could just hang out till late and then head back."

Maxine huffed. "Oh come on, don't be such a geek. We should take advantage of them having that huge house while we can. I want to go back in that pool and hot tub. Don't you?"

She did. She remembered Joe's hand on her thigh.

"Besides," Maxine continued. "Joe likes you. He wants to see you again."

Her heart fluttered. "He said that?"

"He didn't have to. It was written all over his face. Plus, Danny said we were both invited to this little sleepover. That says it all."

Maybe it wasn't such a big deal. She was almost eighteen and could make her own decisions. And she could also say no if Joe tried to push things further than she wanted to go. She wondered just how far her limit would be. It might surprise her.

"Well . . ." she said, warming up to the idea without committing.

"Don't make me go alone. All that guy talk will bore me to tears."

They laughed.

"Oh, all right."

That afternoon a police detective came by the manor.

Joe heard tires on the gravel outside and when he went to the window and saw the white patrol car pulling up he felt a hollow sensation in his stomach, as if his guts had just been scooped out.

He hated cops. He'd been harassed by them ever since he turned thirteen. He was a delinquent, but that wasn't always the cause of their bullying. Sometimes it was just the spiked bracelets he wore, or his shredded jeans, or just because he was walking alone at night. Cops were like any other group of people—a few good ones and a whole lot of rotten ones. In his mind, the bullying jocks of high school were the kinds of dicks who grew up to be cops; egotistical, power-hungry assholes who got off on having authority over others. These pigs made him sick.

The officer got out of his car. He was a heavyset man in his late forties—thick neck, strong jaw line, fat nose. *He's a walking stereotype,* Joe thought, *a TV series cop.* But he was intimidating nonetheless, particularly because Joe had no idea what he was doing here.

Maybe Snowden had asked the local police to check up on them. The idea pissed him off, but it was possible. She had enough money to get them to do it, and she was old and a county native. She probably had connections to people in the department or on the city council.

Maybe someone had seen Danny's Oldsmobile out front and thought someone was squatting or ripping the place off. The rusted car did look entirely out of place against the backdrop of the sprawling manor.

These were the only reasons he could come up with for the pig being there. He hoped one of them was right and he wouldn't be dealing with some berating, law and order bullshit for long. The girls would be by in a few hours and he and Danny were supposed to go shopping for booze and snacks.

The doorbell rang.

Danny was showering upstairs and Robbie was walking the dog. This was all on him. He told himself to stop being a pussy and went to the door. When he opened it, the officer stood there with his sunglasses still on. He didn't smile.

"Good afternoon," the cop said.

"Hello, officer."

"I'm Lieutenant Fred Buchinsky. Do you know why I'm here?"

Am I supposed to?

"Um, no."

The Lieutenant put his hands on his hips. "Linda Lelane left her house on Franklin Avenue at 6:30 last night to go to a concert with friends. According to them, she came here after the show."

Joe gulped. Did they know about how they paid her to bang Robbie? If they did that could mean jail time, whether they were minors or not, couldn't it? He considered lying to him about it, saying she hadn't come over at all, but that would be a mistake. The police were bound to find out he was bullshitting. As soon as they talked to Robbie they'd know the truth. Even if he asked his brother to lie for him, the kid just sucked at it. He'd never been able to get one over with their mom, or teachers, or anyone else. That's how the whole school knew he was a virgin; the stink of his bullshit was clear and pungent.

"Yeah," Joe said. "She came by for a while, to hang out."

"How long was she here?"

"I don't know. Maybe two in the morning. I didn't see her leave."

"She come here alone?"

"Yeah."

"Who else was here?"

"Just my little brother, Robbie, and our friend Danny. We're house sitting."

"Yes, I know."

Can't hide anything from these bastards.

Buchinsky took out a note pad and began jotting things down. "Did she say where she'd be going when she left?"

"No, sir."

"Did she seem distressed?"

What the hell is this about?

"Not to me," Joe said.

The cop squinted, his lips pursed, making a drop of sweat appear at the base of Joe's spine. "Well, Ms. Lelane never came home last night, and this is the last place she was known to be."

Joe blinked and took a small step back. "Oh, I see."

"Do you mind if I look around?"

He did, but he couldn't say no. "Sure, come on in."

Joe moved aside, letting the officer in. Buchinsky looked around and whistled.

"This is some house," he said.

"Yeah. I jumped at the chance to watch it."

"How long is Gladys out of town for?"

"You know her, huh?"

"I'd say all of the police force knows her, son. After what happened, who could forget?" Joe wasn't sure what he was talking about and it must have shown on his face. "Before your time."

"What happened?"

The officer ignored his question. "I'm going to look around here. I hear running water. Who's upstairs?"

"Uh, my buddy, Danny Knox."

"One of our star linebackers. I think they might go all-city this year. Coach Brown has really put a strong team together."

Joe didn't give a fucking shit. He never went to the games or even watched pro sports. He found it all incredibly dull, and thought people who did enjoy them were mere sheep who preferred to be told what to like by the status quo rather than form their own tastes and identity. When he saw a baseball cap with a team logo from any sport, he saw the dope wearing it as someone who'd been branded by their home state, labeling them as effectively brainwashed and easy to manipulate.

"Yeah," he said without enthusiasm.

He wasn't sure if Buchinsky wanted an escort through the house, but went with him anyway. He thought about the weed in his coat upstairs and tried not to sweat because of it. He hoped Danny hadn't left any goddamned molly lying around.

They walked through the living room and the library, the cop whistling as they entered each room. He ran his fingers over the rows of books and gazed all around with childlike wonder.

"I'd love to have a reading room like this. I'm a bookworm, you know? I must read around seventy books a year."

"That's impressive."

"Oh, well. They're mostly just fun fiction. Nothing too dense or challenging."

"What do you like?" Joe asked, trying to keep the talk friendly and make a good impression.

"Scary stuff. Stephen King, Charles L. Grant, Graham Masterton. My son turned me on to this guy named Paul Tremblay. Kept me up all night."

A cop with a taste for horror. It seemed somehow out of place. But then again, Stephen King was a household name and had probably outsold the Bible at this point, so maybe more people were fans of the genre than one might think.

"Of course, my wife hates it," Buchinksy continued. "She only likes romance novels; *Swashbuckling Bodybuilders of the High Seas*, that sort of crap. Between that and her stupid reality shows, I sometimes wonder how we ended up together."

Joe was surprised by the cop's candor. It was as if they were sitting on bar stools instead of doing a routine police search. That was fine with him. If he stayed on the cop's good side, all the better, right?

They went upstairs. The bathroom door was partly open, spewing steam. Buchinsky went toward it and knocked.

"You decent?" he asked, winking at Joe.

"Who the hell is that?" Danny asked.

"This is Lieutenant Fred Buchinsky of the sheriff's department. I'd like to talk to you about Linda Lelane."

Once Danny was dressed they walked through the remainder of the house together, Buchinsky taking his time despite how large the manor was. He even checked the patio and basement. When they came back inside he went through some basic questions with them about Linda, such as what she was wearing, what her mood was, and anything she might have said that would give him an idea where she might have run off to. They hadn't been able to give him much, but it didn't seem to anger or annoy him. He just kept on writing.

"So," Danny asked, "she really is missing?"

Something about this news hit him harder than it should have. It was unsettling.

"Well," Buchinsky said, "nobody seems to know where she is and she hasn't been answering her cell phone. But we're not calling out the search and rescue dogs just yet. She had her mother's Pontiac and she could have gone anywhere."

Pontiac? Danny felt the same chill he'd felt when he'd remembered his dream of driving the car.

Buchinsky grinned. "Truth of the matter is, when most teen girls disappear it's usually just for a day or so. They run off with a boy or take off after having a spat with their parents, then come back home when they run out of cash and get sick of sleeping in their car." He looked at the boys and his grin faded. "Of course, that doesn't mean we won't follow any possible leads." He handed each of them a card with his name and number on it. "You think of anything that might be helpful and you let me know, all right?"

"Yes, sir," Joe said, and Danny agreed.

"Good. You boys have a nice day now. Enjoy that pool. I know if I were you, I'd invite a couple of girls over for a swim."

He winked and was gone.

CHAPTER TEN

THE SETTING SUN CREATED A dazzling light show between the trees, sending tangerine slivers flashing by as she drove toward the manor house. After the blistering summer, Kayla was enjoying the cool air blowing through her open window. Maxine was fiddling with the radio, trying to find a station playing music instead of just blasting frenzied commercials or obnoxious talk shows. She finally settled on the classic rock station—Guns N' Roses's *Sweet Child O' Mine*—as they rolled up and down the hills, enjoying the pretty fall setting all around them. In the eastern sky stars had begun to freckle, encircling a yellow moon as it climbed over the tree line, a ghostly second earth.

Out of nowhere, Maxine asked, "So, you gonna fuck him?"

"Maxine!"

"What? You can tell me."

Kayla couldn't believe how blunt her friend was being. They were close and had been since junior high, but some things were private. "I don't want to talk about that."

"Fine," she said. "But you don't know what you're missing."

Maxine had been sexually active since junior high. She was very comfortable with her sexuality and tended to dress more provocatively than Kayla did, much as she was dressed now in her tight blouse, tighter mini-skirt, and a pair of leather, high-heeled boots. Her lipstick shone, eyes mysterious beneath a dusting of blue eye-shadow, devastatingly sexy.

Kayla stirred behind the wheel. "I'm not even really dating Joe. Not yet."

"That doesn't matter."

"It does to me."

Maxine looked in the mirror above her, checking her makeup again. "Suit yourself."

They drove on, passing the McLeary farm. Rows upon rows of pumpkins lined the field and Kayla remembered how she and her parents used to go to the McLeary's pumpkin festival every year to pick theirs out, get some fresh-popped popcorn, and hop on the hayride that wound through the farm's hundred plus acres. She missed that, amongst other things they no longer did as a family. It made her feel bad for her little sister, who had never gotten to enjoy those traditions. By the time Patricia was born Dad had already dedicated all of his time to his corporate retail career, sometimes working over seventy hours per week. Patricia was growing up without seeing much of her father and was missing out on the fourth of July and Labor Day vacations Kayla had once enjoyed with her folks, when they would ride boogie boards off the beaches of Long Island and listen to the thunder of the tide beneath the boardwalk as they carried ice cream cones to the Ferris wheel. Patricia wouldn't share in fireworks shows over late night rivers, country fairs in lush springs, or jack-o-lantern carvings in the anticipation of Halloween. These moments had created some of Kayla's most precious memories and she pined for them with a painful nostalgia beyond her years.

"I saw Danny practice today," Maxine said. "I think they might go all the way this year with him on the team." Her eyes and smile went wide. "You should have seen him today. He was a monster!"

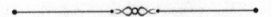

They ate pizza and everyone but Robbie drank beers. Joe thought it would be funny to fill a bowl with one for Horace, but Kayla kept him from doing so. They'd returned to the pool, much to Maxine's delight. Kayla watched her swimming from the hot tub. She had impeccable form, like she'd been born with fins. Kayla, on the other hand, was more of a sloppy swimmer. She couldn't dive or do the breaststroke. She was about as graceful as Horace when it came to water.

In the pool, Danny and the dog were playing catch with a tennis ball and Horace simply could not get enough of it. He retrieved as well as a Labrador and paddled back to Danny each time he recovered the ball, panting with joy. Kayla liked seeing Danny play with him. It revealed a boyish side to the football player. Joe, however, showed no interest in Horace. He was too busy showing interest in her—parts of her, anyway. He kept glancing at her chest as it floated on the brim of the bubbles. That didn't bother her so much, as long as he looked at her face while they were talking, which he did. His hand had returned and it made her feel giddy and playful, and so when he leaned in for a kiss she tilted her head back to receive him. But when she felt his hand move over her breast she pushed it away. Suddenly he pulled back, ending the kiss. Kayla instantly kicked herself. He'd made the first move and she'd been a prude. It wasn't that she was really against making out with him, far from it. She just didn't want to do it in front of the others. She wondered if she should say she was sorry. Joe had gone back to staring at the night sky behind the screened overhang, no longer looking at her. She decided to take his hand. He didn't pull away. Instead, he gripped hers, and she felt a surge of relief. She hadn't blown it entirely. She put his hand back on her thigh, higher up this time, and he smiled at her.

It was only a matter of time before Maxine and Danny went upstairs, and after that Joe would shoo away his little brother. She anticipated their alone time with a combination of nervousness and arousal that crept across all of her private, secret places. The idea of being alone with him, still half-nude from swimming, made her feel energized. She was a virgin, but not without a normal female appetite.

Robbie was once again sitting in the shadows of the patio with only his face showing, glowing blue from the light of the pool. His eyes followed Maxine, never straying. The boy was so shy and withdrawn. Kayla wondered if he'd ever had a girlfriend.

Clouds had formed and swallowed the stars like an angry deity, and the moon that had risen was now just a faint blur. Because it was the Halloween season cable networks had been showing a lot of horror movies, and the other night she'd watched *The Howling*, and now the sight of the smoky moon gave her an unexpected sense of unease. She tried to shake it off, telling herself she was being immature, but the feeling remained, clinging to her like a tick.

A moment later drizzle began to fall, and then the sky opened up and everybody got out of the water, fleeing from the rain even though they were all soaking wet. They wrapped themselves in towels and headed inside, Robbie dragging behind as he dried off the dog. Horace nuzzled into the towel as well as Robbie's jeans, but he didn't seem to mind. Kayla found that very sweet. She'd grown to like Joe's little brother.

Danny wrapped his arm around Maxine, the arm almost as big around as her head. "I'm kidnapping this one." He picked her up at the waist and slung her over his shoulder. Maxine squealed. He winked at Joe and Kayla. "Yous have fun now."

His wet feet squished across the floor and they were off. She heard him clunking up the stairs as Maxine laughed and laughed, Danny singing Rick James' *Super Freak*. Joe snickered as he slid his arm around her waist and she leaned back into him. His bare chest was cool and his wet hair dripped onto her neck.

"Hey," he whispered in her ear. "Maybe we should let Robbie have a little alone time with his new dog."

His hand ran over her bottom.

"We could do that," she said. "I just don't want you to, you know . . . expect anything."

He looked at her. "What do you mean?"

"Let's just take it slow, okay? I'm fine with fooling around a little, but I'm not ready to do everything."

He smiled but she could see the slight annoyance in his eyes.

"Slow," he said. "No problem. I can do slow."

Hazel could hear them from inside the walls.

The moans of the brunette she had chased away the night before and the rhythmic groaning of the big boy. In the other room, the blond girl was breathing heavy as the other boy sucked on her neck.

She grimaced.

This was *her* house; that made them *her* boys.

These girls had their schools and social centers, their dances and clubs and parks. They had all the freedom Hazel had been robbed of. They could find other boys anywhere. How *dare* they try to take these away from her in her own house! It wasn't right, and she'd already given the dark-haired one fair warning.

The whore she'd killed in the shower had been given no warning at all. That was because she had gone after Hazel's very favorite boy of all—the young one, the virgin. This had filled her with a rage so hot and fierce she'd been reminded of the fury she'd felt toward her father.

He was the one who had made it impossible to have normal romances, to splish and splash in lakes with kids her own age the way this group had played in the pool, or to walk hand-in-hand with a boyfriend who picked her flowers and made her mix tapes. She'd never had what every American girl was supposed to have, all because her old man was a bible-brainwashed puritan who would never let her leave the house out of fear of having her mind, body and soul tainted by heathens and atheists. He'd been overly strict, painfully so, and she would never forgive him for wasting her youth in this prison. The house was magnificent, but it held her against her will, and no amount of splendor could compensate for the lack of the very basic freedoms these girls took for granted.

He'd taken it all away from her.

That's why she had taken so much away from him.

Another moan came from the brunette, and Hazel dug her nails into her palms, drawing black blood. She wanted to gut the little bitch and string her intestines down the banister like garland. But she couldn't do that in front of the big boy, Danny. That would send him fleeing in terror, along with the rest of them, and then Hazel would be alone again, crying in the darkness until Mother came home.

She had to be careful. She'd already gotten greedy the night before, collecting the whore's soul and harnessing her image so she could take her form. She'd been unable to wait to take Danny deep inside of her, to taste of his hard desire, and as a result she'd nearly ruined everything. The sudden disappearance of the whore could have been disastrous. It was lucky she'd made love to Danny in that case. It had enabled her to coax him into a spell for a little while and have him take the whore's things and drive her car a mile into the woods. The spell was only temporary (she had not taken full possession of him) but it lasted just long enough to make it appear the whore had left on her own. Still, it'd been a close call, and she told herself to take her time despite the burning within her loins, the hunger of her throat and the manic cravings that gave her rabid foam.

Better to savor it.

There was no telling when she would have such a chance again. Mother had only brought her these boys because it was the right time, the season of the witch. Hazel wondered which side of her the boys would prefer—her petite, teenage form, from when she'd first

mastered the art, or her voluptuous, adult form, which was neither
alive nor dead.

CHAPTER ELEVEN

THE BITCH JUST WASN'T GOING to put out.

He'd gotten as far as getting Kayla to take off her top but she pushed his hand away both times when he went for the bottom. He'd known he wasn't going to get her to go all the way, but he'd expected a little more than just making out. What was this, junior-fucking-high? She wouldn't even touch his dick, let alone suck it.

Joe backed off her, tired of just kissing and touching her tits. He sat on the edge of the bed, trying not to pout and failing. It'd been too long since he'd made it with a girl. He was getting too eager, pushy; he knew that, but at the same time felt like he had to be the aggressor if things were ever going to go anywhere. You had to push a chick a little bit. If they could resist at first then they wouldn't feel like a slut despite what they did once the panties dropped.

But some girls said no and meant it.

Girls like Kayla.

"So," he said, snarky, "wanna watch TV or something?"

He had to let her know he was dissatisfied but didn't want to come out and say it. A little guilt went a long way and it was very obvious she was seriously into him, far more so than he was into her. He wanted to have sex with her, whereas Kayla wanted to *date* him. This gave him an edge over her, making her easier to manipulate. If he worked at her emotions (rather than just her body) he would eventually get the bottom piece of that bikini off. He just didn't want it to take all fucking week.

"I'm just not ready," Kayla said from behind him, pulling the blanket up under her chin. "I hope you're not disappointed."

He could work with this.

"It's just that I thought you were into me," he said.

"I am! I really am." She scooted to the edge of the bed to be next to him and took his hand. "I really like you, Joe."

He sighed for effect. "I just feel like you keep pushing me away."

Kayla's eyes dropped.

Gotcha.

"I'm sorry," she said.

"It's fine," he said coldly, without smiling. It was not given off with a shrug or a laugh. It was the tone of a fed-up spouse in a tired, redundant battle, the same *it's fine* he'd heard so often from his mother when she was either disgusted or defeated. "It's fine, I just thought, you know . . ."

He purposely trailed off, letting her fill in her own blanks. She looked bottomed out now, like she'd been winning at a craps table in Vegas but had gotten just a little too greedy and lost it all in one roll of the dice. He could see the regret in her eyes.

"You sure you're not mad?" she asked.

"No." It was true enough. "Just disappointed, like you said."

Kayla excused herself to the bathroom but not because she needed to use it. She just needed to cry. That's how mad at herself she was. Tears came to her not just when she was sad or moved by something emotional like a romantic movie. She cried whenever she got frustrated, especially with herself, just as she was now.

She sat on the toilet and tried to be quiet as she sobbed, but the bathroom was large and echoed every sniffle, even with the faucet running to drown it out. She only hoped no one was close enough to the door to hear her.

Idiot. You're such an idiot. You're gonna blow this if you don't make more of an effort.

She was still in her bathing suit, the top back on, and she looked at the scars on her arms. She got off the toilet and went to the drawers under the sink. There were scissors, but she needed something sharper, something that could make a quick, clean cut that wouldn't bleed for too long. She would have to make the incision somewhere other than her arms, somewhere she could keep hidden from the others, even Joe, who had gotten nearly all of her clothes off.

You should have let him take the bottom off too. What would have been the harm? He just wanted to touch her there, and it wasn't like she didn't want him to. Well, to be honest, she did and yet she didn't. His hands had felt so good over the rest of her body, his fingertips gently raking her stomach and pinching at her nipples; having him touch her in the same place she sometimes touched herself would probably be nothing short of amazing, maybe even life changing.

But that was where the real fear came from.

She just didn't feel ready to take such a huge plunge, not even with a guy she was crazy about, especially not this early. But she so wanted to be with him, so wanted to make it work. She hated that he felt as if she was pushing him away. Perhaps she had physically, but not emotionally. But with guys there was rarely a difference. It wasn't Joe's fault for feeling snubbed. *She'd* done that. *She'd* made him feel unwanted while she was trying to get him to be interested in her. It would be funny if it weren't so pathetic.

Such an idiot.

In the top drawer she found toothpaste, a bag of floss swords, and some disposable razors. She took out a fresh one and used the scissors to snap off the plastic and free the blade, and then went into the shower with it and sat down on the bench. It would be easier to clean up blood in there. She pulled down her bathing suit bottom and ran the blade just above her vulva, through the top of the blond tuft of hair. The pressure in her chest gave way to a hollowness that let her breathe again. The cut was sharp, clean, and the blood came quickly. There was more than she'd expected. She'd gone too deep again. Taking the showerhead, she sprayed down the wound. While the tears still rolled down her cheeks, her body stopped heaving and her nose dried. The tightness that had made her face ache went slack, and a sense of calm came over her, as soothing and serene as a summer breeze, and even the shame she felt for hurting herself couldn't outweigh the quick relief it provided.

Behind the tile of the shower's wall, something thudded softly.

She heard a quiet sound like a woman's voice. It sounded like a moan of pleasure. She thought of Maxine, but she and Danny's room was all the way down the hall. This noise was coming from the other side of the wall.

She put her hand up to the tile, still holding the razor blade. It made a smear on the tile so she reached for the showerhead to wash it off, but when she looked again the blood had disappeared, as if the cracks in the tile had absorbed it all in the split second she looked away.

The water turned ice cold and Kayla jumped out. She stuffed a bit of toilet paper between the cut and her bikini bottom to stop the bleeding and got out of the bathroom as fast as she could, trotting down the hallway to find her friends.

Downstairs, Robbie was passed out on the couch.

Maxine smiled. The kid was cute. A dork, but cute.

Normally she tried to avoid late-night snacks, being weight conscious even though she had no need to be, but all that sex had given her an appetite. Danny had dozed off. She'd heard Kayla and Joe talking quietly in the other room but didn't want to disturb them. It was high time Kayla stopped being such a fuddy-duddy and went all the way. It would be good for her. It would finally launch her into full womanhood and Maxine would feel like she was hanging out with an equal instead of with a girl who was just a hair above playing with dolls. She knew her judgment of Kayla was a little harsh, but she couldn't help but find her lack of sexual activity immature and a little irritating. It made her feel like she was some sort of tramp by comparison.

She giggled thinking of what she'd just done for Danny with her mouth and anus. She'd grown to enjoy the latter now that she'd learned to relax.

Maybe I am a tramp, but I know what I like and I'm not afraid to go after it.

In the cupboard she found a box of Ritz and a jar of peanut butter. When she closed the door the Rottweiler was there, staring up at her. She gasped. The dog had seemingly appeared out of nowhere. Once the initial shock wore off, it was almost cute. He must have heard the pantry open and come running in the hope of scraps.

"Oh," she teased, "piggy wants a cracker, huh?"

The dog growled and Maxine stopped.

Shit.

She was alone with it. The closest person was Robbie, but he was back in the living room. Besides, he was a runt. She would have a better chance of fighting off the dog than he would. Still, he seemed to have formed a bond with it. Maybe he could get it under control.

"Um, Robbie?"

Why the fuck hadn't they gotten rid of this fucking mutt?

She took the open jar of peanut butter and held it out to him as an offering. Though she knew little about dogs, she did know they were all crazy for peanut butter.

All but this one.

He snapped at her, his teeth nipping the jar as she withdrew.

"Robbie!"

The dog was snarling. Drool hung from his mouth. His yellow teeth flashed, and there was something about his eyes now, something off. They looked different in the soft light of the kitchen, almost red.

"Robbie! Help me!"

There was a sudden rumbling of the walls that wasn't thunder, and the sound of it brought the horror she'd seen last night back into the front of her mind.

Blood. Gore. Eyes.

The dog barked and bucked, his front paws coming off the ground with each snap of his jaws. He wasn't jumping on her, but he soon would be. Maxine was about to scream.

Robbie came into the kitchen, rubbing his eyes.

The dog went silent and immediately lost interest in her. It went to Robbie, his stubby tail wagging happily as if he hadn't been vicious just seconds ago.

"What's going on?" Robbie asked.

He looked at her and his eyes went wide.

She'd forgotten she was wearing only her bra and panties.

"We need to get that dog out of here," she said.

"What? Why?"

"He was about to attack me."

Robbie actually laughed. "What?"

"I'm not kidding. Didn't you hear him growling and barking at me?"

"I heard him bark, but look at him. He's harmless."

He scratched under the dog's jowls and it slobbered on him as its hind leg began to kick uncontrollably.

Maxine stewed. "Just keep him away from me. We need to find out who the fuck he belongs to. I mean, we don't know shit about him. He could be rabid or something."

Robbie started to laugh again but swallowed it when she shot him a hateful look. "Okay. I'll try and keep him out of your hair."

"See that you do."

She took the snacks and headed upstairs, the dog watching her until she was out of sight.

Silent flashes of lightning gave her pale snapshots of the bedroom. The shadows stretched to the ceiling, moving as if headlights were driving down the road even though the house was too far away from it to be affected by passing cars.

Kayla wanted to wake Joe, but didn't dare.

They were in the same bed, even though they hadn't gone any further. He seemed to have lost interest and she was too afraid to initiate anything. He'd drunk another beer and passed out, and she shut off the light to try and get some rest. Tonight had been more stressful than fun, and she was ready for it to be over.

But the lightning kept her on edge, just like the shadows that seemed to move. They did so in short bursts, just enough to make her doubt what she had seen. They were quick, so it was hard for her to trace what was causing them. She told herself there must be some external light source causing it to happen, but couldn't think of what. The window faced pitch-black forest. The shadows seemed unnatural, alive and trying to hide that fact.

She drew the blanket up higher.

Beside her, Joe's occasional snores helped drag her back to reality, and when she watched him sleep she didn't see the shadows creeping. But that was more frightening to her because she knew they were there even when she wasn't watching. As long as she watched, they couldn't fall across her. She wasn't sure why but she didn't want that. The thought chilled her.

She chose to stare out the window, looking at the treetops swishing like animal tails. She could just make out the clouds that embossed the sky, and when the lightning flashed she could see through them like an X-ray. It was time for the world to sleep, but the night was alive, feverish. It whirled with its own dark power, the trees crackling like radio static, the storm clouds devouring the sky with hungry tongues, the electric strobes energizing the night's very essence, giving it an edge as sharp and tantalizing as the razor when it ripped through her flesh.

Kayla's chest rose and fell. A moan escaped her throat. The night stirred, almost beckoning. She rose from the sheets, dressed in her jeans and sweatshirt now, grabbed her jacket and slipped into her shoes. Even as she walked downstairs she could hear the call of the black thicket outside, and when she made it out to the porch she walked to the screen door and out into the yard facing the unflinching shadow of the mountain. The night thrummed, trees shaking like flailing limbs, leaves crackling like burning wicker, dried grass writhing into whips. A cold wind kissed her and her teeth began to chatter, but still she walked on, toward the lure of the woods. There was something within them, something dangerous yet beautiful. She could not see, hear, or smell it; she could only feel it, just as one feels the presence of someone lurking over their shoulder. The soft fuzz on her flesh stood erect and the smell of something earthy and pungent struck her. With each step the air grew colder and drier. It caressed her like the hands of a lover, slithering up the cuff of her jeans to find all of her private places. Another moan escaped her, even though she hadn't intended it to.

And then she saw them.

They moved behind the trees in shadows somehow darker than the night itself. They were spindly and tall, their legs birdlike, arms swinging by their sides like giant sloths. They moved soundlessly through the piles of dead leaves, not even crackling them, and they were quick, darting from tree to tree with the agility of frogs.

Kayla held her breath and did not move.

The shapes shifted in the thicket. She couldn't tell if they'd spotted her but knew in an instant it was they who had roused her from bed, entrancing her somehow. They were hypnotic as they flowed through the woods as if swimming through the air, almost impossibly graceful, their bodies all long shadows.

Kayla trotted backward, still watching the trees, and when she was sure they weren't coming after her she turned and ran back up the hill toward the patio, slamming and locking the screen door behind her. She stumbled over the mat at her feet and barely caught herself before crashing into the pavement.

Groaning, she got to her knees and saw a different shadow, this one floating beneath the surface of the pool like a dead body bound by chains. She gasped and bolted upright, her body chilled and taut.

The shadow was more human in form than the ones in the woods. It had long hair and feminine curves but was hard to make out because it seemed to be at the very bottom of the deep end of the pool, and the heat of the water created a veil of mist that rose from the edges like cemetery fog.

Something was thrumming below.

Kayla worried Maxine had taken a night swim and had somehow gotten stuck. She could be drowning. She could be dead already. The thought made Kayla rush to the edge, and as she got closer the shadow shifted and changed, becoming nothing more than a black smudge created by the light at the end of the pool.

She breathed a sigh of relief.

Jeez, girl, you're getting to be as bad as Maxine with all this seeing things.

But the shadows in the woods must have been real, right? She bit at her lip and looked at the pool again, waiting for any sign of strangeness, but all she saw was stagnant blue water. She started back to the house, not noticing the pale face as it emerged from the waterfall.

CHAPTER TWELVE

"I THINK THERE ARE PEOPLE living in the woods," Kayla told him.

They were having breakfast and Joe was more than ready for her to leave. He kept glancing up at the stairwell, hoping Maxine would come down and the girls would get out of here. He still liked Kayla and certainly still wanted to fuck her raw, but the company of females easily wore him down, particularly when they weren't putting out. He had no interest in hovering in the friend zone like a chump.

And now she was talking this bullshit.

"Last night," she said. "I went outside and ... well ... I'm pretty sure I saw people moving around out there. It was really creepy."

"Maybe they're vagrants." He wasn't committing to the idea. He just wanted her to shut up. He slurped at his cereal.

"Well, I guess they could have been. But why would they be all the way out here? It's not like they can ask for spare change out in the country."

Joe shrugged, milk dribbling down his chin. "Maybe they're schizos and don't know where they are."

She sat back. "That's scary, Joe."

"No, scary would be if they were a pack of cannibals come down from the mountain."

"Jeez, stop that. You're freaking me out."

He snickered. Finally the others shuffled down the stairs, first Danny and then Maxine tailing behind him. Her hair was like a hurricane and blanket lines streaked their faces.

"Don't you just love my new do?" she asked, showing off her bed head.

Kayla giggled. "Fabulous!"

"God, that bed is like the most comfortable thing ever. Felt like I was sleeping on a cloud in heaven."

She stretched and Danny slapped her ass on the way to the fridge. A moment later Robbie came around the corner with the dog trotting alongside him. Joe was about to tell him he needed to take it to the pound when the doorbell rang.

"Shit," he said, thinking of the police officer.

They hadn't told the girls about the officer's visit, of course. Doing so would mean they would have to explain about Linda having been there, and that was not something they wanted to do. Joe hadn't even told Robbie the cops had come around. He didn't want to give his little brother a heart attack by making him think the police were on to his paid-for handjob.

"Isn't somebody going to get that?" Maxine asked.

Joe stood up. "Yeah, sure."

He nodded to Danny, insinuating he should come with him. He wasn't sure it was the cops but had a feeling whoever was behind that door wasn't bringing good cheer.

He opened it.

A young girl with dark hair and amber eyes stood before them.

"Hey," she said.

Joe blinked at her for a moment, not responding. She looked about sixteen, petite and pale, and there was a haunted look to her purple, sunken eyes, one that didn't match her warm smile. She wore a button sweater over a flower-patterned sundress.

"Hey," Danny said, as if she were an old friend.

"I'm Hazel."

There were no cars in the driveway other than Danny's Olds and Kayla's Charger. Joe didn't even see a bicycle.

"I saw your cars out front," Hazel said. "I wanted to say hi and see what you were up to."

The boys stood there, dumbstruck.

"It's cool," she said. "I used to live here."

The moment he saw her, Danny felt a tug within his chest. He was a carp and she'd snagged him with a hook. She reminded him of someone he could not place, like he'd seen her in a movie he couldn't fully remember. But the sight of her oval face and flowing locks sent a warm quiver through him, making him semi-hard.

Maybe I've seen her in a porno?

She didn't look the type. Besides, she was young.

Maybe she had a sister that went to school with him. If anyone else had recognized her they didn't show it. Danny felt she brought something to the mix the other girls didn't, like a single flower growing out of a field of mud. She was not classically beautiful but still there was something to her lips, eyes, and high cheekbones that made the other girls invisible. He could feel Maxine's jealous stare burning into the back of his head and he didn't even care that everyone, including Hazel, knew he was gawking at her. She gave him a wry smile.

"So," Maxine said, "who are you exactly?"

Hazel continued petting Horace. He'd run to her side the moment she'd come in. "My name is Hazel Snowden. I used to live in this house."

Joe cocked his head to one side. "So, you're Gladys's grandniece or something like that?"

She smirked. "Something like that."

Danny was envious she was talking to Joe instead of him, and he stepped closer to her, a goony grin on his face. "We're house sitting the place for her."

"You checking in on us?" Joe asked.

"No. Just stopping by. I miss living in this old house sometimes. I visit Gladys now and then but was kinda excited to see you guys hanging out here. She's stuffy and old fashioned, too motherly, you know? She doesn't know how to have any fun. This house is made for fun, don't you think?"

"It's cool," Joe said.

Danny saw his friend was loosening up. That was fine, but he didn't want him hitting on Hazel. Though he hadn't been able to call it yet, he wanted dibs, Maxine or no Maxine. These sudden feelings were weird, and he didn't quite understand where the intensity of them was coming from, but he felt them nonetheless. Strangely, he knew he would get rough with Joe if it meant winning Hazel's attention.

"Do you know this dog?" Kayla asked.

Hazel patted him on the head. "Don't mind him. He's a wanderer. He comes and goes as he pleases."

"What's his name?"

Hazel tilted her head, her eyes falling darker. "Well, what have you been calling him?"

"Horace," Robbie said.

"Well then, that's as good a name as any, isn't it?"

She stepped toward Robbie and held out her hand. She hadn't done this with anyone else and Danny felt a twinge in the base of his spine. Sweat bubbled at his hairline like lava.

"And what's *your* name?"

"I'm Robbie."

"That's a good name too. Full of ... *life*."

Robbie's face revealed anxiety and arousal and Danny had to bite the inside of his mouth to hold his rage in. He shook his head, trying to get a grip on his own thoughts. Why was he so possessive of this girl he'd just met? She wasn't *Playboy* material or anything. Her fashion wasn't even up-to-date. Besides, he'd been trying to help get Robbie laid. Wasn't it a good thing she was showing a little interest in the kid?

"So," Joe said. "Why didn't Gladys ask you to watch the joint?"

"She thinks I can't handle it. I'm not responsible enough." Hazel walked to Joe and the dog came with her. "If I had this place, I'd throw a big party. I like things like that. I like to get *wild*."

Danny was fully erect now and he clasped his hands in front of his crotch to hide it.

"Well, we're down with partying," Joe said. "Ain't that right, Robbie?"

An empty-headed "Yeah, bro" was all the young boy could muster.

"It's a little early for partying," Maxine said, hands on her hips. "I mean, don't you think this was a bad time to stop by?"

Hazel's face darkened for a moment but then the smile returned. It seemed synthetic though, as if it was painted on, a costume.

"I was on my way to church," Hazel said. "My father's a minister."

That's funny, Danny thought. *Didn't Gladys say her husband was a priest or something? Religion must run in the family.*

"Well, don't let us keep you," Maxine said, making Danny flinch at her bitchiness.

Hazel ignored her and looked to Kayla. "I hope you don't mind me saying so, but you're very beautiful."

Kayla blushed. "Oh, um, thank you." She ran a hand through her hair self-consciously.

"You seem sweet too, unlike some girls I know."

Danny held in a laugh. Maxine said nothing, only glowered.

"You too," Kayla said.

Hazel moved to the counter and tucked her hair behind her ear. The slight movement was so erotic to Danny. The urge to touch her pecked at him like an insect.

"Well," she said, "I'm off to the chapel. Father gets ever so angry when I'm late. But maybe I'll see you all later?"

"Hell yeah," Danny blurted out.

Joe gave her a thumbs up. "Every night is a good night to party."

She went back through the anteroom with Horace trailing behind her and turned around one last time, her eyes seeming to sparkle without any light for them to catch.

"I'll be seeing you," she said.

And then she was gone.

The girl had really gotten to Robbie, and he couldn't help but notice how the other guys were into her too, especially Danny. He'd done everything but drool, and the look on Maxine's face had been hilarious and yet terrifying. Robbie did not envy the wrath Danny would endure once they were alone.

There was something about Hazel that was very different, and not just the fact that she had shown a genuine interest in him. She was aloof, sure of herself in a way that defied her age, and her curious charms had drawn the attention of everyone in the room. He hoped he would see her again.

As they drove toward town, Danny at the wheel and Joe riding shotgun, they listened to screeching heavy metal, the older boys smoking a joint, Robbie watching the bloats of fog that had slid down the mountain and were now sluicing through the trees like white worms. He was in the backseat, Horace lying on the floor.

The girls had left, but promised to come back later in the afternoon. They just wanted to check in with their parents so they wouldn't get in trouble. The afternoon light was muted to a somber, funereal gray, the heavy clouds hovering like doom, swollen with the threat of rain. Black crows spun through the air in slow circles as the McLeary farm passed by in an orange blur.

"So what do you think of Hazel, dude?" his brother asked.

Robbie felt pressure in his chest, as if he was holding in a burp.

"I dunno. She seems cool, I guess."

"Last night it was three guys and only two girls. Maybe we'll be a little more evened out tonight. That is if Maxine ever forgives Dan-o, here."

"It's fine," Danny said in a cloud of weed.

"She looked like she was ready to cut your balls off and skip them across a pond."

"Yeah, she talks shit. She'll get over it. It ain't like I did anything."

"Well, we shouldn't worry about hunting down Linda anymore. Hazel had eyes for lil' old Robbie here. I could almost smell her pussy getting wet."

Danny turned. "Hey, shut the fuck up!"

Joe forced a laugh. "What the hell is with you, man? You got a crush on her all of a sudden?"

"No, man. I'm just . . . I dunno."

Robbie twiddled his thumbs. Their conversation was making him nervous for more reasons than one.

"Come on," Joe said. "Just the other day we were gonna drop a shitload of cash for Robbie to get some. Now we got a girl who looks like she'll do it for free. What are you getting so uptight about?"

Danny watched the road intently, his knuckles white on the wheel. "Let's just get some pizza, all right? I don't want to talk about pussy anymore."

Now Joe laughed for real. "Shit. That's a first."

Horace didn't know why the master had come and gone so quickly. He was not allowed to cry for her when she left, nor was he allowed to jump in circles when she appeared. The urge to do so had shaken within him, but the pleasure of obeying her outweighed all other emotions. She had come to them in her younger form, the one that was the most like flesh, and there was a new smell to her that was rich and tantalizing. It smelled of the yard and the trees, of unearthed dirt and decaying leaves. He'd delighted beneath her scratching hands, cherishing the affection he received for trapping that girl in the shower so master could take her away.

He'd done a good job. He was a very good boy.

She assured him he was a great familiar, an effective and obedient spirit. And that was all he wanted to be, an animal guide to his master. She was his world, his everything, and if she so wished he would rip the faces off everyone in the house, the boys as well as the girls, even the ones he liked.

She was the master.

She knew best.

CHAPTER THIRTEEN

KAYLA WASN'T SURE SHE WANTED to go back.

She didn't think it was asking too much to be invited to dinner and a movie. The first fair of the fall was happening too, and she loved carnival rides and the sad magic of their swirling lights. That would be a good date, not just making out in a hot tub again and again and then having a guy who wasn't really your boyfriend trying to get in your pants.

And yet she still liked him.

Stupid.

She enjoyed the splendor of the house just as much as Maxine, but after two straight nights with the boys she was ready for a break. She wanted to put some distance between her and the manor and the shapes she'd seen last night. She'd been cold sober and fully awake. The shadow in the bottom of the pool was probably made by the distortion of the light within the water, but there was someone, or something, in those woods, and it wasn't alone. Part of her wanted to know what they were, but another, larger part of her was afraid to find out.

And then there was Hazel.

Was Kayla the only one unsettled by this girl's sudden appearance? Maxine had certainly taken a dislike to the girl, but that was more due to Danny's slack jaw and staring eyes than anything Hazel had done. Kayla didn't exactly dislike the girl but her innocent looks combined with her sly and seductive nature reminded Kayla of the evil brat from *The Bad Seed*. Somehow her quaintness seemed like a cover for an inner devil. Kayla wasn't so sure she wanted to hang around to see if she came back, particularly not at night, when the shadows lurked and the azure glow of the pool played tricks on her brain.

She decided to stay home tonight. As she disrobed for her bath she noticed the scab that had formed above her sex. She had almost forgotten about cutting herself last night.

All over Joe. All over stupid, pig-headed Joe.

It would be funny if it weren't so pathetic.

She'd been so good about not cutting herself. Although she wasn't over it, she'd adjusted to her father's regular absence, and now that her grades had picked up she wasn't feeling as stressed because she didn't have the pressure of getting into a good college hanging over her head like a pendulum. Her self-abuse had been under control. She'd almost felt like it was behind her now.

Over a stupid boy.

It was like being an alcoholic. She was starting all over now.

The hot water felt nice on her feet. She liked her baths near scorching. Not as another form of self-punishment, but as a way to open up her pores and separate her consciousness from her body. Disassociation could be so sweet. The tub was her way of meditating and she sank into it whenever she had too much on her mind, always emerging with a new perspective. It helped her make all the tough decisions.

She went in slowly, hissing as her buttocks hit the water, and splashed her upper body in preparation. She slid all the way in then, gritting her teeth against the sting, and busied herself with the inflatable pillow to keep her mind off it until her body adjusted. The soapy bubbles made hills around her jutting knees and settled her bones when she closed her eyes. She had lit scented candles, filling the dimness with the autumnal smells of pumpkin spice and cedar. Her mother had taken Patricia to the park, so the sweet silence thrummed.

Kayla sank deeper.

The shadow people scattered across her mind.

Her eyes opened again, resisting. She didn't want to dream of them. She closed her eyes again, trying to force away the images of spindly bodies and flailing limbs. But they kept returning to her, her mind insisting she work this out.

Had they really been vagrants? People living in the woods?

They might have set up a shantytown of some sort. God, she'd hated Joe's suggestions of cannibal maniacs. It made her skin crawl. None of the theories made much sense to her. They didn't explain the people's oddly shaped bodies or the way they'd appeared blacker than any night she'd ever seen. Maybe they were monkeys escaped from the zoo. No, that was even more stupid. But they had to be something.

Unless she was losing her marbles.

She thought of the cut.

It's not like you have it together, kid.

Robbie was restless.

Dusk was falling, the gloom of the day was accelerating it. He stood in the backyard, tossing the tennis ball to Horace. The dog lunged, his paws creating a swirl of dust around him as he charged after it. It gave Robbie something to do other than think about Hazel.

Would he see her again tonight?

The night was bringing a meaner chill with it and he zipped up his hoodie. He loved fall but was a thin boy and felt the cold deep in his bones. It almost felt like winter was coming, and if the air had been wetter he might have anticipated early snow. Above him, leaves rustled in a galaxy of gold, reminding him of Hazel's eyes.

Was his brother right? Could she really be interested in *him*?

He was almost too afraid to believe it, sure he'd only be proven wrong and made a fool of once again. He didn't want to climb a mountain only to be pushed off. But she'd been nice to him, hadn't she? He'd had girls cozy up to him before because they wanted something from him (sometimes to make him the butt of a joke) and he'd almost always fallen for it. But what did Hazel have to gain from manipulating him? Wasn't it more likely she had honestly flirted with him?

"What do you think, boy?"

Horace sat before him, tennis ball in his mouth, dripping with slobber. Robbie put out his hand and Horace dropped it, and he chucked it away again and wiped his hand on his jeans. The dog charged ahead, chasing the ball as it rolled downhill toward the woods. Above them, tucked under the churning clouds, a bone-colored moon hung full and fat, rising to the beckon of the coming night.

Who are you kidding? You couldn't land a girl like that, not in a zillion years. The best you're gonna do is have someone paid to do it, like Linda.

He thought of her hand tugging him and how he'd covered it with his release. It was a memory he already treasured and he knew it would stay with him until he was a withered old prune limping around a nursing home. When at last he died, he'd think of his hand on Linda's vulva and dream of touching it one last time.

Horace hadn't returned from the edge of the woods yet.

"Here, boy!"

Robbie stared down the slope, his hands in his pockets against the cruelty of the night wind. He thought he could see Horace sitting at the edge of the tree line, but from where he was it was only a black shape.

"Come here, boy!"

The shape moved and two eyes shimmered before the head turned away from him again. It was Horace, and he was staring into the woods, unresponsive to his calls. Robbie kept after him, trotting a little faster. He called the dog again but this time Horace didn't even turn around, looking straight up, at full attention, his butt planted on the ground. It was as if an invisible man was holding a treat. He wasn't barking or panting despite all the exercise he'd just had. He was sitting perfectly still, silent.

What is he doing?

Robbie couldn't see anything in the woods, just a thickening darkness settling like leathery wings. But as he got closer he felt a presence. He saw and heard nothing, but still he sensed something beyond the tree line, waiting, watching. He'd never felt such a strange sensation. It wasn't a hunch, but a certainty.

"Hello?"

The state park was not far away. Hiking trails curved through the hills and up toward the mountain a few miles behind the house. Someone might have wandered off a trail and gotten lost.

What if it's a bear?

Robbie took a step back.

Wouldn't Horace bark if it were a bear? Wouldn't he be making some sort of move if it were a lost hiker, either barking or running over to say hello?

"Is someone there?"

Only the soft whistle of wind.

He tapped Horace. "Come on, boy."

The big dog looked to him and then to the woods again. Robbie saw the ball on the ground and threw it back toward the house.

Horace didn't budge.

A black shape moved behind the trees. Robbie gasped. It was large but spindly, a shape unlike any living thing he'd ever seen, not quite animal and not quite man. There was no sound. The thing swayed through the trees and Horace's head turned, watching it. Robbie wanted to run but was oddly hypnotized. He could not see the shape very well, and yet he could not look away. It seemed somehow out of focus, like he was wearing glasses that did not belong to him. Everything else was clear, despite the growing dark, but the shape was a blur, impossibly black like distant space, and Robbie was suddenly colder, as if a freezer had been opened beneath his feet.

He heard a woman's voice calling from the hill behind him, back near the house.

"Here, boy," the voice called.

Horace ran faster than ever. He ripped up the grass with charging claws, sending tufts into the air, spraying Robbie's jeans.

Who's up there?

He trotted behind the dog, squinting in the dark as it disappeared into the night. For a moment he could see a silhouette, then it vanished. When he finally reached the top of the slope where the patio was, he saw Horace standing by the door, butt wagging, waiting for him with a big, goony look on his face.

There was no one else there.

Joe was as bummed as he was bored.

Kayla had decided to stay home, telling him she had a big math test tomorrow. He'd actually forgotten it was a school night. Maxine was still peeved at Danny for making goo-goo eyes at that chick Hazel, so it was just he and the boys tonight, sitting around the house, watching TV. They'd sat through a *Simpsons* rerun, Danny stoned and cracking up, and then Robbie had turned it to the movie channel. They were playing non-stop horror movies through October, and Robbie was a big fan of the '80s fright flicks. They'd watched *Halloween 3: Season of the Witch,* which Robbie loved but Joe found slow and corny (where the hell was Michael Myers?), and now they were halfway through the 1988 version of *The Blob.* Joe sipped another beer, watching the pink slime attack a woman in a phone booth. He laughed when he saw the dead sheriff floating within its shifting, pink mass.

He thought about Hazel.

She hadn't come back. It was past ten now and what little party the boys had in them was slipping away. There was something different about her. She carried an air of seduction he'd only seen in older women. There was confidence in her movements and a comfortable familiarity with her own body. She knew how to swagger her hips when she wanted to draw men in, how to brush ever-so-softly across them, letting them smell her to the point of almost tasting her. She wasn't the sexiest girl he'd ever seen, but she radiated sex effortlessly.

And she wanted Robbie.

That much was clear.

Joe hoped she would come back. He wanted her to be at the Halloween party this weekend.

Danny began snoring and Joe took that as a sign he should call it a night too. He stood up, stretched.

Robbie looked up. "Crashing?"

"Yeah. You should soon too if you wanna make it to school tomorrow. Danny'll drive you."

"You going?"

"Haven't decided yet."

He bopped Danny on the head with his empty beer can.

"Bedtime, macho man."

Once in his room, Joe flicked on the light before getting undressed. Remembering the cool silk of the sheets from last night, he decided to sleep in the nude and draped his clothes over the back of a chair. They'd only been there a few days and already he'd made a mess of the room. Now and then he was taken back by the house's decadence, as if he was seeing it all again for the first time, and for some reason his reaction to this was to sling his belongings all over the place and decorate the floor with beer bottles. Perhaps he was marking his territory just as the Rottweiler would have.

He flicked the light off and jumped onto the unmade bed, thinking of how he'd awoken late last night and looked at Kayla lying next to him. She had dressed, but he still felt her up a little bit while she slept. Her jeans were too tight to get into but he cupped her buttocks and slid his hand under her sweater to squeeze her big breasts again. She'd stirred but hadn't woken up, so he caressed her between her legs. All he managed to do was give himself a hard-on, which aggravated him. Then he'd fallen back asleep to dream of the sex that reality was so cruelly denying him.

Rain spattered against the windowpane, creating a peaceful white noise. Soft shadows climbed the walls like huge insects, the branches outside creating strange shapes as they clicked against the side of the house. Joe breathed deeply, his heart rate steadying as his mind drifted away.

He was almost fully under when he heard the door creak open.

He looked toward it, expecting to see Danny or Robbie, or even the butting nose of the dog. Instead he saw a small, human shape drifting into the bedroom, seeming to move without stepping.

"Who is that?" he asked.

Whispers seemed to come from every corner of the room, saying nothing. Joe tensed as he clenched the sheets. The shadowy figure lurched and swayed, disappearing and reappearing in the dark folds of the bedroom.

"Who's there?" he said, less confident.

The voice was low, soft. "I told you I'd be back."

He sat up, squinting in the dark. A pale oval of a face appeared, lips parted and wet, eyes impossibly auburn in the darkness. Long, black curls covered her bare chest, matching the dark tuft at her sex.

"Hazel?"

The girl smiled a rictus grin. "I want you, Joe."

He rubbed his eyes, wondering if he was actually awake. This certainly seemed dreamlike. But no, he wasn't sleeping. The rictus smile flashed in the darkness like crooked stars.

"How did you get in here? Did Robbie let you in?"

She put one knee on the bed and leaned down, putting her palm on the mattress. Her hair swung, revealing small, ghostly breasts. Her breath was cold on his neck.

"I want you inside me."

She reached for the sheet and drew it back, exposing his nudity. He didn't resist. His erection waved and he scooted over to make room for her.

"I thought you wanted my brother," he said.

The smile returned, big, bizarre. "I need you first."

CHAPTER FOURTEEN

KAYLA FELT LIKE SHE'D DONE well on the test today, so she rewarded herself by putting off her homework. It had warmed up and the foliage was at its peak, the forest looking like a postcard image as she made her way up the trail that wound through Black Rock Park. She was a little agitated Maxine had canceled on her at the last minute. She was just going to see Danny so they could have a make-up screw. It wouldn't be the first time her friend bailed on her for a boy. She supposed she should be used to it by now but it always managed to sting. She wasn't going to let it ruin her afternoon hike. In a way, she thought it would be even more enjoyable to spend it alone.

A blanket of leaves crunched beneath her boots, the only sound in the woods. There was a pleasant silence now that the bugs of summer had gone away. There were no more singing cicadas or chirping crickets, only Kayla's own sounds. There were other people out hiking, but it was a weekday and she had this particular trail to herself for the time being.

Appreciate this.

She'd been taking mental snapshots of home now that the reality of going off to college next year was sinking in. She'd go away somewhere and would only see her hometown for the holidays, maybe spring break too if she weren't partying at Coney Island. Even though things weren't perfect at home, she loved her family and would miss them. She wouldn't be around to see her sister grow up. Even when she was done with college she would be moving on to a career and a place of her own and doubted that would mean a return to upstate New York.

She pushed her way up the last few steps to the clearing and decided to rest for a minute, sitting down on a large rock as she took the water bottle out of her bag. Before her was an expansive view of the forest, the trees flowing in a tapestry of red and copper. Where they ended, Snowden Manor loomed, enormous and magnificent, like an ancient, French cathedral. She'd passed it on her way and thought of Joe, wondering where their relationship (or lack thereof) was headed. Maybe she would call him later, but right now her own peace of mind was her priority. This moment was for her. She owed it to herself to not lend him any of her current headspace.

She started on the next section of trails, still alone in the wilderness. She could hear no other hikers, only the occasional scatter of squirrels hoarding acorns for the coming winter, and she stepped into a heavily shaded patch and felt the temperature drop. The day's mildness had all been thanks to the abundant sunshine, a relief after yesterday's drear, but under this canopy of trees a deep chill struck her. She hugged herself and stuck her hands in her armpits, her breath making amorphous ghosts.

Something moved ahead.

She figured it was just another hiker, but they weren't on the trail. Whoever it was moved through the thicket, behind the cover of the trees. She stopped in her tracks, thinking of the shapes she'd seen two nights ago, moving about at the end of this very batch of woods. She thought about saying hello, to see if it really was just another hiker, but something held her back, something cold and hard within her chest. Her mouth was dry but she did not reach for her water bottle. She stood perfectly still, ready to run back the way she'd come.

The shape lurched, all long legs and swinging arms. It was soundless despite the heavy piles of leaves. Kayla turned around to head back but saw another shape moving up the trail behind her. It was smaller than the other one, but closer. Much closer. And it was sticking to the trail, coming toward her, blurry and cloaked by the shade. It seemed naturally camouflaged, like it was manipulating the trees to conceal itself.

Kayla stepped back, deciding to go the other way. She didn't want to get a better look at whatever the shadow was, she just wanted to get the hell away from it. Turning toward the trail she saw three shapes coming toward her on this side, one leading the way while the others flanked its sides, blocking the path entirely.

Kayla screamed.

The forms were pitch black, faceless, inhuman.

She ran into the woods, frantic, running so quickly she collided with hanging branches, snapping them away with her shoulders, throwing her hands up to protect her face.

She tripped.

Getting up, dirt fell from her knees and she looked around again. She was alone. She didn't see any shapes or shadows near her or on the trails.

Am I going crazy?

She couldn't have seen what she thought she saw. It wasn't possible. But she'd seen those things twice now—by day and by night. They'd lured her, subconsciously, when she'd been at the house. Now they seemed to be hunting her down. They'd circled around her like wolves, closing her in, coming at her now that she was alone and could easily get lost.

Her phone didn't work so well up on the mountain, and she didn't have a compass. If she strayed too far from the trail she might not be able to find it again. The nights were cold and mean now and she didn't want to spend one outside. She had to go back to the trail. It was right there, and no shapes were lurking anywhere near it.

Unless they're hiding, lying in wait.

She told herself she was being ridiculous, but she didn't believe it. They must have been real, even if she couldn't explain what they were. Taking a deep breath, she stepped past the row of trees in front of her, shrieking when she saw the woman in black standing before several of the tall shapes. Hair so blond it was almost white flowed behind her, blowing back from the sudden gust of wind.

Her blue eyes locked on hers.

The woman had Kayla's face.

CHAPTER FIFTEEN

HORACE HAD DETECTED THEM IN the woods yesterday afternoon.

He knew every one of them and remembered which ones had been nice to him and which ones had not. They were so different now. He didn't see them as much as he *sensed* them. Ever since the master banished them to the black forest, they'd become confusing shapes. They looked different every time he saw them, but he could identify each of them from their individual smells. The odors were fainter now that there was no flesh, no muscle, not even bone, but he was still able to pick them out.

But then there were the others, those he could see but could not smell. They made him whimper and wine. They too were black shapes, like the others, but their forms were more like humans, even though they did not feel like humans. They seemed like reflections in water. They were seen but not heard or smelled, and that frightened him in a way little else could.

But he was supposed to stay there.

That's what the master wanted.

She was after the boy. The one who gave him meat treats under the table and scratched behind his ears. The boy was his favorite. He would miss him and the light-haired girl who smelled like flowers and soap. But the master wanted them, and that was that.

He wondered if he'd see them again one day, moving in the trees.

Master knew best, but he liked being free, and he liked the boy.

He did not want to be alone in the wall again.

She'd passed out.

When Kayla awoke she was lying in a pile of leaves. Slivers of a bright sky poked between the branches above as her eyes began to adjust, and as her memory came back she jolted upright. She scurried like a crab, fleeing from nothing, looking left and right for the shapes.

The woman.

She had my face.

Had it not been for her cloak, it would have been like looking in a living mirror. The woman was not like the other shapes. She had a normal body—Kayla's body—and she was easier to see, although there was a faded blue glow to her. Behind the woman, Kayla thought she'd seen other white faces, but she'd passed out before getting a good look.

She stood and brushed herself off. She was dirty and bits of leaves were in her hair. Grabbing her bag, she took a better look around.

Alone again.

She headed for the trail quickly. Hiking time was over and would be for a long time.

Did I dream all of that?

She remembered tripping over a root. Had she banged her head and blacked out? Had it all been a figment of her imagination?

No.

It was all clear to her. There were no holes in her memory the way there were after most dreams. She'd seen the shapes again, this time in broad daylight, and she'd seen her doppelganger.

What is going on?

She didn't want to stand around thinking about it. She sprinted through the brush until she reached the trail and started running, the fear still fresh. But her mind was in overdrive, horror throttling her, sending one thought to topple another before the first could finish.

Oh my god, I really am going crazy.

She rounded the curve, coming around a row of trees, and when she found the shadowy people standing there, waiting for her, she was hardly surprised, but a yelp escaped her anyway, tears brewing in her eyes.

Her own double reached for her, smiling, her incisors protruding. "Don't be afraid."

The others weren't the gangly shapes Kayla had seen earlier. They were human forms, like her double, and they too were in cloaks of changing color, blue and black and gray, their faces half-covered by drooped hoods.

"We're here to help you," the double said.

Kayla couldn't speak. Couldn't even move.

Her doppelganger inched closer. "This is not a dream. You're in great danger, Kayla. You must heed our warning."

She put her hand on Kayla's shoulder and a warm current moved through her. It had an opiate effect on Kayla, calming her immediately, making her frazzled thoughts slow so she could concentrate.

"Who are you?" she asked.

The woman's eyes gave off a light that reminded her of the glow of the pool.

"I am a part of you. I am your wraith."

A gentle wind blew and the double's hair fluttered across her face, just as Kayla's did.

"A wraith?"

"Yes. I am your spiritual double."

Kayla swallowed. "What, like . . . a ghost?"

"More like a reflective shadow. I come as a premonition. We appear when our true selves are in mortal danger, much as you are now."

A male voice chimed in. "Much as we all are."

The male figure drew back his hood. Robbie. Or rather, Robbie's double, his wraith. Had it not been for the slight glow around him, she would not have been able to tell the difference.

"What . . ." she muttered. "What's going on?"

"There is darkness here," her wraith told her. "It draws its power from the mountain. It lives in the manor house."

"Darkness?"

"Yes. A spirit that is neither alive nor dead."

Kayla blinked, her eyes still wet. Her hands rolled over each other.

"She is a thing of evil," the wraith said. "A succubus, a sorceress.

She is in the walls of the house she lived in when she was still mortal—Snowden Manor."

"Who . . . who is she?"

The wraith lowered her head, eyes dark and hollow.

"Her name is Hazel."

The tale the wraith told was incredible and terrifying. Had it not been told to Kayla by a supernatural force—her own spiritual double—she never would have believed it.

In the early '80s, Hazel Snowden was a teenage shut-in, forced to stay inside the manor by her overbearing father, renowned priest Arthur Snowden. She was not allowed to have friends, certainly not boyfriends, and was not allowed to go to school, her father insisting they were dens of iniquity that would taint her purity and tempt her away from the Lord. So her parents had homeschooled her, most of the responsibility falling on her mother, Gladys Snowden, who was not as strict as Arthur but abided by his wishes for fear of his cutting words and sudden fists.

The only contact Hazel had with the outside word was with the people she saw at her father's church and the wild dogs that lived in caves up on Black Rock Mountain. Sometimes they would come sniffing and scrounging onto the property when she was raking leaves or mowing the yard, and she snuck them food carefully, for her father hated dogs and animals of all kinds. He threatened to leave out bowls of antifreeze to poison them if he caught her giving mongrels the food he worked so hard to provide. These dogs were her only friends however, and she felt a special bond with them, particularly one big Rottweiler.

At seventeen Hazel had begun to notice the looks she got from some of the boys in church, particularly Drake Pender, whose brown eyes were like windows to another life. They often spoke after the services but never got much time to do so. Her father was usually busy with the congregation after mass, but they didn't linger long and whenever he saw her talking with Drake he scowled and she knew she would be in for a lecture once she got home.

"Boys only want one thing from you!" he'd yell. "I will not have my daughter deflowered by some towheaded nitwit. I won't have you spitting out a bastard from between your legs. You will stay pure! You owe it to me, you owe it to your mother, you owe it to *Christ!*"

But Hazel hated Christ.

She'd grown up being threatened by him, and she associated him and everything Christian with pain, oppression, and sadness. Her father had seen to that. She hated Christ almost as much as she hated her father, and sometimes she wondered if they were really one and the same, a single pretentious, capricious man who thrived on being worshipped, obeyed, and feared.

But she liked Drake Pender. He made her feel funny in a way she didn't quite understand, having never truly had sex explained to her. It'd only been hinted at during her father's vile rants and branded a terrible thing indeed, which only furthered her excitement. She thought about Drake when she peed, but she could never tell him that. She could never tell anyone how funny he made her feel. Her mother would think she was disgusting. Her father would bring out his belt and would even use the buckle on her, much the way he'd done when she'd spilled grape juice on their white sofa. But she kept on thinking about Drake whenever she peed, and those thoughts soon carried over to her baths, and once she started touching herself she couldn't stop. She knew she was sinful. Knew she was so dirty she was pure filth. And she liked that. She liked the idea of being an affront to God, spiting him, going against everything she'd been forced to listen to since the day she was born. And if her self-pleasure was an abomination, she could only imagine how sinful it would be if she made her fantasies a reality.

It was a cold night in October when she snuck Drake into her room.

She'd invited him earlier that day as they'd held hands in the field behind the church, carefully ducking behind a row of trees so her father didn't see. Her room was on the second floor, but her window was beside the rain gutter and Drake was able to shimmy up, supporting his weight by planting his feet on the planks of the house.

Once she got him inside she wasted no time, pulling off her nightgown to show him her naked body in the blue light of the moon. Then she started undoing his belt. By the time her father walked in, Drake was deep inside her, thrusting his hard cock, her legs wrapped around his waist like a vice, wishing he'd never exit her, wanting to keep him within her as long as possible, forever, taking him, possessing his infinite desire. When she saw her father's face appear over Drake's shoulder, teeth bared, eyes like a soulless shark, she smiled at him and her throat filled with mocking laughter. Her father's hand went around Drake's neck and he flung him off her and into the wall.

"Jezebel!"

Her father backhanded her then returned his attention to Drake, whose face was the color of chalk.

"This is a house of God!" her father said. "How dare you befoul it, you filthy bastard!"

Arthur pounced on the boy like a maniac, fists flailing as blood spattered through the shadows, wetting the walls. Hazel screamed and ran to her father, but he was in a rage as blind as his faith, and he continued to pummel Drake, kicking him as he lay curled up on the floor.

"Filthy bastard!"

Hazel panted. The sudden violence, combined with her lust for Drake and her pent-up hostility toward her father, caused a fracture in her sanity. She jumped upon his back and sunk her thumbnails deep into his eyes. He cried out and tried to shake her from his back but she wrapped her legs around his waist, just as she had done with Drake. She pushed farther, thumbs sinking in as she felt the eyes pop and leak. He grabbed at her wrists but she held fast, empowered by the freakish strength of the mad, heart raging against her ribs, teeth snapping, eyes rolling. Her father ran backward and slammed her into the dresser, knickknacks crashing to the floor, but she held on. Somewhere in the shadows, Drake screamed.

Her father fell backward, landing on her and knocking the wind from her chest. As she struggled to breathe he writhed free and spun over to look down at her with eyes filled with blood. He began swinging, punching her in the face. He'd beaten her on many occasions but usually hit her where the bruises wouldn't show, pounding her stomach and back. Now he was cracking her jaw and sending spurts of blood from her nose as it broke in half. She felt her lip split against her teeth as one of them came loose, and her father grabbed her hair in both fists, babbling incoherently about Christ as he slammed her head into the floor over and over again, rattling her brain, splitting her scalp.

He stopped so suddenly Hazel knew something serious had happened. Through the one eye she could get open, she saw a look of horror on her father's face. His mouth was open, as were his red eyes. He was gasping for air. A slim shadow appeared behind him, and Hazel watched as the knife was pulled out of his back, glimmering before it was sent back in with a sickening, wet sound. In and out, in and out, more and more blood splattering the walls and floor as Hazel watched her mother stab her father to death.

When at last his body hit the floor, he splashed into a thick pool of blood that had formed below him. The steaming gore covered his face. Hazel looked up at her mother and even in the dim light she could see the tears running down her face. Gladys helped her daughter up and held her close to her chest like she had when Hazel was just a child.

Standing in the corner trembling, was Drake. His face was bloodless, his limbs vibrating. Gladys watched him with iron eyes and everything went silent.

She handed the blade to her daughter.

"He's seen too much," she said.

Hazel's mouth fell open. "But, Mom . . ."

"No buts. He's a witness, and we cannot have witnesses."

Her mother's eyes, naturally brown, had turned green. They seemed to glow slightly in the dark, like emeralds by candlelight. The sight of them made Hazel gasp.

"Please," Drake said, "I won't say anything. I mean, you had to do it, right?"

Gladys did not reply. She only stared at her daughter.

"I can't," Hazel said. "I want him. I need him."

Gladys brushed Hazel's hair over her ear, eyes shimmering. "He's just a boy. One of many."

"But Mother, he wants me. He makes me feel special."

"Trust me. They're all the same, my dear. Every last one of them."

Drake crept toward the door.

"There will be other boys," Gladys said. "Mommy will make sure you get all of the boys you need. Now do away with this one before he tries to escape."

Drake lunged for the door and Gladys blocked his path, but he was fast and she didn't see the punch coming. She bent forward and held her stomach where she had been struck, knees buckling.

Hazel saw red and not just from the blood dripping into her eyes.

She only meant to slice him, but she lunged with too much force and the knife flashed as it came up, plunging into the soft flesh of the boy's belly, sinking into his kidney. Blood sluiced, hot upon her clenched fingers. Drake screeched like a fox in a trap, then collapsed as she withdrew the blade. From the corner, Gladys' eyes burned like stars, watching. Drake remained on the floor, making it easy for Hazel to send the blade into him again, this time through his throat. Blood pooled in his mouth and spilled over the sides, his lips moving but only garbled words coming out. He slid on the floor, the knife sticking out of his neck, having split his Adam's apple like a ripe peach. The coppery stink of gore filled her nostrils.

The heat of the moment passed and the cold October air hit her again, accompanied by a deeper, more personal coldness. She shook uncontrollably as the evil of what she'd done sunk into her heart, where it would make a home forever.

"That's a good girl," her mother whispered, eyes a soft brown again.

They buried them in the packed earth of the cellar floor. Gladys knew the importance of burying them deep, and they worked until the morning light came, digging and digging and digging with the frantic energy that had come to them on the heels of the killings. Hazel felt the beginnings of panic, but her mother's calm demeanor and soothing words kept her from a full breakdown. Once they had the earth packed over the seven-foot hole they'd dug, they moved old boxes and crates over the spot. They went upstairs with the mops and bleach, spray bottles of 409 and SOS sponges in hand. They did not stop for breakfast or lunch. They scrubbed every crack and crevice and threw the bloodstained clothes into the fireplace.

That night they ate dinner in silence.

Missing posters for Drake Pender went up all over town, but Gladys didn't report her husband missing. She told his assistant to take over sermons, explaining that Arthur had caught the flu. She would eventually report him missing but not at the same time as the Pender boy. No one had known about the kids' secret rendezvous, so no one had come knocking on their door. And when a few weeks went by she came up with a story about Arthur having recovered from his flu but still having trouble with his voice. She decided he'd gone to see his doctor but had never arrived there and had never come home. She filed the police report over a month after Drake's disappearance had stricken every parent in town with terror.

Gladys was a well-known, well-respected member of the community. She was never suspected of foul play. In time, the search for Arthur Snowden and Drake Pender came to a silent, inconclusive close.

By December, Hazel was no longer worried.

But she did miss Drake. She still desired him, and now that she had tasted the full pleasure of a boy she wanted more, so she tried to hold her mother to her promise. Her desires were abundant and with her father gone she wanted to attend public school so she could meet more boys. But her new, promiscuous attitude worried her mother, and she was forced to remain the shut-in she'd been before.

"You promised me boys," Hazel would say. "All the boys I could ever want. And I want them, Mother."

Having less control over her daughter than her husband had had, Gladys changed the locks so a key was needed to get out of the house. Bars went up on the windows, not to keep out intruders but to imprison her daughter like a princess in a Grimm fable. Trapped and isolated once again, Hazel decided that if she couldn't partake in her lustful leanings and offend the god she loathed with such vehemence, she would have to find another way to sin, something more powerful than stealing, coveting, or taking his name in vain.

She had killed. The ultimate sin. And after the fear of being caught had faded, Hazel found she had liked it. By killing Drake, she'd claimed him as her own, forever and ever, possessing him just as she had wished to, only spiritually instead of bodily. It was the only kind of commitment that could last. Despite her tender age, she knew this to be true.

Murder held more power than love.

Murder was forever.

All that winter, Hazel read through her father's books. One of the worst sins, according to her late father, was to put other gods before the Lord, so she wanted to do exactly that. Arthur had been a professor of religion and lost cultures. Not only did he have multiple forms of the Bible but also had books on Zoroastrian deities, Greek mythology, Nordic gods and the rituals of the ancient druids.

The latter was what she found the most intriguing.

To the Celtics, she learned, the world was a magical place. Otherworldly forces ruled it, every element having its own spirit. Every tree, puddle, and pebble had its own soul, and various deities were everywhere, as were fairies and other mystical creatures.

The idea of a world ruled by magic enthralled her.

She read of the fire festival of Beltane, a celebration of fertility, and of the sacred celebration of Samhain that welcomed the darkest time of the year. Though not much was known about the rituals themselves, there were many nods to folklore as well as human sacrifice. Almost all of them pertained to appeasing local gods and obtaining supernatural power. But Imbas Forosnai, the ceremony that most intrigued her, involved a druid entering a sensory deprivation hut to remain under a pile of skins while other druids chanted. After several days, the deprived druid would be tossed out of the darkness and into the broad light of day. It was believed this ritual brought on a higher state of consciousness.

Hazel became obsessed.

She read everything she could on the druids and particularly enjoyed the books on their folklore, such as one large volume about Stonehenge and the many takes on the strange monument different cultures had attributed to it over the years. Though the formation was constructed by a culture that left no written records, the rocks were believed to have healing properties, and although they were not exactly tied to the ancient druids, some scholars had made a correlation, and popular culture had done the rest.

She soon began her own rituals in the same vein.

In her room at night she would align candles and recite chants. She prayed not to the devil but to the spirits of the earth, focusing on Black Rock Mountain, which she could see from her bedroom window. And as she continued to study, her rituals became more accurate. Soon she moved them to the cellar, to perform them over the bodies of the boy she had slain and her own dead father, a man of the cloth.

The sin of this thrilled her.

The effects came gradually. First she developed heightened senses. In her backyard, she could smell fish swimming beneath the river. She could hear slight creaks from inside the mountain. She could see around the other side of stars.

But most of all, she could feel.

She felt the spirits beneath the snow, felt them in the rocks, the branches, the reeds. They were all around her, filling the valley with a force that trickled down from the haunt of the mountain. If she was going mad, then let her go mad. What she felt was bliss and she would not allow anything to take it away, not even sanity.

The dogs became more obedient. She was able to communicate with them without words. She had read of such spirits being known as *familiars*, who did the bidding of witches. They were often cats or serpents, but Hazel had always loved the dogs, so the Rottweiler became her familiar, guiding her into a world of untouched power. She gave him a name that could not be spoken, one that came to her from the mountain.

And then the darkness came for her.

With the inverted star painted on the cellar floor, which her mother had since had tiled over to seal in their secret, and the half moons drawn on by a finger dipped into a bowl of her own menstrual blood, the tiles began to loosen under her knees. They became jelly-like, then aquatic. Blue light peeked out of the cracks and devoured her body, flushing her with rich ecstasy, frosting her flesh, her nipples, her mouth, and her sex. She fell onto her hands and knees, and when she opened her eyes she saw the blackness churning in the center of that unholy light. It was a vortex darker than darkness, emitting an arctic chill that made her skull ache and her body curl inward. The hole widened, and she began sinking into it like quicksand.

She entered the floor.

And swam through the walls.

The darkness gave her the power to move through the house to the outside world. She could escape. And what's more, she had her familiar, the spirits of the earth, and a newfound power within her that burned in her heart like a hot coal. She could will her body to change, making her look older, fuller. She could move with the grace of a cat or the speed of a gazelle. And she was strong. She could bend steel rods and had been able to lift one end of her mother's Cadillac.

But she kept these new gifts a secret. She had private plans. Plans that would satisfy the desires she had once feared were insatiable. She had the ability now, the touch of evil she'd needed. There were no longer any rules or restrictions. Nothing would or could deny her.

She would have all the boys she wanted.

And oh, how she wanted them all.

Hazel started with the boys from church. She lured them to her window, just like Drake, parting the bars for them, letting them ravage her, allowing them to be on top even though it was she who was in control. She initiated everything. She *dominated* everything. These dirty games were hers. And the boys never said no. They loved on her, worshipping at the altar of her body all through the night and coming back for more during the ones that followed. Soon she developed a following, and this harem of choirboys and local hooligans became her new obsession. She owned their bodies, and the more she drew their lust and devotion, the closer she came to owning their souls, even without the mess of murder.

Her dark gifts made it possible.

One by one, she foraged her collection.

CHAPTER SIXTEEN

"SHE BECAME MORE THAN HUMAN," Kayla's double said. "An *anti-being*. Her soul remains restless because she's never been able to get her fill of earthly pleasures."

Kayla stared, overwhelmed. "So if she's not a ghost, what is she?"

Her double's eyes shimmered. "A witch."

"A *witch*?"

"Hazel Snowden is a sorceress, a succubus that feeds on the affection of men. Having been deprived of them for so long, her desire brought her into the heart of madness. But the arts she mastered became more demanding and she became more possessive. She grew paranoid, believing other women would tempt her boys, so she had them beg for her love, and when they offered themselves to her completely she took their souls and stored them in the walls of the manor. But she worried they would try to escape if she left the house. So she became a shut-in again, this time by her own will.

"For years she's been satiating her appetite for male souls by seducing whatever men visit the house. She particularly enjoys taking men of faith, to further insult her father. But she has not lost her preference for teenage boys, because her teenage self has never fully matured. She grew to have the body of a woman, but her dark spirit will remain seventeen forever. So now, as the hour of Samhain strengthens her black magic, she is growing more powerful, and she's hungry for fresh boys, fresh souls. And the darkness that gives her that power wants souls of its own. They want *virgins.*"

Kayla felt faint. "They want me?"

"They want us both," Robbie's double said.

"And she will go to any lengths to take all of you," said her wraith. "She'll take the souls of the men and feed the women to the darkness beneath the mountain."

As she spoke these words her cloak went from black to red, the color flowing from top to bottom. The cloaks of the others changed similarly.

"She's going to kill me?" Kayla asked.

One of the other figures stepped forward.

"No," he said, pulling off his hood to reveal his face. "I am."

She gasped, seeing nothing but blackness in Joe's double's eyes.

"There's still time," her wraith said. "Fate remains uncertain. But you have to get everyone out of that house before it's too late."

Kayla tilted her head. "Wait a minute. If you're my double then how do you know all of this when I don't?"

"Because *the others* have told us; *the shadow people.* They know the secrets."

At the sound of their name the spindly creatures moved behind the spirit doubles, lurking in the hollow like smoke, having been there all along, but unseen, bending the light like black holes.

Kayla took a step back. "What are they?"

"They are all that remain of the ones Hazel has taken, but hasn't imprisoned behind the walls of the manse, those she's killed but does not desire. Every victim has had their soul stolen, and Hazel has stolen their image so that she may use it to lure further victims. Without their souls and images they are forced to become shadows of their former selves. They too are neither alive nor dead and cannot rest until they are freed, but some don't even want to be free; some are still seduced by her and totally devoted. They're trapped in the purgatory she has created—their souls in the house, their shadow selves banished to the forest of Black Rock Mountain, the source of the power."

Kayla put her fingertips to her temples. "This doesn't make sense." Tears of frustration brewed in the corners of her eyes. "I don't understand. Why would Joe kill me?"

"Because that's the way Hazel wants it. She will seduce him and he will become her slave. Once she has his undivided devotion she will make him prove his love by killing you, thereby surrendering his soul to her while offering yours to the dark forces within the mountain. She will keep your body image, and you will become one of the lost, one of the shadow people, banished to these woods for all of eternity."

Kayla took a deep breath, her skin tightening.

"What about Mrs. Snowden, who hired Joe and Danny? I mean, she must have found out what her daughter was doing. She must know what she's become."

The wraith nodded. "She does. She fears her daughter but still loves her. She's all she has in this world now, and while she didn't lead her daughter to the dark arts, she too has dabbled in sorcery, long before Hazel did. Her maiden name is Breen. She comes from a long line of Celtics, many of them masters of the craft. It's in the Breen blood. They cannot escape it."

Kayla crossed her arms. "So the bitch set us up?"

"Yes. *The bitch set you up.*"

Tubular music echoed through the hills like owls calling. The city clock chimed, ringing once for each hour of the day, and with each clang of the bell the wraiths receded into the leaves that spun into dust devils at their feet.

"Wait!" Kayla cried out.

But they were already vaporizing behind the veil of leaves, a gray froth finding the afternoon shadows and nestling there.

"Our lives count on you," Robbie's double said.

Joe's wraith looked at her one last time. "Don't let me do it, Kayla."

The sky dimmed and the wind picked up, fiercer, more serious. Leaves filled the air in a dizzying display of gold and the wraiths became as blurry as the shadow people as they blended into the dim hollow.

"Save me," added her wraith. "Save yourself."

CHAPTER SEVENTEEN

IT WAS THE BEST SEX Joe had ever had.

Hazel had done things to him he'd never imagined, even in his most twisted fantasies. Her fingers were silken, yet she had an incredible grip. Her mouth and tongue brought him to the edge of ecstasy and then pulled him back, teasing before giving her all. Her vulva was tight and hot, and she had total control of the muscles within it, her vaginal strength milking him. She'd taken him in every position, taunting and devouring him, draining every last drop of his lust.

What she'd done was nothing short of magic. His body was sore but his spirit was still willing. But as he awoke he found her side of the bed empty. He punched the pillow. She hadn't even said goodbye.

Did I do something wrong?

Self-doubt foreign to him raked his nerves like broken fingernails. He tried to think if he'd done or said anything that could have offended her. *We had such an amazing night. What could have ruined it?* He was normally confident with his abilities to please women. Had he failed her? Was she disappointed? He hoped he hadn't blown it with Hazel. After only one night, he was completely smitten. He wasn't *in love* with her but desired her with a ferocity that surprised him. Normally, once he had made it with a girl he quickly lost interest in her and grew more and more annoyed by her presence. But the opposite was true with Hazel. He wanted to know more about her, *everything* about her, and he wanted it without having to wait.

He hadn't gotten her number.

Shit!

Maybe Mrs. Snowden had it. He'd been meaning to check in with her anyway, to show her he was responsible. Now he had added motivation. He couldn't lose track of Hazel. He *had* to fuck her again.

Danny had gone to school, taking Robbie with him. Joe had the house to himself and as he walked through it he was once again struck by the enormity of both its size and its luxury. The bookshelves in the library were monolithic and stacked full with books, many of which looked like they predated the 20th century. He browsed them but didn't open them for fear they would fall apart in his hands. He'd never seen so many different bibles. He hadn't had any idea there were so many versions of it. It made him laugh, thinking of just how gullible people must be to believe a book is a sacred text when there were so many interpretations. How could the word of God need so many editors?

He kept walking, making sure the house was in good shape, just as he'd been paid to do. The girls hadn't screwed with anything. Hazel was a Snowden, and he trusted her, but the other girls could have been snooping around. They could have damaged or stolen something. He hadn't felt suspicious of them before, but this morning he had a newfound distrust. He couldn't explain it, but overnight he'd come to be slightly annoyed by Kayla and Maxine. Maybe it had to do with Kayla not putting out, he thought.

He began cleaning up the living room, throwing out empty potato chip bags and beer cans. There were ashes in the fireplace so he swept it out and went on to the kitchen. He unloaded the dishwasher and put all the plates away, then wiped down the counters. To his surprise, he was enjoying the chores.

All the while he thought of Hazel. Her flesh flashed through his head, her nubile body blossoming before his mind's eye. He recalled the wet lashes of her tongue on his balls, her flushed pussy against his mouth as they went into a sixty-nine. He could almost smell the soft meat of her breasts and heard the animal moans she'd made.

Satisfied with the inside of the house, Joe went to the back porch to clean the pool and hot tub. The tables were lined with a glistening assortment of green and amber bottles. The water of the pool was a liquid mirror, reflecting the perfect blue of the sky. He broke it gently with the skimmer. He remembered Maxine elegantly swimming through the water and a feeling of anger filled his chest. It was unwarranted, but it burned there just the same.

Why am I so pissed at her and Kayla?

He cleaned and thought of Hazel, imagining how beautiful and graceful she would be while swimming under the stars, her body silhouetted by the eerie glow of the pool. In that moment, he realized that only she was really worthy of the pool's azure decadence, that Maxine and even Kayla would ugly it somehow, taint it. The pool belonged to the Snowdens. It was *meant for* Snowdens, first and foremost. Snowdens like Hazel.

Only Hazel.

He thought of her tight around his cock and almost dropped the skimmer. After dumping the bottles in the recycling bin he went back inside and decided he should check the cellar as well. No one had been down there since he'd started watching the place, but it would be best to check on the entire house.

He went through the doorway where wooden stairs sank into freezing darkness. He turned on the light—a single yellow bulb that hung above him from a wire, which surprised him because it seemed so cheap and out of place. He reached the floor and took a look around, the dim light throwing thick shadows, obscuring every corner. Boxes and crates were stacked against the walls and along one side, better lit, was the long rack of wine bottles. Joe had never been much of a wine drinker, but he wasn't going to turn down free booze, especially when it was supposed to be so fancy. He was a Miller Lite and Jack Daniel's kind of drinker. He had not developed a sense of what was quality and what was swill. He might as well develop his pallet on someone else's dime.

He turned the bottles to look at their labels and color. Most of them were covered with a fine layer of dust, others draped in cobwebs. He wondered which would most impress Hazel and hoped he would be able to share one of the bottles with her soon, hopefully tonight. Stepping around to the other side, he heard a rustling in the dark behind him.

He stopped there, a mannequin staring into the shadows. Only his fists moved, clenching shut. A few moments passed in silence before his shoulders relaxed again.

Probably a mouse.

The cellar smelled of mildew and dirt and age. It was a forgotten world down here, the black belly of the house. The bulb above flickered briefly, causing the shadows to twitch like figures drawing nearer. Joe bit the inside of his cheek, chewing it the way he always did when he got nervous. He walked around the rack and across the tile at the center of the cellar, not noticing the blood that had seeped up through the cracks, making thin, red streams that ran across the floor in square patterns.

He climbed back up the stairs and closed the door just as a gravelly voice whispered.

"*Filthy bastard . . .*"

Danny couldn't concentrate.

He zoned out during all of his classes, even history, which he'd always found fascinating. Somehow the life of Oliver Cromwell couldn't compete with his thoughts of Hazel. She ruled over his mind, never leaving the forefront for more than a minute. Even when he overheard people talking about Linda's disappearance, he didn't chime in.

Nearly all of his thoughts were sexual.

He found himself fantasizing about Hazel taking him over and ravaging him. It was an uncommon daydream for him to have because he usually preferred to be the one on top, to have total control of a girl and the pace and positions of sex. But in these savory fantasies he would submit to Hazel with a welcomed powerlessness. He wanted her to dominate him, rule him, to put him in the thrall of her sensual dictatorship.

To possess him.

He wasn't sure why, but when he fantasized of her he replayed everything that had happened in bed with Linda. It'd been incredible sex, but for some reason he'd begun to associate it with Hazel Snowden instead of Linda Lelane. It wasn't something he could explain, but he felt he didn't have to. Good sex was good sex, and something about Hazel's sly style and breathy tone assured him she would offer nothing short of bliss in the bedroom, bliss so intense it would fucking hurt.

He was equally distracted at practice. Everyone kept slipping past him as he spaced out, his eyes getting lost in the swaying trees and the bruised sky beyond them. Last practice he had excelled, and today's sudden change sent Coach Brown into fits, veins bulging in his neck.

"Damn it, Knox! What the hell is wrong with you out there? You stoned or something?"

He was berating him in front of the rest of the team and Danny could see their mocking smirks out of the corner of his eye.

"No, Coach. Sorry, I'm just . . . just not feeling well today."

"You sure ain't *playing* well, I'll tell you that! You play like this at our next game and Polk is going to cut through us like butter!"

"Don't worry. I'll be ready for them on Friday."

Brown took a deep breath, and Danny resented the look of judgment the man was giving him, but he didn't let it show.

"Three more days till the big game, son," Brown said. "Don't let the team down. Hell, don't let *yourself* down."

"I won't, coach."

But Brown was already walking away.

Joe decided against telling Danny and Robbie he'd fucked Hazel. Though he was usually the type to brag, this time he chose to keep his late night rendezvous clandestine. He wanted to keep the memory as his own private treasure, much like he wanted to keep Hazel, at least until they became an official item. Then he would shout his love for her from the top of Black Rock Mountain.

Love?

Had he really just thought that? About a girl? He wasn't a stranger to the word. He'd say he loved heavy metal, weed, and motorcycles. But he'd never used the word in relation to a girl. He always found the idea sweet to the point of disgusting, like when a couple would use baby talk with one another.

Love, he laughed, and yet he knew it was what came next, after obsession. And obsessed he surely was.

His phone rang. Kayla.

He sent it to voicemail.

CHAPTER EIGHTEEN

WHERE TO BEGIN?

How was she supposed to tell them? She could hardly believe it herself. But Kayla couldn't deny it. To do so would be to admit to herself she was going crazy, that she was some sort of schizophrenic, and that thought was even more frightening to her than believing in witches and wraiths, of people without souls or shadows confined to the mountain by some sort of black spell.

When Joe's phone went to voicemail she hung up, not knowing what to say. She hadn't been planning on coming right out with it. She wanted to talk to him in person.

Somewhere other than Snowden Manor.

The thought of returning to it filled her with abject horror. She was sure if she and her friends were to die it would be in that damned house. The wraiths made that pretty clear. Kayla thought again of Maxine's vision of blood. Her friend had not been hallucinating after all.

Maybe that was where to start. Maxine, having seen the evil in the house, or a glimpse of it at least, may be more open-minded when it came to hearing Kayla's story. It would have to be done in person, so Maxine could see she was serious. Kayla knew the panic in her eyes wasn't going to go away anytime soon, nor would the redness if she didn't stop crying.

She lay on her bed, holding onto one of her pillows as if it were a stuffed animal. Downstairs she could hear her mother shuffling around the kitchen. It was past six now, which meant she would be in a drift of valium and wine, so Kayla was confident she wouldn't have to deal with her, but a moment later there were footsteps on the stairs.

Kayla cursed quietly. Her bedroom door came open and she turned, expecting to see her stoned mother, but there was no one there. She sat up, fearing some sort of supernatural being, but instead she saw a tuft of blond hair. Her little sister Patricia was coming toward her, a popsicle in hand, fudge surrounding her mouth like clown makeup.

"Want some ice cream, sissy?" the child asked.

Kayla chuckled. "You got it all over yourself."

Patricia looked at the fudge running down her arm and giggled.

Kayla got up. "Come on, you little silly head."

She took her sister's clean hand, walked her into the bathroom, and used a wet washcloth to clean her up. Patricia grinned up at her with plump squirrel cheeks, and Kayla suddenly envied her for how a simple popsicle could give her such joy.

"You look sad," Patricia said. "Don't be sad, sissy."

She held out the popsicle and Kayla smiled, shrugged, and took a bite.

"Tell me again what you saw," Kayla said.

They were sitting at the booth furthest from the counter so they would have privacy while they ate their pizza. Maxine seemed aloof. Her sunglasses were mounted on top of her head and she wore giant hoop earrings. Somehow this carefree look made Kayla feel like her friend wasn't taking the conversation seriously.

"I was just tripping," Maxine said.

"But all you had was some weak ecstasy and beer."

"Well, it must have been enough."

"You came downstairs *screaming.*"

Maxine looked away, embarrassed. "I just got scared. You don't have to mock me for it."

"I'm *not.* Really, I'm not. The only reason I bring it up is because I think . . ." She trailed off, unsure how to proceed.

Maxine leaned forward. "What?"

Kayla released the breath she'd been holding. "There's something in that house, Max. Something evil."

She felt better having said it, despite the look her friend was giving her. Kayla looked down at her soda and stirred the ice with her straw.

"What're you trying to say?" Maxine asked.

"I'm saying there's someone else in that house, and they're not exactly human. Not anymore. I think what you saw that night is part of it."

Maxine's face pinched. "But, all I saw was a bunch of blood and eyes."

"Didn't you say it was trying to grab you?"

Maxine was reluctant but then said, "It seemed that way."

There was a moment of silence between them, their eyes locked, friends suddenly a little uncomfortable with each other.

"Come on . . . ." Maxine said with a shake of her head.

"I'm serious. That woman who hired them, she had a daughter. That girl who came by—"

"No way. She's our age and Mrs. Snowden's really old."

"I know, but that girl is older than she looks. She's some kind of evil entity, like a witch." Kayla tensed as Maxine snorted out a laugh. "I know it sounds crazy."

"A witch? You're serious?"

"She's like, an evil spirit, you know?"

"Kayla, this is—"

"No, listen. You saw that thing, *whatever* it was—don't you think it's possible it was something supernatural?"

Maxine looked toward the ceiling, but there was something in her eyes that told Kayla her friend was on the fence, despite her denial.

"That's only in the movies," Maxine said.

"Maybe not."

"There's no such thing as ghosts and goblins. We're not seven anymore, you know."

"What if it's all true though?" Kayla said, leaning across the table. "I think it is. I didn't before that house, but now . . . you're not the only one who saw things, Max. I saw these black shapes in the woods. And then I saw these . . . wraiths."

"Saw what?"

"Wraiths. They're like the ghosts of people who aren't dead but are in danger."

"Ghosts of people who are still alive?"

"Yeah."

A short laugh of disbelief. "Jesus, do you hear yourself?"

"What you saw didn't make sense either. That's what I'm trying to tell you. It's supernatural. How else could we have both had strange visions?"

Maxine sat on that for a moment and her eyes went wide, her lips curling.

"Son of a bitch!" she said.

"What?"

"Joe and Danny. The bastards must have spiked our drinks!"

"I don't think they would—"

"It must have been Joe's idea, that little shit-stain. He must've used roofies or something so he could try and get in your pants."

Kayla threw up her hands. "But why would Danny drug you?"

"Because he likes to be in control. He probably did it just for laughs."

"For *laughs*? I don't think so. And Joe may be a little pushy, but he's no rapist. Besides, I saw what I saw on two different days. The wraiths I saw this afternoon and I haven't seen Joe at all today. He wasn't even at school. I saw the wraiths today while I was hiking. They warned me about the house, about Hazel."

"That girl."

"Right. Only she's not really a girl. She's a woman. She just changes her shape and her looks."

Maxine looked exhausted now, as if her head hurt from thinking about it all. "Kayla, this is nuts. You know that, right? Please tell me you know that."

"I need your help on this. The wraiths told me we're all in danger."

"They spoke to you?"

Kayla nodded.

Maxine put her palms flat on the table, leaning in. "Christ, you're hearing things as well as seeing things? You should get your head examined. Seriously. Something could really be wrong with you."

"I'm not insane!"

A family a few booths away looked at them and Kayla reeled herself in.

"I'm not saying that," Maxine said. "I'm just worried about you."

"Max . . . please."

Her friend sighed. "Look, even if I believed all of this—and I'm not saying I do—what the hell are we supposed to do about it?"

Kayla gazed out at the parking lot. The night had swallowed the world and the streetlights in the parking lot fought in vain against it.

"I'm not sure. Not yet."

Horace could smell the master on the tall boy, and her scent lingered in one of the rooms. It was the smell of sex. She was conquering them. It would take more times, but they would fall, and he would be there to help drag them down.

In the yard, the youngest boy tailing behind him, Horace sniffed at the grass, following the equally rich smells of the others that lived in the woods. They were restless tonight. He could feel their strange energy. But unlike a hare or stray cat, the creatures in the dark did not make him want to give chase. He liked to watch them move about, but they were not prey. Not anymore. They were soulless, and without souls they were hardly alive. To hunt them would be like hunting an animal that was already dead. At best, these creatures were crippled, and that alone removed any excitement. They'd already been taken. Now the boys in the house were being taken too.

The master had already touched the older boys. She'd marked her territory and would continue to work on them until they were as obedient as he was. The youngest boy would be next. Horace liked him and would be sad to see him go into the walls with the others. But there was nothing he could do to change that. The master took what she wanted, and Horace helped her. No matter how he felt about what she asked him to do, he was obedient, a good familiar, a good boy.

He hoped the girls would come back soon.

He liked the way they smelled.

CHAPTER NINETEEN

WHY HASN'T SHE COME BACK?

Joe bit his nails for the first time since sixth grade. He paced around the dining room, treating it like the track in the schoolyard. Sometimes when he needed to get his head straight he would trot along the track. It was the only exercise he ever really got. It helped him to think, and he found that pacing around the giant table had a similar effect.

It was night now, close to ten.

He hadn't heard from Hazel.

His teeth ground in his skull like a cement mixer, his hands as clammy as his underarms. The beginnings of a stress headache pinched his temples. Even his bones ached, as if he was going through withdrawals, as if she were a terribly addictive drug.

Maybe she is one, he thought. *Lady Heroin. Miss Morphine, USA.*

God, he wanted her.

He bit his thumb's cuticle away and wished he could contact her somehow, wished he had telekinetic powers and could sneak into her thoughts to make her feel how he felt. He'd not been able to get through to Mrs. Snowden. He left a message telling her the house was fine, but he didn't know how to ask about Hazel, so he just left it at that. Now he wished he'd asked her to call him back. It was too late to call her. He didn't want to come off as weird or creepy by calling her up late at night to ask for her niece's phone number.

He went to the window again and stared into the night with a choked longing. The stars were out but their beauty offered no peace. Joe made his way to the back porch for some fresh air. The insect songs of summer had gone, leaving only the rustle of leaves and the horsewhip clacking of the reeds. The air was crisp and he could see his breath. At the edge of the property there was movement, and looking closer he realized it was Robbie and the dog. The two had become inseparable. Joe realized he almost never saw the dog when Robbie went to school and wondered where it went.

Horace barked upon seeing him.

Damned dog.

Robbie started running so Horace would chase him up the hill to the patio where Joe stood. When they reached him Robbie smiled, even though Joe couldn't see any good reason for him to.

"Nice night, huh?" Robbie asked.

Horace snorted in dumb agreement.

"Not bad, I guess."

"This kind of weather makes me want to go camping. Remember when Dad used to take us?"

Joe groaned. "Don't talk to me about Dad."

It was always a sore subject, seeing how the old man had run out on them, and tonight, in particular, Joe didn't want to think about the son of a bitch. He had enough bugging him.

"Okay," his brother said.

Robbie's tone was sheepish, and his weakness annoyed Joe worse than usual. He just wished the kid would grow up already. He'd gotten sick of holding his hand, especially because he never seemed to learn anything from him.

"I was thinking," Robbie began, "about what you said. I know you've been trying to help me with girls, and I do appreciate what you tried to do with Linda. I think you're right about that girl Hazel too. I mean, maybe she really does like me. Maybe I should ask her out, you know? If you'll give me some tips."

There was a searing heat in Joe's head. He turned to his brother, all teeth, snarling. "Oh, is that so? All of a sudden you're ready to put on your big boy pants, yeah? You think you've got the balls to actually ask a girl on a date?"

Robbie looked away, hurt, fragile.

"Don't give me the tears now," Joe said.

"I'm not, jeez."

"You want pointers from me? So far you haven't taken any of my advice. You still act like you're fuckin' twelve, you little puke."

Robbie glowered and stepped back. "Why are you so angry?"

This set Joe off and he got in Robbie's face. "Maybe I'm sick of your bullshit—all your comic books and horror movies. No drinking or smoking, and too scared to screw. Maybe I'm sick of having a little *faggot* for a brother."

The thought of Robbie even trying to ask Hazel out had sent Joe into a rage, giving him a hatred for his brother he'd never felt before. Everything about Robbie that had always just irked him now seemed like the absolute worst things a person could do. He was surprised by his own surge of anger, but it didn't stop him from unleashing it.

Robbie stepped farther away and started toward the patio door. He said nothing.

"That's right," Joe said. "'Just run away."

Maxine thought about calling Kayla's mom. She was concerned for her friend's mental state and thought it would be a good idea to involve her parents. Her mother could get her to a shrink or a special hospital, get her on medication so she wouldn't believe in ghosts and witches anymore. It really would be the best thing for her, to keep things from getting worse.

But she didn't call. Because, in a way, she thought Kayla could be right. Maxine had never been able to fully swallow the idea that what she'd seen on the ceiling had just been in her mind. She wanted to believe that, but couldn't. What she'd seen was so graphic and lifelike. So maybe Kayla was right, at least in some way. Maybe there was something going on in Snowden Manor, something supernatural, diabolical. But if that was the case she certainly didn't want to go back there. But they would have to find a way to convince Danny and the other boys to leave. It wouldn't be easy to get them to bail on such a high paying job, but they had to try. If even some of what Kayla had said were true, they would have to get them out fast.

A witch.

Maxine thought of the petite girl who had come to the house so suddenly. She'd looked so lithe and breakable. Was it really possible she was some kind of witch that was going to kill them all and take their souls? It was farfetched to say the least, but no more than a blood monster with a dozen eyes watching her having sex.

So what the hell are we gonna do?

After pizza, Kayla dropped her off at home to check in with her parents and let them know she would be staying over at Kayla's. But tonight they weren't going to watch movies and eat raw cookie dough. Their days of toenail-painting slumber parties were over. Tonight they were going to figure out a way to save the boys and, from the sound of it, themselves. Kayla would be back to get her by ten-thirty. It gave Maxine just enough time to take a shower, gather her things, and think long and hard about all this craziness.

Maybe she should just call Danny. Tell him she didn't want him to stay there anymore. She could use sex to coax him into doing what she wanted. It had always worked for her in the past. But there were still many days to go, and he'd told her Mrs. Snowden was probably going to extend her visit. Leaving would mean forfeiting his share of the money. There had to be some way to convince him to get out and not go back, but if they went to the boys with this story of witchcraft and wraiths they would think they were a couple of psycho bimbos. So what did that leave them with? Lying? What would they tell them, that the place was full of toxic mold and they all had to vacate?

She thought of Mrs. Snowden again.

Maybe we should call her and get her to come home.

That could be the easiest thing to do. They could convince her to return, saying the house was in shambles. It would screw the boys out of the deal but it would get them out of there, wouldn't it?

It wasn't much of an idea, but it was something.

She hoped her friend had a better plan.

Gladys was afraid.

It was the right time for this to happen, the right time of year and the right circumstances, but still she felt a strange vibe, one that had started as unease and worked its way up to a quiet, lingering terror. She'd changed hotels in the hope of shaking the feeling off, but it clung to her like a starved tick, refusing to let go.

And it was worse at night, much worse.

She would watch the sun go down from her room, and a smooth fear would roll over the ridges of her weary spine. Even all these miles away she could sense the house and the decades old malevolence that festered inside it like disease. She could feel the walls swarming with imprisoned souls, the woods beyond the property ravaged by shadowy beings, and could smell the dog's wet fur and taste the rising blood that tickled the back of her throat.

She knew her daughter's every move. She was growing more powerful, more unstable.

The boys were there for Hazel's pleasure. It was a terrible need but a necessary evil. Gladys had no qualms with that, and had perfectly good alibis here for when the boys disappeared. So it was not what her daughter was going to do to the boys that worried her, but the strength she would harness from each new devotee. Even though her victims were few and far between, they still filled Hazel with the most sinister, venal force, making her power-mad and giving her grandiose delusions. Instead of utilizing the magic, her daughter was now convinced she was *the keeper* of it, that without her there would be no sorcery at all.

Gladys reflected on everything that had happened, that dark, blood-slathered night never leaving her mind for long. It had been the beginning of the end. She had just been so tired of Arthur's cruelty and religious mania. So she'd returned to the dark magic she'd learned from her grandmother, ancient Celtic rituals designed to cause harm to another. Arthur even had books on it for her to reference, and she'd used them to practice a sort of voodoo against her husband. It had worked, but not in the way she had hoped it would.

When she'd found them wrestling in Hazel's room, the first thing she'd noticed was how Hazel had ripped into her father's eyes. For weeks Gladys had been performing a ritual with a skull she'd purchased from a medical supply store. During it, she shoved knives into the skull's eyes because she wished blindness to fall upon her husband in an ironic twist because she had always loathed his blind faith. She'd gotten her wish but with a twist of its own, her daughter inflicting the wounds instead of some unnamable force.

She'd made sure Arthur and the boy's corpses were buried deep and performed another ritual to assure they would never be found. She offered herself completely to the hungry spirits of the earth and offered her daughter to them, to keep her safe behind the shield of their black magic. So Hazel had never seen a court room for what they had done, but once inside the sphere of the magic, she was drawn to it and her insatiable lust made her an ideal sorceress. Now it had all gone too far, much further than Gladys had ever intended.

And it was getting worse.

She held herself, looking for a comfort nothing could offer.

He didn't want to stay there anymore.

At first Robbie had been glad to be considered part of the party, when Joe and Danny first got the job and had the girls come, but the party was certainly over now, and he had grown bored of the house's opulence.

And his brother was being a real jerk too. One minute Joe was trying to match him up with a girl and the next minute he was tearing his head off over nothing. Robbie appreciated how he was trying to take him under his wing in the absence of their father, but when Joe got like this he reminded Robbie of their father in the worst way.

The only reason he hadn't left yet was Horace. Mom would never allow him to keep the dog. Robbie had spent most of his life with only few friends that he felt a bond with the way he did with this dog. Beside him in the bed, the big dog sighed and rolled his head onto Robbie's chest, looking at him with exhausted eyes. They'd played all afternoon and were worn out. He put his hand on Horace's head, scratched him behind the ear, and the dog let out a rumble of pleasure as his tongue fell out. He wrapped his arms around him and brought him closer, hugging him, feeling happier than he'd been in a long time.

Horace licked at his face and Robbie laughed until he heard a girl's voice.

"He likes you."

He started and sat up as Horace jumped from the bed and ran into the darkness where the voice had come from.

"Who is that?" he asked. He couldn't see anyone, not even a shape in the shadows. "Kayla? Maxine?"

A soft breeze came through the open window, fluttering the curtains, and he heard the leaves rustling outside as the cool air fell across him like stroking fingertips. And while he did not see her, he could sense the girl, as if they'd locked eyes, as they had earlier.

"Hazel?" he asked. "You're there, aren't you?"

First there was only darkness, closing on him like a fist. Then a white face emerged from its depths, hovering like a harvest moon, disembodied. Robbie licked his lips. The night breeze made Hazel's hair into a writhing animal, and her auburn eyes seemed somehow darker, wider. Her mouth opened and her breath smelled of lilacs and dreams.

"What are you doing here?" he asked.

Her face moved forward, bringing her body with it. She was nude, magnificent. Robbie's body tightened as he looked at hers. She was creamy pale with an ideal young girl's body—slim waist, shy breasts, small shoulders, and a thin triangle of dark hair between her thighs. It seemed to glisten, something wet beneath, moist and hungry, waiting, opening.

"Robbie," she whispered. "I want you."

He couldn't move. Anxiety and excitement glued him to the sheets. Oddly, he glanced to Horace, as if for answers. The dog stayed behind Hazel, sitting in the expanse of shadow she'd emerged from. Robbie looked at her body as it drew near.

Did her breasts just get bigger?

There was something to her face too. It looked more filled out, as if she was ten years older. When he looked down her hips had widened, giving her more of an hourglass frame. Suddenly she looked a lot less innocent. A womanly strength radiated off her, giving her authority. He attributed her mature look to the dim light and his own nervousness but still wondered how she had blossomed before his eyes.

She pressed her breasts together with her arms. They were no longer bashful but full and heavy, and as they pressed against Robbie's chest he nearly gasped from their touch. Her hands snaked around his waist and pulled him into her with a desire on the edge of starvation.

"Do you want to give yourself to me?" she asked.

He did, but couldn't seem to find any words.

"Tell me," she said. "I want to make love to you, Robbie. But you have to give yourself to me. You have to give me your virginity."

He became flustered and thought about protesting the fact that he was a virgin. Her knowing mortified him. Christ, how did *she* know he was one?

Joe, that's how.

This had to be his doing, of course. Just like Linda. How else could he explain this beautiful girl being all over him? It wasn't an everyday occurrence, that was for sure.

"You want me, don't you?" she asked.

He mumbled. "Ye-yes."

She reached into his pants and gripped his semi-hard cock, fingers slithering around him, feeling boneless and cool.

"Give yourself to me."

He wasn't sure what she meant by all of this, but then again he'd never gotten very far with a woman. Maybe this was all part of foreplay. He didn't know what to do, so he just went along with her, hoping he wouldn't look too stupid.

"Tell me you want to fuck me," she said, her lips glistening, revealing teeth that looked somehow reptilian in the light of the moon.

Robbie swallowed hard. "I wanna . . . fuck you."

Behind them, Horace whimpered.

Hazel slid his pants down and drew one of his hands to her engorged breast. It yielded to his cautious touch and his heart palpitated. This was really happening.

"Tell me you want me to take your virginity."

He nodded emphatically. "I do. I do."

"Say it."

"I want you to take my virginity."

Horace let out a *yip* and Hazel turned toward him. It sounded like she hissed. The dog fell silent and she turned back to Robbie, pushing the head of his erection against her slick vagina.

"Tell me you give yourself to me."

Robbie's legs began to shake. "I . . ."

Horace began barking. Hazel spun around, snapping at him like a fellow dog would. "Hush! You will obey me! He is *mine*. He is not for *you!*"

Robbie was confused but too aroused to care. He would try to figure out Hazel's relationship with Horace later. For now he just wanted her to keep doing what she was doing. He would give anything for it to not stop. Hopefully he would last longer than he had with Linda.

Horace groaned and shrank back into the blankets of the shadows, Hazel staring at him until he was out of sight. She looked back at Robbie, her eyes burrowing into him like rusted drills as her hips rocked in his lap, still teasing.

"Say it," she said, almost angry.

Hitching up one leg, she grazed his shaft along her wet opening, and Robbie was lost to her then, completely and hopelessly, with no regrets. Not yet.

"I give myself . . . to *you*."

The shadows deepened as she slipped him into bliss.

PART II

SEASON OF THE WITCH

CHAPTER TWENTY

THEY REACHED THE MANOR HOUSE at a quarter to midnight. They hadn't called, deciding a sudden visit would have more of an effect. Kayla got out of her car, a tremor coursing through her as she gazed upon the towering manse. With only a few lights on, the glowing windows made a grim face like a jack-o-lantern: two square eyes, a nose, jagged teeth. The night brought a cold front and the earth sighed with rising mist. She took cautious steps. Maxine was still in the car. Even in the gloom Kayla could see the pale reluctance on her friend's face.

"Come on," Kayla said. "We'll just get them to come out."

Maxine opened her door slowly and stepped out into the night. She held herself as she moved toward Kayla.

"I hate being here now," Maxine said. "I'm still not sure I believe it all, but it creeps me out anyway."

"That's okay. I saw it all myself and even I don't want to believe it. But we have to do something."

Maxine's eyes held heavy worry. "You think they'll believe us?"

"Probably not. But like you said, we can use our womanly wiles, right?"

Maxine's eyebrows dropped. "What the hell are womanly wiles?"

"Charm, seduction, manipulation. All the stuff we do to get men to do what we want."

Despite the circumstances, Maxine giggled. Kayla was trying to lighten the mood so they wouldn't scare themselves stupid before they even got to the door. It wasn't working very well.

"So," Maxine said, "we're going to try and lure them out first, right?"

"Right. I don't want to spend any more time in there than we have to."

They moved toward the front porch, briefly hesitated, and then walked up the steps together. Kayla rang the bell. They waited, each second seeming like an eon. She could hear Maxine's teeth grinding.

Danny opened the door, swaying like he'd been drinking. His eyes were bloodshot and his brow was slick with sweat. He looked pale and bloated, his hair tossed like he'd been napping. Seeing them, he smiled but not with his eyes. The door opened wider.

"Hey ladies. You've come back to the pleasure palace?"

Maxine forced a smile of her own. "Came to see you, big boy. Kayla and I have a surprise for you guys. You wanna take a ride?"

Danny squinted. "You don't wanna hang out here?"

"We have something set up," Kayla said, adding a little huskiness to her voice. "Something special."

"You know me and the boys need to watch the house."

"Come on, babe," said Maxine. "We just want to take you out for a little while."

Danny's face soured like he'd just bit into cat food. He seemed uncomfortable, even a little nervous. "No. We have to be here ... we're *supposed* to be here. *Always.*"

Maxine scoffed. "Not twenty-four-seven. Gimme a break."

"Look, something could happen. Besides, we're waiting."

Abruptly, Kayla felt cold. She resisted the urge to take Maxine's hand.

"Waiting for what?" she asked.

The large boy looked at her like she was the village idiot. "For Hazel, of course. She could come back any minute. We need to be here when she does."

Kayla's chill deepened, bones trembling beneath icy flesh. It was as if something had overpowered Danny. He was weirdly married to the idea of not leaving the house. And in mentioning Hazel he gave her a clear glimpse of how he was slowly succumbing to whatever strange hold she had over him, as well as the others. Beside her, she could feel Maxine's jealous wrath brewing, but she kept it together, still trying to coax her boyfriend out of the house.

"Forget her. *I'm* your girlfriend, remember? She's just some chick you barely know. You don't need to wait on her."

"Of course I do," he said, astonished.

Maxine frowned. "Why?"

He didn't answer.

"Danny," Kayla said, "where's Joe?"

On cue, she heard his boots clicking on the tile beyond. He appeared as a long shadow, and then emerged into the light of the porch. The boys stood there in unspoken alliance. Like Danny, Joe had a strange look to him. There was hollowness in his eyes that had not been there before, as if something inside of him had been pinned down and suffocated. The boyish grin that had flirted with her was gone, replaced by tight, colorless lips. He looked like a statue of himself—expressionless, lifeless, undead.

"Hey," she said, forcing a smile, trying to blush girlishly. "I've got a little surprise for you. Something you've been . . . *waiting for.*"

This was her ace in the hole, her Hail Mary pass. She hoped that by alluding to sex she could get him out of the house and snap him out of whatever grim state he was in. Once his head was straight she could tell him the truth. There was a chance he might believe some of it. For now, she had to play the part of sex kitten.

"We have a job to do," Joe said. He was curt, his voice low, monotone, expressing no friendship between them. "But you're welcome to come inside."

"Baby . . . we have a great surprise set up for you guys. We can't bring it here. Trust us, it'll be worth it."

She raised her eyebrows and bit her lower lip, holding her hands together, right across her crotch, turning up the schoolgirl sensuality.

"Why don't you just come into the house," Joe said, stepping aside to make way for her. "We'd love to have you. *All of us* would."

The emphasis made her mouth dry. Was it Joe who wanted her, or was he merely a puppet now, something shiny to lure them into a trap? She hoped things hadn't escalated to that degree. If they had, it would be easy enough for the boys to overpower them and drag them into the house. No one was around to hear them scream. No one knew where they were.

"We've partied this place out," Maxine said. "Come on. Let's try something new."

Danny shook his head. "Nah, we like it here. But you can come in. Especially *Kayla.*"

Kayla went rigid.

What the hell was that all about? Is he trying to make Maxine jealous?

Her friend's face contorted. "You don't want me anymore? Is that it?"

Danny shrugged. Tears of shock brewed in Maxine's eyes.

"Cut the waterworks," he said. "You can come in too, but we'd really like Kayla to join us."

Kayla looked to Joe. He was smiling now and she found it worse than his deadpan. "You okay with Danny showing this new interest in me?" she asked. "I thought I was *your* girl."

Joe crossed his arms, popped vertebra in his neck. "Well, we haven't *consummated*, now have we? Besides, Danny's right. We would rather have you."

"Why?"

"Because *you're* the virgin."

Under any other circumstance, she would have slapped him. But there was something very wrong with them, something that would only get worse if she didn't help. Hazel had them under her spell, and the longer the boys stayed with her the more twisted they would become, transforming into her frothing slaves.

"Yeah, I'm a virgin," she said. "But that can change."

Joe's eyes opened wider.

"But not here," she added.

"Suit yourself," Joe said, and began to close the door.

"Wait!" She nudged the door open. "Goddamnit, will you just listen to us?"

"You wanna talk? Come inside."

"No!"

"Why not? You scared?"

"Are you scared to leave? I never thought you were a chicken shit, Joe. Was I wrong?"

His face darkened and for a moment she was worried he might hit her. "You're not gonna get me with that double-dog-dare crap. Now get inside."

He took her arm and she pulled away fiercely but he snatched her wrist. Maxine smacked him and he let go, a look of shock on his face as a pink handprint blossomed on his cheek.

"Not the face!" he shouted, pointing at Maxine. "You just want me to look bad when Hazel comes back, don't you? That's it, isn't it? You bitches are jealous! All jealous! Every last fucking one of you!"

"One skinny bitch is enough for both of you now?" Maxine

asked.

"Don't you talk that way about her!" Danny said. "You don't know what we have together, what we—"

Kayla broke. "Listen to yourselves, you guys! Don't you see she's got you brainwashed? She's not fucking *human*! She's a part of this house! She's going to take all of you. She wants your souls!"

The guys fell ashen for a moment and she thought she might be getting through. Then they erupted in laughter and her heart sank, a block of cement in a tepid bog.

"*Souls*?" Danny said, cracking up. "*Not human*?"

"You've lost it, Kayla," Joe added. "Get a grip."

"She's not fucking around!" Maxine said. "You guys are in serious trouble. This house is . . . *evil*."

Joe shook his head. "Christ. You sound like one of those dumbass movies my brother is always watching."

"Where is Robbie?" she asked. "Maybe he'll believe us."

"Upstairs, probably asleep. But even he wouldn't buy this horseshit."

"Guys, please," Kayla said. "This house has a dark history . . . people have died here, and Hazel is a part of that, she—"

The door slammed shut, though neither Joe nor Danny had grabbed the handle. It seemed to have slammed all on its own, as if by the gust of a hurricane. She and Maxine stood there for a moment, breathless, but the boys did not open the door again, even when the girls started knocking. One by one the lights in the house turned off, disfiguring the jack-o-lantern face until it was gone completely. No noise came from the house now, only the wind that blew gently around it, ensnaring it in fallen leaves with high, ghostly, musical saw whistles.

They stepped off the porch. Maxine was wiping her eyes.

"What do we do now?"

Kayla had no answer, but as she looked upon the great manor, she noticed the ridges in the climbing slats, which had once been used for gardening. The rows jutted out, all the way to the second floor on the side of the house facing east. A tangle of vines clung like Velcro.

"We have to get inside."

Maxine blinked. "What? Are you crazy? I thought the wraiths said our lives were in danger."

"They did. But the guys' lives are too. We can't just abandon them."

"They just laughed in our faces!"

"Not Robbie. He's a sweet kid, I'd never forgive myself if we didn't try to get him out."

Maxine looked at the ground, tears falling with more frequency. "I can't believe Danny said those things."

"It's not him, Max. Not really. He's under the spell of that damned witch. We can still get them out, but we should get to Robbie first. If we can convince him, maybe he can help us convince the others."

Maxine looked up at the house as if it was a grizzly bear about to pounce. Fear had its giant hands around her throat. "How the fuck are we going to get in there?"

"Look at those slats sticking out. We can scale this side of the house. It'll be just like the rock climbing wall down at the gym."

"I hate that wall."

"We have to do it, Max. We can't leave Robbie here."

"Did you see how that door closed?"

"Yeah, I did."

"That wasn't them. It was her, wasn't it?"

"I think so, yes. She heard us talking bad about her and cut us off."

Maxine bit her lip. "Seems like a warning."

"Guess it does. But we can't let her scare us off."

"Why not? Maybe that's the only warning we're gonna get."

"Look, if we go home and the guys die, will you really be able to live with the fact that we didn't do everything we could?"

Maxine exhaled, long and slow, and wiped the last of her tears away. "No. I won't. Let's start climbing. Just promise you'll stay close to me."

They moved up the side of the house with relative ease, both girls being young and fit. Kayla went up first with Maxine below her, each of them taking ginger steps to maintain the silence. The nearby maple tree scraped the side of the house with its branches, drowning out what little noise they made. When they came to a second floor window, it was partly open, leaving only the screen as a barrier. She peered inside but saw only blue-black shadows draped across an empty, unmade bed. She took her car keys from her pocket, used one to cut into the screen, then reached through and pulled, bending the frame. The screen popped out. She put both hands on the sill and lifted herself through the window and tumbled into the darkened room. She crouched, letting her eyes adjust. Behind her, Maxine came through and crawled up beside her.

"Are we alone?"

"I think so."

"Look." Maxine pointed to the dresser where Robbie's backpack was. "We got lucky. This must be his room."

"But where is he? They said he was sleeping."

"Maybe they lied. Or maybe he got up to use the bathroom."

Behind them, the window came down so slowly they didn't notice. Silently, the lock snapped into place on its own.

"Should we look for him?"

Kayla didn't answer. Someone else did.

"*You won't find him.*"

It was a woman's voice, husky, intimidating. Maxine whimpered and grabbed for her friend's hand. Kayla took it and looked around the room, seeing no movement, no shadowy silhouettes. The disembodied voice seemed to be coming from every direction at once, circling like a predator. The girls drew closer, huddling for shelter.

The voice cut the silence. "He is inside, with *us.*"

Somehow Kayla mustered her courage. "Let him go, Hazel."

There was a hush, and Kayla knew she had shocked the witch by identifying her. A ripple of confidence went through her.

"He gave himself to me" Hazel said. "I possess him."

"You can't own him."

"He is one of my boys now!"

The voice was wet, a gurgling in a hoarse throat. With each word the room pulsed slightly, the walls like a sleeping creature's ribcage, breathing.

"What do you want?" Kayla asked.

"Same thing every girl wants—love, adoration, devotion. I want *boys.* All the boys Daddy would never let me have."

"Don't you have enough souls already?"

"There's never enough; especially not virgins. You and Robbie are so pure and clean. Your delicious innocence delights me."

A pink light grew in the center of the room, blooming like a drop of blood in a rain puddle. Its core brightened, casting the room in a bubblegum glow like a discothèque. There was a stifling warmth to it, as if it turned the bedroom into a giant womb, and Kayla had the sudden urge to lie down and submit to Hazel, but she fought against it, knowing the witch was trying to lull her with black magic.

"You can't have me!"

"Oh, but I can. Your body will serve me well. Boys can't resist a nubile, blond virgin."

"No way. Maybe Robbie gave himself to you, but I won't. Now let him out."

Hazel's laughter was garbled. "He *wants* to be in here with me."

The light intensified and a shadow appeared in front of them. It was the form of a woman, much more voluptuous than Hazel had been when they'd met her. Kayla knew this must be Hazel's adult body, even though she could not make out the face.

"You tricked him," Kayla said. "You seduced him, didn't you? He didn't know what you really meant by *giving himself* to you. He just wanted to get laid."

The curvy silhouette's hair stormed and a hot windblast spread across Kayla's cheeks. Hazel's hair contorted, growing thicker and longer, looking like braids or dreadlocks. Kayla gasped. The witch's head was now swarming with slick, fuchsia tentacles and hissing snakes. The feelers of the tentacles had razor-like teeth, all snapping like mucus-smeared bear traps. Covering Hazel's body were deep cuts in the shapes of stars, moons, and other symbols that seeped blood turned purple by the light. Maxine screamed and Kayla hoped it would get Joe and Danny's attention so they'd come into the room and see this nightmare for themselves. Maybe it would snap them out of their trance. Hazel's face came into the center of that fuchsia light. It was more mature, the face of a beautiful woman, a model's face. Her smile was sharp and her eyes had an eerie glow, like a beast in a truck's headlights. She was feline and exotic, something from beyond the tangible world.

"Robbie is mine!" she howled. "Soon Joe and Danny will be, wholly and utterly . . . mine, mine, *mine!*"

"No!" Maxine cried. "Not my Danny! He's *my* boyfriend, you *bitch!*"

A gust blew them back, spinning them across the floor like so much debris. The dresser quaked, sending Robbie's things clamoring to the floor as the walls rippled and heaved, swelling like pregnant bellies, and faces began to appear beneath them, pushing their way out. They swam behind a thin veil of wall, but their features were sharp and distinctive. There were dozens of them, some smiling while others had gone wide in a silent scream. The hardwood floor began to stretch and creak as an army of wooden hands, gloved by the wood, climbed up Hazel's calves, caressing, worshipping at the altar of her sex.

"See how they adore me?" she asked. "You little girls are nothing compared to me. I am the goddess. Your precious boyfriends have felt my touch, savored my pleasures, and now that they have, you won't be able to satisfy them."

"You don't need more slaves," Kayla said.

"It's not about what I need. It's about what I *want*. And I want these boys. I want *all* the boys. And you, my little virgin princess, are going to bring them to me."

Again Kayla felt the urge to submit. The rosy aura all around her was comforting and somehow arousing. Part of her wanted to step into the glow and fall on her knees before the goddess. She held Maxine's hand tighter to keep her grounded in reality. She had to fight this black magic.

"I can take your body," Hazel said. "Just like I took that slut, Linda. I can rip your precious little heart out, princess. But it would be so much sweeter if you just let me in. I can show you ecstasies beyond anything you could feel in this world."

Kayla gritted her teeth, hissing out the word. "No . . ."

"Yes. You know you want me to take over. I can give you all the boys you want, all the love you need. You won't have to worry about being an awkward virgin anymore. Let me in, Kayla. Let . . . me . . . *in!*"

Kayla's vision blurred as her heartbeat slowed. Something slithered up the ridges of her spine, making her muscles loosen. Her nipples hardened, her mouth watering. A smile came across her face as euphoria flooded her, and Maxine grabbed her by the shoulders and shook her violently.

"Kayla! No! Snap out of it!"

She came out of her reverie, and as Hazel came at them Maxine pulled Kayla's arm and they ran toward the doorway. Maxine flung it open and they spilled into the hall. Strange things stirred within its walls. Faces pushed out of the drywall, some mocking with vicious grins, others seeming to cry for help or encouraging them to keep running. Overhead, bits of the popcorn ceiling fell upon them like snow as pale arms appeared, covered in the chalky bits, lit only by the moonlight that poured through the six-foot window at the end of the hall. The pink light from the bedroom began to stretch out into the hallway, pursuing them, slowly turning the passage into a Technicolor nightmare. They ran, pounding on the doors for Joe and Danny's help even though they weren't sure whose side they would be on. The wood of the doors seemed weaker now, gummy and rotted, and they splintered and bowed with each knock. A hand grabbed at Kayla's ankle and she used her other foot to stomp on it. The floor was swarming, alive.

"Oh my God," Maxine said, and Kayla looked up.

From out of the floor, Linda Lelane's head appeared at the end of the hallway, sailing through the hardwood like a shark fin parting a brown sea. The head cackled, Linda's eyes shining like rubies in the sun. Her teeth were rows of serpentine fangs and her nose was missing. As she came at them, more and more of her emerged. Her breasts were swollen and bruised and the nipples pumped out black blood that spattered across the rest of her body. Her bellybutton was a gaping wound, opening and closing like a second mouth, and she walked upon broken, contorted legs, feet twisted backward on snapped ankles, knees buckled and thighs ballooned from swelling, making her move like a spider.

The girls turned and lunged for the staircase, taking two at a time, racing for the ground floor. Even if the front door was sealed they could break the glass of the doors leading to the pool and make it to the backyard. But as they ran the banisters burst into flying splinters and the steps smoked as if a fire was growing below them, climbing up. They made it to the last ten steps just before the stairs began to buckle beneath them. They jumped and hit one of the Chinese rugs just as the staircase collapsed in an orange heap of flaming detritus. Smoke and flame writhed like lovers, the room thundering.

"Joe!" Kayla cried. "Danny!"

Maxine's hands went to her head. "Where the fuck are they?"

"I don't know. Come on . . ."

The fire was spreading. They got to their feet. Kayla was ready to throw a lamp through the patio doors, but they opened easily when she turned the handle. As they passed the hot tub and reached the pool, she realized why. Terror filled her throat, choking her. She tried to scream but gagged, tears rolling down to her mouth.

Maxine did enough screaming for both of them.

The pool was overflowing, a tide of azure waves splashed across the porch and out past the screen covering. The pool itself was bubbling, boiling, but the mist that came off of it was so cold the tears on Kayla's face turned to frost. Gunmetal-blue light seized the darkness, illuminating the terrible scene like a second moon as the surface of the water revealed dozens of rolling eyes. They weren't dislodged and floating; these eyes were alive, blinking, part of the water itself but undoubtedly human. As the center of the pool sent waves in each direction, the naked bodies of several men emerged, groping the night air like unearthed ghouls. They were of all ages, the majority of them young. Looking upon them Kayla realized they were all the men who had come to the house—delivery men, census takers, eagle scouts, Jehovah's witnesses. They were gardeners and pool cleaners, salesmen and plumbers, repairmen and solicitors.

And they were all Hazel's now, serving her blindly for they had no eyes. Their eyes belonged to the water, the ceiling, and the walls. They were part of the house, part of its security, as watchful as any surveillance camera, each reporting back to the master.

The girls made a run for the screen door. The eyeless men groaned as one entity, creating a desperate, metallic thrum, and as they rounded the end of the pool a tall figure came out of the shadows, moving fluidly and floating across the concrete. Long, gray hair blew about his head and he bared his bloodstained teeth like an animal. The hollow pits where his eyes should have been were encrusted in dried blood and they swarmed with tiny black tongues. His body was all shadows, broken and spindly, and at his neck was a row of thorns. From the drifting smoke of his body six skeletal hands sprung, and Kayla tried to swat them away but her hands went right through them, making them ripple and vaporize. Maxine stumbled backward, screaming, and as the ghoul pulled back into the shadows she slipped on the gushing water, and then she was falling, falling, gone.

CHAPTER TWENTY-ONE

WHILE KAYLA AND MAXINE WERE trying to escape Hazel's devotees, Hazel was recruiting new ones. She was ubiquitous within the house, in many places at once, so while she and her worshippers hunted the girls she was also in the master bedroom with Joe and Danny, continuing their seduction.

She made the room silent despite the chaos beyond it, so only she could hear the wonderful music of the two girls screaming in terror. She smiled now that everything was going her way, despite the obvious interference of the wraiths and the cursed shadows of the souls that were rightfully hers, just as these two boys were soon to be. All they needed was some more coaxing, some more spell-binding erotica.

They were all naked. Danny was pressed against her back while she pressed against Joe's front. Their young flesh was so taut and smooth; it electrified her senses, imbuing her with the power of their fledgling desire. The football player's arms were strong and the rebel's hands were knowledgeable of the female body and worked magic of their own. An erection pressed against her bush and another slid between her buttocks. Their lips chewed at her neck and breasts, their hot breath reminding her of the mortal form she'd abandoned long ago.

They'd been jealous at first, especially Joe. He went on the offensive when he saw Danny in the room. Hazel enjoyed that. Danny went on the defensive. His obsession was growing at a rapid pace. The boys had been on the verge of a fistfight when she got between them. It took some convincing to assure them there was enough of her to satisfy them both, and if they wanted her they would simply have to share because she desired each of them and would settle for nothing less.

She would have the virgin girl. The other was disposable. But the boys were her priority and she grinded them now, punishing Daddy, shaming him in his own home by wetting cocks and rubbing scrotums and chewing nipples and tonguing assholes. The depths of her depravity never ceased to excite her. She couldn't get enough of sin. She wanted more and more, and now that her mother understood who was really in charge, there would be no end to her growing harem, no limit to her army of supple young flesh.

He was in the walls.

Robbie understood this despite the impossibility of it. He moved through them as if he were shifting through quicksand, writhing in a state of consciousness resembling sleep. He could not feel his body and had the strange sense someone had taken it from him. He also felt he was being lured away from the house now. The woods beyond the property were beckoning him, the clacking tree branches and rustling brush giving the woodland a voice that called him by name, telling him to join the others.

But there were *others* in these walls too. He was not alone here, but he did not know how to communicate. All he could do was drift as he tried to better understand what had happened, what was still happening.

He remembered making love to Hazel and how sweet it had been—long and slow, Robbie not ejaculating prematurely as he'd feared. He credited that more to Hazel than to himself. She'd been in control of the sex and knew how to make him last, slowing and hushing him when he got too excited. Her body was like a bandage for a wound he'd had all his life, and losing his virginity to her felt so right he'd nearly wept at the beauty of it, knowing the moment would forever live inside him, shining like sunlight on a summer lake. He remembered a deep somnolence falling over him as soon as their lovemaking had ended and Hazel's fingernails grazing up and down his back, lulling him. He cradled against her like an infant and felt no shame as he moaned gently into her breast, surrendering to a rich, dark slumber.

Now there were only the endless caves within the house and the fear that this was not a dream. It seemed too real, too detailed. And he felt totally cognizant. There was none of the out-of-body perspective or watching as a third party he often felt in dreams. All his conscious desires and anxieties were present, and the fear he felt now was beyond any nightmare. It was pure and true, the worst fear he'd ever had to swallow back, and as he flew through the walls like dust he felt a sick, hollow panic course through whatever form he'd taken and was now a prisoner of.

The woods beckoned.

He had to find his way to them.

The Dodge roared as Kayla pressed the pedal to the floor, the cool wind whipping her hair, tears flying from her eyes like torrential rain. Her body was still shaking and she struggled to keep the wheel straight. Her mind was racing even faster than the car, making her scream as she headed toward the police station.

The image of Maxine's horrified face as the men in the pool dragged her into the water flashed across Kayla's mind like a spray of acid. She'd reached for her friend and took her hands, but the shadow men overpowered her and Maxine's wet limbs slipped from her grasp. Still she tried, getting on her hands and knees at the edge of the pool with no regard for her own safety. As Maxine screamed blue bubbles beneath the water, Kayla threw her arms into the murk, reaching but grabbing nothing, as if Maxine was now just smoke and shadow, just like the men who'd taken her. And as Maxine sank deeper into the pool, the men drifted back away from her as the silhouette of a young woman came fluttering across the orb of azure light and clung to Maxine, pulling her down like an anchor. The shadow woman's eyes glowed, several mucus-drenched arms growing out of her sides like baby sharks being born, encasing Maxine as Hazel dragged her deeper and deeper into the bottomless pool until there was nothing more to see.

Kayla nearly dived in after her, but the shadow men were approaching, rising from below like zombies. And so she'd gotten to her feet and ran toward the screen door. She didn't even waste time trying to open it; she just ran at full speed, *crashing* through the door, making it snap back on its hinges as she stumbled into the yard. She charged through the darkness alongside the house and got into her car as fast as she could.

Now she was speeding into town, wishing the sun would come up even though it was only just past one. She figured the police station would be open twenty-four hours. That only made sense, didn't it? But she just wasn't sure.

And just what are you going to tell them?

She certainly couldn't say there was a witch in Snowden Manor that was seducing her friends and taking their souls. They'd throw her in the loony bin, and while she was rocking back and forth in a padded room Hazel would be taking Joe and Danny, just as she'd taken Robbie . . . and now Maxine.

But she had to get adults involved. She needed the police. How else could she take on the horrors she'd seen in that hell house? Hazel was far more powerful than she'd imagined. If Kayla was going to go back there she needed assistance and some sort of plan. The wraiths had given her warning, but they hadn't given her the knowledge or tools she needed to combat the witch. She thought about returning to the trails when daylight broke, so she might get another chance to talk with them. For now the police would have to do.

I can tell them Linda Lelane was there and that Maxine is trapped somewhere in the house, she thought. Hazel had taken both girls. Linda had been missing for some time now and Maxine would soon be too. If she could lead them to anything that might imply the house was involved, she might get them to search the place, even gut it, and Joe and Danny would *have* to leave then, wouldn't they? She hoped the boys wouldn't be brought up as suspects in the disappearances, but that was a risk she would have to take. She knew they weren't at fault for Maxine and liked to believe they'd had nothing to do with whatever happened to Linda, but given their brainwashed state anything was possible. If she didn't hurry they'd be lost to the witch forever, and there would be no way to get Robbie back, if there still was one at all.

Just get the police out there, she thought. The house was torn up now. The damned stairs had burned down. The cops would see that and call Mrs. Snowden back from her trip. If the boys hadn't vanished the way Robbie had, then hopefully the cops would see how strange they were acting and could get information out of them pertaining to Robbie.

She pulled up past town hall and parked on the street. Walking toward the police station, she threw her coat around her to shield her from the late-night chill. When she reached the station she saw the lights were on and sighed with relief.

Someone can help me. Someone has *to.*

The station served as the local jail and was open at all hours. Kayla had never been inside one before and as she walked in she immediately drew everyone's attention. Two cops looked up from their desks, and along the wall three dirty-looking men in cuffs sat on a bench, leering at her like the urban predators they were. She moved as far away from them as she could and approached the counter where a black female officer was watching her with a stoic gaze.

Kayla did her best to rein in her panic. She tried to think of what to say but was at a loss for words. The events of the evening raced through her head like heat lightning, muddying her thoughts.

"Are you all right?" the officer asked. Kayla shook her head *no.* "Can you tell me what's wrong?"

Kayla was embarrassed as her lip curled and tears spilled from her eyes, but she couldn't help it. And once the levee broke, she began to sob, causing the officer to come around the corner and put a hand on her shoulder.

"It's okay," she said. "Why don't you just come with me, honey. You're safe now, everything's going to be all right."

Lieutenant Buchinsky wasn't thrilled to be called so late, but he was already up. Despite the different meds the doctor kept giving him, his insomnia continued, and once again he was wasting away a night in his recliner. Too blurry-eyed to read his Tim Lebbon novel, he was watching an infomercial for a special sponge. He'd been hoping it would bore him to sleep but now he was actually thinking about buying the damn thing.

The phone buzzed on the end table. The ID told him it was the station. Maybe it was an emergency, he thought grimly, but he still didn't like the assumption he was always on call, even if it was true. But missing teenage girls were a different matter altogether. He found those cases more pressing, even if most of these kids turned out to have run off on their own. It always broke his heart when he found the others. Sometimes murders, sometimes suicides. He had two teenage daughters of his own, and every time he saw the crushing heartbreak on the faces of the parents, he thought of Erin and

Tracy, and something cold and tight centered in his chest and didn't fade for weeks. When it came to missing girl cases, he'd told the station to call him at any hour if they got a good lead.

He picked up the phone.

In less than an hour he was walking into the station with a tall cup of black coffee to make the before-dawn morning a little easier on him. He stepped up to the counter where officer Tanner was typing something into the computer.

"Mornin', Lieutenant," she said.

He nodded at her and waited.

"Wallace's office," she said.

"Thanks."

He walked down the hallway, nodding at officer Rowan as they passed one another. The station was eerily quiet this time of night, with the exception of the murmurs of the DUIs in the drunk-tank and the ramblings of the mentally ill vagrants that got dragged in from time to time. The fluorescent lights hummed overhead like bug zappers, their pale illumination making his eyelids pinch. When he reached the third room on the right he knocked on the door and Wallace opened it up, his eyes looking tired over the bent nose and gray moustache. They said good morning and Wallace stepped aside, and as he entered the room Buchinsky saw the pretty blond girl sitting on the couch in front of the desk, her face still pink and wet from crying. A blanket was around her shoulders and she had her legs tucked up to her chest. There was a look in her eyes that he'd seen many times but could never get used to.

"Hello," he said, extending his free hand. "I'm Lieutenant Fred Buchinsky."

"Kayla Simmons," she said, shaking his hand. His was so much bigger that it swallowed hers entirely.

Wallace cleared his throat. "Her mother's on the way."

Buchinsky sat on the edge of the desk and put his hands on his knees, leaning forward. He tried to seem relaxed so the girl would feel comfortable.

"I've been told that you have some information for me about the Lelane case," he said. "That you know where she is."

"I do," she said in a near whisper. "She's in Snowden Manor."

Buchinsky tensed, remembering his visit. He thought of the two boys, Grant and Knox, and how he'd read no guilt in their eyes or demeanor. But he'd been wrong before.

"You're saying she's still there?"

"Yes."

"From the look on your face, I'm guessing something bad has happened."

She nodded and tears returned.

"Okay," he said. "We're going to wait until your mother gets here before—"

"But there's no time!" she said. "The boys are in danger. She already took Robbie."

"Who's Robbie?"

"Joe's brother. She took him."

"Who? Linda Lelane?"

"No ..."

The girl was hesitating. He wanted to press her but he would have to wait for her mother before taking a full statement.

"Would you like something to drink while we wait for your mother?"

"You don't understand! This is an emergency! Why won't anybody go out there?"

"Well, we need to know what's going on first."

He looked to Wallace who seemed sluggish as he leaned against the wall. He made a face that told the lieutenant he didn't think the girl was all there.

"There's another girl," Kayla said. "She ... *took* Linda, and she took my friend Maxine. Now she's after the boys."

"What do you mean by *took*?"

"I think she killed them."

"You *think* that?"

"Yes. I saw her drown Maxine in the pool, and Linda was there, all bloody like she'd been stabbed or ripped up."

With a knock at the door Tanner came in, leading a woman in an expensive coat and bed-head hair into the room. Tanner introduced her as Mrs. Simmons then left the room to return to his post. Simmons was a pretty woman about Buchinsky's age, but the worry on her face made her look older. Stress wrinkles crept at the corners of her eyes and outlined the sides of her mouth. She'd left the house without makeup, which caused her pale skin to whitewash her features. She went to her daughter and they embraced.

"Oh, my baby."

"I'm okay, Mom. Where's Tricia?"

"She's at home asleep. I went next door and woke Mrs. Stapelton. She was nice enough to come over to watch her, given what was going on."

The girl looked to the floor. "Oh, Mom. I'm sorry."

"Don't worry, love. As long as you're okay."

Buchinsky leaned forward. "We're going to take a statement from Kayla. We needed you to be present."

"Statement? Is she in some kind of trouble?"

"She claims to know the whereabouts of a missing girl and says her friends are in danger."

"Oh, I see. Perhaps we should call our lawyer."

Kayla groaned. "Mom, no."

"You're within your rights," he said. "But we just want to ask her some questions."

Kayla nodded. "It's fine, Mom. I need to tell them so they can help."

"You weren't just at Maxine's house tonight, were you?" Simmons asked her daughter. "Where did you go tonight? Is Maxine with you?"

Kayla teared up again. Buchinsky butted in. "Mrs. Snowden, may I ask Kayla some questions?"

The woman sat back on the couch, still holding both of her child's hands. "All right, Lieutenant."

"Thank you." He turned to Kayla and began by having her state her name and basic information. Then he got into the meat of it. "So you and Maxine Brownstone went to Snowden Manor tonight?"

"Yes."

"What time was that?"

"Around 11:45."

"And Joe Grant and Danny Knox were there?"

"Yes. They're still watching the house."

The girl's mother stirred, disapproving.

"What was the nature of your visit?" he asked.

"We were worried about them and Robbie."

"Why is that?"

The girl hesitated again.

"You need to tell me if we're going to help you and your friends."

Kayla's face turned a deeper shade of red. "I don't think you'll believe me."

"Just tell me what happened, then we can act on it."

"Hazel," she said. "Hazel Snowden, the daughter of the woman who owns the house. She's brainwashed them or something. And she's *possessive* of them. She got jealous of Linda and Maxine, so she did away with them."

Buchinsky's teeth began to grind at the mention of Hazel Snowden. He hadn't heard that name in a long time. "How did she do that?"

"She drowned Maxine in the pool. I think she cut Linda up or something."

"And you saw all of this?"

"Just Maxine. She slipped and fell into the pool while we were trying to escape . . ."

"So are you saying that she fell, or Hazel attacked her?"

"Hazel was in the pool. She dragged her down."

"And what did you do?"

"I tried to pull her out, but I couldn't."

Tears leapt from her eyes. If the girl was lying, she certainly believed the lie.

"What did you do then?"

"I ran away so they couldn't get me too."

"They?"

The girl breathed heavily as she looked away. He'd caught her in something she hadn't meant to say.

"Who is *they*, Kayla?"

"It's gonna sound crazy . . ."

"It's all right. Just tell me the truth."

"I am! Hazel Snowden has some kind of power over them. She seduces boys and keeps them in the house. They're everywhere, or at least their souls are. The *rest* of them are in the woods, but she keeps their souls. That's who *they* are. They do her bidding and they tried to kill me just like they helped Hazel kill Maxine and probably Linda too."

Buchinsky didn't reply at first. He turned to Wallace, understanding the look he'd given him earlier. Beside her, the girl's mother's mouth hung as wide open as her eyes.

"I know it sounds crazy," Kayla said. "But you have to believe me. I was told this was going to happen and now it is. We have to go there, there isn't much time."

Buchinsky looked at the ceiling. "Kayla, how do you know all of this business about the souls? Who is it that told you all of this?"

She paused again. "The wraiths."

"The what?"

"*Wraiths.* They're like premonitions, the ghosts of what's to come. They warn you when your life is in danger, so they told me about Hazel, told me if we didn't save Joe he was going to murder me."

Mrs. Simmons began to sniffle and pulled a handkerchief from her purse. Kayla was tense on the couch now, her entire body taut like a high wire, as if on the edge of mania. "I'm not crazy and I'm *not* making this up! I swear! Maxine saw it all too."

"But you're saying she drowned."

"Yes. Hazel pulled her under the water."

Buchinksy stood, rolled his shoulders. "Well Kayla, if your friend did drown, then you probably should get your story clear or get your lawyer involved after all."

The girl blinked with fresh tears. "What?"

"Hazel Snowden couldn't have drowned anybody. She's been dead since 1989."

CHAPTER TWENTY-TWO

SHE WISHED SHE HADN'T TOLD the truth, but it all had just come pouring out. If she'd tried to keep things from the police it would have seemed like she was lying, trying to hide something. But now they obviously thought she was nuts, that she'd had some sort of mental breakdown. Even her mother seemed to be of that opinion, judging by the way she looked at her. The policeman asked if she'd taken any drugs recently, and Kayla was so insulted she insisted they give her a drug test. They chose to forgo that, deciding to act upon her information instead, crazy or not. It appeared the lieutenant thought there might be some truth underlining her wild story, so he drove them all out to the manor. The ride was silent with the exception of her mother's soft sobs.

Kayla clenched her fists as they approached the giant manse. The first thing she noticed was that it looked completely normal from the outside. There was no psychedelic light coming from the bedroom windows or illuminating the rear by the pool. Thinking of the fire that had started on the stairs, she wondered if Joe and Danny had somehow put it out, for she saw no trace of smoke or flames in the bottom floor windows. The stillness of the house made her uneasy. She feared they might be stepping into a trap. But she couldn't back out now. She owed it to Maxine, and there might still be hope for the boys.

Maybe.

As they stepped out of the car the merciless October wind came, whipping her hair and making the tails of the lieutenant's trench coat flutter like battle flags. Her mother's arm slipped around her and she stuck close in a way she'd not done since she was a little girl. The police went up the steps and they followed behind, every muscle in her body flexing as something other than the breeze made her flesh pimple. Suddenly she felt like they were making a terrible mistake. Hazel had power that went beyond anything the police could do. How could they possibly arrest someone like that, especially since she was legally dead?

The news of Hazel's death stunned Kayla. The wraiths hadn't made everything clear. They'd only said she was between life and death, that she was some sort of living phantom. But according to Lieutenant Buchinsky the death of Hazel Snowden was well documented. In the winter of 1989, Gladys Snowden found the body of her teenage girl in their cellar. She'd committed suicide, bleeding to death as a result of multiple self-inflicted wounds. He would not elaborate on the nature of those wounds, but thinking of the symbols she'd seen carved into Hazel's body, Kayla had a good idea of what they'd been.

Hazel must have been participating in some kind of ritual when it happened. The engravings in her flesh were emblems—tokens of her sorcery. That much was clear. Had Hazel truly died, or had she only *transformed,* leaving behind her physical body and its earthly limitations? Maybe that was why the wraiths hadn't told her Hazel was dead, because in the true sense of the word she wasn't. She was not a human being, and she was not a ghost. She was something else entirely—a black witch, a vicious succubus, a fiend.

The Lieutenant rang the doorbell and knocked three times. They waited with the same thick silence that had hovered over them in the car. A light came on inside and they could see someone moving around behind the glass. Kayla could not tell who it was, and remembering Hazel's black silhouette, she felt a chill go through her blood.

The door opened.

Joe stood there, looking half awake but otherwise fine, certainly better than he'd appeared earlier that night. He was shirtless and his jeans hung low on his waist. He swayed slightly, giving them a confused look.

"What's all this?" he asked.

Buchinsky flashed his badge. "Mind if we come in, Joe?"

"Um, sure."

He moved aside and Buchinsky entered first. Wallace nodded toward Kayla and her mother, telling them to go in before him so they would be sandwiched between the two lawmen. She stepped with caution, half expecting the floor to turn to quicksand beneath her feet and the walls to explode into a swarm of greedy hands.

"Who else is here tonight?" Buchinsky asked.

"Danny's upstairs."

"There are no stairs!" Kayla said.

Buchinsky gave her a look that said *let me ask the questions* and then he turned back to Joe. "How about Maxine Brownstone? She here?"

Joe blinked. "Um . . ."

"Yes or no, son."

"Well, I mean, she might be. It's a big house." He snickered but Buchinsky glowered and that put a stop to it. "She's Danny's girl. She comes and goes."

"Kayla says that she and Maxine came by earlier."

"That's true, but they left."

"Mind if we look around?"

Kayla sensed Joe's reluctance, but what could he do? Deny them access? Demand a warrant?

"Sure," he said.

"Let's take a look at the stairs."

Kayla trembled. Now they were getting somewhere.

As they rounded the corner to the next room, Kayla was shocked to see the staircase was fully intact, without so much as a smoke stain. Her heart plunged into her abdomen, boiling in the tension there.

Buchinsky pursed his lips and turned to her. "You said these were burned, correct?"

"There was a fire, I swear!"

He made a closer inspection. "They look okay to me."

Had it been a hallucination? Had Hazel played a trick on her and Maxine's minds?

Buchinsky's face soured. Clearly he was starting to believe she'd wasted his time. He looked to Joe. "I don't suppose you've heard anything from Linda Lelane."

"No, sir. I would've called you."

"Where's Danny Knox? I'd like to speak with him too."

"Upstairs, asleep. I'll get him."

Joe hopped up the stairs two at a time, showing off how secure they were. He disappeared across the balcony and Buchinsky grumbled.

"Anything you want to tell us while he's not here?"

This isn't working. They think you're crazy.

Maybe you are.

The idea that she may have imagined all of this hit her like a hammer to the back of the skull. She'd read about different mental disorders, how they could completely alter one's sense of reality. The distortion could begin without anything triggering it and the ill person often had no awareness of their condition, causing them to believe their delusions no matter how outrageous they were. Was it possible she really was schizoaffective or something? Was she clinically maniacal? Her eyes began to water.

"Maxine is here," she said. "We need to check the pool. She was . . ."

Just then there were footsteps at the top of the stairs, and Kayla gasped at what she saw.

"Look who's here," Joe said.

Beside him stood Maxine.

She waved to them all and smiled as she came down the stairs. Danny followed a moment later, looking bleary-eyed and exhausted. Buchinsky gave Kayla another hard look but didn't say anything. He didn't have to.

"Hey," Maxine said.

Once she reached the bottom of the stairs she gave everyone a nod and a glance, and when she came to Kayla she looked at her for an extra long time. She was smiling, but her eyes were mean, and Kayla felt a coldness coming from behind them that served as a warning. They seemed to say *who do you think you're fucking with?*

"Miss Brownstone?" Buchinsky said.

"That's me."

"Feeling all right tonight?"

She was all peaches and cream with him. "Yes, sir. Why wouldn't I be?"

"No *accidents* in the pool?"

"I haven't even been in the pool tonight. It's too cold, you know?"

Buchinsky grunted. "Suppose so. But Kayla here told us you fell in, or more so that someone pulled you in and was trying to drown you."

Maxine snorted a laugh. "You okay, Kayla? You been getting

enough sleep?"

Kayla saw the coldness in Maxine's eyes begin to freeze, the pupils taking over the irises. There was no doubt as to what was going on.

"This is not the real Maxine Brownstone," she said.

Beside her, Kayla's mother started to cry again. Wallace frowned and shook his head as Buchinsky turned on his feet, leading the way back to the living room.

"I'm worried about you, Kayla," Maxine said, and only Kayla could detect the mockery. "You've been acting so weird lately."

"Yeah," Danny agreed.

Joe nodded, his face like a sad clown.

Kayla seethed. "Shut up!"

"Hey now," Joe said. "Calm down. We just don't want to see anything bad happen to you."

The threat in his words was clear, but no one else picked up on it. The policemen wouldn't listen to her now. Neither would her mother.

"Please," she begged them as they led her through the living room. "You have to listen to me!"

"I've heard enough out of you," Buchinsky said. "The only reason I'm not going to haul you in on making a false statement to the police is because there is obviously something wrong with you." He turned to her mom. "Ma'am, I strongly recommend you take your daughter to a behavioral health center to be examined. She needs psychiatric help, not the help of the police force."

Her mother blinked. "Yes. I will, Lieutenant."

Panic nestled. "But Mom!"

"Quiet now, honey. Let's get your car at the station and get you home."

"Wait!" she said. "What about Robbie? He's missing. What about him?"

"He went home," Joe said with a shrug, "where he *wants* to be."

He and Danny and Hazel (as Maxine) watched her with dead eyes as the adults led her toward the front door, no longer listening to her pleas. The door came open and when she hesitated Wallace took her arm.

"Let's go, kid."

She tried to protest but her mind was overloaded; all that came out of her mouth was a stream of gibberish. Her mom cried beside her, louder now, unashamed.

Once home, her mother told her she would be going to a shrink in the morning. One of Mom's friend's husbands was a reputable one and could get Kayla in quickly. While part of her wanted to object to this, Kayla began to believe, more and more, that something may very well be wrong with her after all. She knew she had some emotional problems, being a cutter; perhaps there was more to it than just self-mutilation. Maybe her mind was as scrambled as an egg. When she saw Maxine at the house, she'd been so sure that it wasn't really her, that Hazel had taken her image. But Maxine *did* look and sound like Maxine. And Hazel Snowden was supposed to be long *dead*. Kayla's only reference for all she'd believed had come from the wraiths, and that didn't help matters much. Here she was, alive, and her own ghost was giving her warnings and advice? How much sense did that really make?

Jesus, this really could all be in her head. But if it wasn't, didn't that mean that time wasted thinking she was insane was time that should be spent saving everyone, before it was too late? But wasn't that the sort of thing a crazy person would think? Don't they have delusions of grandeur, believing they have super powers or connections with spiritual beings and that the fate of something truly epic rides upon their shoulders because only they are capable of fixing it?

She was so depressed. All she could do was lie there and cry as she watched the sky turn bright purple outside her window, the sun just beginning to rise on another confusing and terrifying day. Her body ached to sleep, but she knew it would not come. She couldn't keep her hands from shaking or get her eyes to close.

I don't feel crazy. *I'm stressed out, but I feel like I'm making sense, no matter how farfetched my story is.*

Pulling the sheet to her chin, she replayed everything that had happened since she'd first gone to the manor. It was so much like a nightmare. She tossed and turned for two more hours, dozing off before snapping awake again, and then there was a knock on her door. She tensed, but it was just Mom. She looked haggard and much older than Kayla had ever seen her, and Kayla was pained by it.

"I was going to make some breakfast," her mother said. "How about some bacon and eggs?"

It'd been a long time since her mother prepared a breakfast for her. Normally she was left to her own devices and only Patricia was treated like a daughter. Mother had been treating her more like a roommate, and while she appreciated being respected as a young adult a big part of her missed being nurtured.

"I'd love some, Mom."

"I talked to Tina. She got us an appointment with Dr. Bruce at nine. Okay?"

"Okay."

Her mother seemed relieved. "Thank you."

The door closed and Kayla heard her little sister puttering around.

"I want to wake up sissy!" she said.

"No, honey," she heard her mother say. "Sissy needs rest. Lots and lots of rest."

CHAPTER TWENTY-THREE

A BLACK VOID.

Not the dark passageways of the walls, but an endless oblivion where he levitated, surrounded by nothing at all. Robbie would have gulped if he had some sort of form, other than the shadow of his former body that blended in with the darkness all around him. He was disembodied, weightless. He could only move like smoke through the house, but now he was inside a nothingness he could not remember having entered, and the ever-increasing strangeness of this world he'd been thrust into was torturing his mind, making him fear for his sanity.

"Where are you?" he called out. His voiced echoed on and on. "Hazel!"

A faint noise came from all directions. It sounded like a whimper, followed by scratching.

"Hello?" Robbie called.

The scratching continued, the whimpers growing louder.

"Who's there?"

A bark.

"Horace! Where are you, boy?"

More barking, but Robbie still saw nothing. It sounded like the dog was all around him, panting and barking excitedly.

"Come, boy! Come here!"

The vortex emitted a hollow sound, like wind, and though he was formless Robbie began to feel colder. The scratching was faster now, desperate sounding, and Horace wasn't just whimpering, he was mewling.

The dog clawed at the door to the cellar, so Joe nudged him with his foot.

"Get lost, mutt!"

But the dog returned to the spot and continued to cry. Joe was worried he was going to tear up the door, so he shrugged and opened it, letting the dog trot down the stairs.

Fuck it. Let him stay down there all day.

He went to close the door but realized he would be leaving the Rottweiler alone with fragile shelves that housed extremely expensive wine bottles. Regretting his decision, he went down the stairs, looking for the dog in the dust and dank of the cellar.

"Here, boy."

What had they named the dog again?

"Henry! Harry!" he tried. "Where are ya?"

The cellar was large, filled with dark pockets even after he turned on the overhead bulb. Stacked boxes made weird shadows on the walls and ceiling, and spider webs created a silken fog.

Maybe I should go get some food to lure him out.

And maybe while I'm in the kitchen, I'll sharpen the butcher knife so it'll be perfect for cutting Danny's throat.

He thought of his friend's neck opening like a second pair of smiling lips and how beautiful his blood would look leaving his body. Ever since he'd realized Hazel loved them both, Joe had been thinking of little else than the murder of his best friend. Jealous rage coursed through him like a drug, and even as they'd enjoyed the threesome he'd seethed on the inside whenever she took Danny inside of her. Hazel was his one and only, his *goddess*, and he wasn't keen on the idea of sharing her. He was more in love than he had ever dreamed possible, and there was no fucking way he was going to let some big, dumb jock get between him and his dream girl.

But Hazel had plans for them. She was going to take them places they'd never known. All they had to do was prove their devotion by making passionate love to her again and again, until they reached some sort of pinnacle she'd alluded to. But Joe had a better idea. He would prove his devotion by killing for her, murdering his best friend to show he would let no one come between them. She might be upset at first, but he was confident she would come to realize just how dedicated he was to her. How could she deny his love when he was drenched in the blood of his oldest friend?

And he would get Kayla for her too. He was sure of that. Hazel wanted her, so he would fetch her. She would be a gift. Then *they* could have an orgy, one he would enjoy much more, even if he really didn't want to share Hazel with a woman either. It was better than a man, but it was still something he would not be okay with in the long term. If it came to it, he'd gladly kill Kayla too. He'd decorate the halls of the manse with her viscera if it were Hazel's will. It would probably be best to do that sooner rather than later. She'd already brought the cops, and they would be back once Maxine's parents began to wonder where she was. Hazel had wanted Maxine. Kayla was out of line by trying to interfere. She was just lucky Hazel was still after her for her virginity, just as she'd been for his brother, otherwise Kayla would have suffered the same fate as her friend. And if Joe had his way, she soon would.

"Homeboy!" he called out for the dog.

He heard a shuffling and when he came to the center of the cellar he saw the dog digging at the floor. It was tiled and he was getting nowhere, but he kept trying.

"Stupid pooch." He nudged it. "Come on, upstairs."

But the dog kept pawing and whining.

"What? What's your problem?"

When he saw the first bit of blood in the cracks, he thought the dog had ripped off a toenail. But when he looked closer he realized the blood wasn't dripping down on the tile, but rather rising up, seeping out of it.

"What the fuck?"

The room grew colder until he could see his breath. At his feet, the blood began pooling, and the dog was barking now, going berserk. Joe stepped back but the blood kept coming, a rising, crimson deluge.

"What the fuck is this?"

Filthy bastard, a voice seethed in his ear.

He spun around, seeing only the thick curtains of the shadows.

"Who is that?"

This is a house of God. How dare you befoul it.

He spun in circles, unable to find the source of the voice.

"What? Who in the *fuck* is that? Show yourself."

A deathly quiet thrummed. Even the dog shut up.

"Danny? Is that you? Come on, quit fucking around!"

Something slick was at his ankles and when he looked he saw his feet submerged in the growing, red pool. The dog splashed through it, still trying to reach the same spot beneath the floor. The smell of rotting flesh filled Joe's nostrils, pungent and raw. He nearly gagged.

I will not have my daughter deflowered by some towheaded nitwit!

Joe swung his fists in the dark at his unseen provoker. "Fuck you! Who the fuck are you?"

The blood at his heels grew thicker, congealing around them. He pulled at his feet and they made a popping noise like he was coming out of sucking mud. But with each step he had more trouble moving, the blood forming into tendrils that climbed up his shins, constricting around him like snakes.

If you should die before you wake . . .

The blood tentacles squeezed his kneecaps, rose higher, and then coiled around his waist in tacky, oozing belts. Joe cried out as the pool heightened, expanding like a pup tent, the center becoming a ball that dragged the rest up with it in a pyramid formation. He gasped as the ball sunk inward in spots, creating two hollow eyes, a nose hole and rivets of jagged teeth, forming a crimson skull. The blood beneath its neck turned darker, then black, making the mass of the body into a shroud. Around the ghoul's throat Joe saw a blood-streaked preacher's collar. Skeletal hands rose from the skinless ghoul's sides.

Filthy little bastard!

Joe screamed and put his hands to one knee and pulled on it with all his might. It came loose and he swung it to his side, and then pulled out the other one before the goo could once again ensnare the first. The blob-ghoul breathed and hissed, bloody spittle flying from between his teeth, red fingers clutching the air. The dog barked and splashed; for some reason he wasn't sticking to the floor. Joe ran to the stairs and charged the doorway. The dog followed behind, probably just as freaked out as he was.

I will not have my daughter . . .

Joe slammed the door behind them and slid to the floor, shaking, and realized he'd pissed his pants.

"Because I want you here, with me," Hazel said. "I keep the souls of the others but let their shadows roam the mountain, which holds the power. But you? You I want to keep here, as my treasure. Your virginity has pleased the mountain, and I am being rewarded."

Robbie had asked her what they were doing in this darkness, which had begun to fade with soft pink light. Hazel appeared, as if beckoned by his and Horace's noise. She looked older and more voluptuous, her nude hips swaggering as she approached, breasts like a new mother, eyes like razors catching skin.

Robbie shuddered. "What's happened to me?"

"You're mine, Robbie. As per our agreement."

"Agreement?"

"Don't play dumb. You gave yourself to me."

"Yeah, but—"

"There's no *buts* in an agreement like that."

She wrapped a long leg around him, defying his formlessness. Somewhere inside himself, he felt the old stirring of loins no longer there. Or were they? In some other form? She pressed into him and he leaned backward as if he was lying on an invisible, adjustable hospital bed. Once horizontal, Hazel straddled him. Her body rippled, a reflection on a pond, and the soft pink light encased them in fluid warmth. And just like that he was inside her, but *she* was also inside *him*. They didn't join in the traditional sense; they filled each other's entire bodies, or what was left of them. It was a sexual embrace, but one that went beyond mortal sexuality. Under different circumstances the effect would have been euphoric, but now that Robbie was lost in the walls, hovering in darkness without a body, he was overcome by a sickening fear. But that didn't stop Hazel. She kept on thrusting, loving him, raping him.

"You're mine now, Robbie-boy. You're . . . all . . . *mine*."

Horace was so confused.

He knew he should not disobey her, but knowing what she was doing to the boy made him antsy. More than that, it made him unhappy. The boy had become his best friend, and while Horace longed for the rules and guidance of the master, he felt a powerful kinship with the boy, as if they were from the same pack. But the boy was in the walls now, and worst of all he was in *the cellar*. Horace knew what else was down there, and now the taller boy knew too, and by the moist stink at the older boy's crotch it was clear he knew the danger of it.

Horace didn't want the boy he loved to be trapped forever with the master. Even if she let Horace back in the walls to be with the boy, it would not be the same. They could not enjoy the smells of the night and the chase of the critters in the woods. There would be no ball. No belly rubs. Only darkness, forever.

The master hadn't come to scold him. Perhaps she hadn't heard him clawing at the floor in search of the boy. He'd been bad, he knew, but if he could get away with this much, perhaps he should push it again, maybe even further. He did not want to disobey the master, but she was not paying attention to him anymore. Maybe she didn't need him. Maybe she didn't want him. The pain of this thought made him want to howl, but the thought of never being with the boy again hurt even worse.

He loved the boy.

He had to get into the wall.

CHAPTER TWENTY-FOUR

MAXINE'S FATHER ANSWERED THE PHONE with a clearing of his throat. He was a gruff man, a bulky mechanic that stood six foot three when he wasn't slouching from a bad back. Kayla knew very well how grouchy he could be from seeing him curse at the television while watching sports, complaining the players just didn't have the heart the ones from his youth had had.

"Hello," he barked.

"Mr. Brownstone?"

"Yeah, who's this?"

"It's Kayla. Kayla Simmons."

"Oh. Well, Maxine ain't here . . . Wait a minute, I thought she was with you."

Kayla took a deep breath. She knew no other way to get the police to take things seriously than to get the Brownstones involved. She wasn't sure, but she believed Hazel couldn't leave the manor. Even if the cops brought the Brownstones to the manor to prove Maxine was there, they would know it wasn't their daughter, just as Kayla had known. It was in the eyes. Hazel couldn't replicate them, perhaps because she was so heartless and sociopathic, or perhaps because she was not quite alive. Once Maxine's parents saw that the girl in that house was merely a ringer, Kayla would not be alone, and hopefully everyone would stop thinking she was crazy.

"That's why I'm calling, sir," she said. "The last time I saw her was at Snowden Manor."

"Manor? What are you talking about?"

"I'm worried. I think she's in trouble."

The man's voice rose. "What kind of trouble?"

By this point, she knew better than to tell the whole truth. She didn't need another adult treating her like she ought to be tossed into a rubber room. What she needed was someone else to be concerned for Maxine.

"She's hanging out there with some boys . . . I think they're doing drugs. I couldn't get her to leave. I thought you should know."

There was a long pause before he finally spoke. "Where the hell is this place?"

She gave him the address, hung up, and went to her dresser to change into something she didn't mind getting dirty. That morning she hadn't been sure how to dress to see the shrink, so she'd put on a nice blouse and black skirt. But once there she felt overdressed and stuffy, as if she was trying to put on airs for someone she didn't have to impress.

"Tell me about the wraiths," the doctor had said.

Obviously mother had given him a play-by-play of last night. At first Kayla tried to manipulate it into something less irrational, but that wouldn't get her anywhere. She talked to the shrink for an hour, not just about her "delusions" but about her stress level, how she felt at school, how she felt about her parents and friends and boys. After just one session he gave her a note to stay home from school for the week and a prescription her mother filled immediately. Kayla wasn't shocked when she Googled the drug and found it was an anti-psychotic. She hoped she could get away with pretending to take it.

Talking about the wraiths made her realize what she had to do.

She had to go back to the mountain. Talk to the wraiths again.

Perhaps fate had changed after her initial warning. There may be some new course of action. She needed more information than they'd given her the last time. That had been a history lesson. Now she needed advice.

She slipped out of the skirt and put on faded jeans with holes in the knees. She tossed on a t-shirt and hoodie and stepped into her sneakers. Her mother was in the kitchen, reading on her laptop, and Kayla had no doubts about what she was reading up on.

Schizophrenia.

Her mother looked at her with tired eyes and Kayla realized she wasn't the only one who hadn't slept. Sadly, Kayla wasn't surprised she hadn't heard from her father yet. He obviously had more important matters to attend to.

"I want to go for a walk and clear my head."

Her mother nodded. "Okay. Well, I think we could all use the exercise. Give me a moment and Patricia and I will go with you."

Kayla shifted on one foot. "Well, I'm gonna go hiking."

"You think that's wise right now?"

"Nothing strenuous. I just feel like I need some time to myself, to try and sort things out."

Her mother looked waxen, sour. The moment of silence between them stretched out like a dog day, and her mother put her forehead into her palm, her elbow on the table supporting her. "All right. I can understand that. But will you promise me just one thing?"

"Sure, Mom."

"You have to make a sincere promise."

"Okay. I will, I will."

Her mother stared at her. "Promise me you'll be careful ... and that you won't go anywhere near that house. Just leave it alone, honey. Leave it alone."

Kayla nodded. "I promise."

And then she was out the door.

While gloomier, there was no humidity to the air, no smell of rain or early snow. Above her, amongst the riot of the dying trees, a single crow cawed, the only sound on the desolate trail. Leaves lined the path in brown and tangerine disarray, looking like the arched backs of angry cats. Kayla zipped up her hoodie but kept the hood down so not to block her peripheral vision, just in case a sasquatch-like shadow strolled past or a ghostly, familiar face emerged from the bushes like a masked slasher in one of those '80s horror movies. The overcast sky had cooled the earth. It was Tuesday afternoon, and yet the trail was as dark as dusk and sorrowful as a funeral song.

She was alone.

But she hoped she wasn't.

"Where are you?" she called to them.

She'd reached roughly the same spot the wraiths had come to

her. She wished there was some sort of talisman to get in touch with them, like a genie's lamp she could rub or a flute she could play to make the wraiths appear. Considering the fatality of their message, it irritated her that they'd given her no way to seek further guidance from them. She waited on the spot, eventually sitting on a boulder. The breeze chewed her face as it tossed her hair about. The air had been still when she'd gotten on the trail, but now the wind was picking up, making the fallen leaves roll like wagon wheels through the dirt and stones. When the dust devils began tossing the leaves, Kayla stood, sensing they were getting close.

First she saw the shadow people. They emerged from behind skeletal branches in murky, fluid movements. Then the red cloaks appeared, and the ghastly white faces of the wraiths, framed by hoods. They floated toward her, a cold wind carrying them, pushing them along like sails. Kayla was less frightened than the first time. In fact, seeing this living reflection was a relief. But then she remembered—if she was seeing her wraith, that meant her own death was still pending.

"The moon is changing," her doppelganger said. "By Friday night it will be both a harvest moon and a super moon."

Kayla blinked. "Okay . . ."

"It wields great influence over the mountain. The fuller it becomes, the more power the mountain possesses, and the stronger Hazel Snowden gets. She already has the virgin boy. That alone has intensified her power. Soon she will be strong enough to leave the manor."

The wraith beside her removed his hood. Robbie's face, white as winter, stared at her. "There's still hope. You have to save me, Kayla."

"How? I don't know what to do."

"There's only one way to stop Hazel," her wraith said, drawing closer. "You must beat her at her own game. You have to become seductive, sensual, just as she is, so you can draw the adoration of as many boys as possible, particularly the ones inside the manor."

Kayla's eyes went wide. "What?"

"If Hazel sees that you are more lusted after than she is, it will weaken her. She will no longer be able to hold Robbie in her world or keep Danny and Joe under her spell. The power of the mountain will leave her, and transfer over to you. Then, and only then, will you be able to destroy her."

Kayla put her hands to her head. "How am I supposed to do that? You mean I have to become a slut or something? I can't do that!"

"You don't have to sleep with the boys, you just have to make them *want* to sleep with you over Hazel. You must get past your self-doubt and recognize yourself as a sexual being. If you are confident and flirtatious the boys will come. Remember, you are a virgin. Boys are drawn to that like moths to a flame."

"But what if I can't—"

"You have to," her double interrupted. "You still have time. Hazel needs a few more days to continue her seduction of the boys. She won't want to take them all the way into her world until Friday's super moon. That's when she will be at her most powerful. She will offer the souls of all her boys up to the mountain as a sacrifice, so that she may be granted the power to leave Snowden Manor and move amongst our world."

Friday, Kayla thought. That's when Joe was planning to throw the Halloween party at the manse. The house would be filled with boys. But she would have to start working on getting male attention now.

"If I manage to get other boys interested in me, and gather them at the manor, what then? Won't Hazel be enraged?"

"She will, and that's when you will be in danger most, both from Hazel and all those she has under her spell. Joe will be almost completely lost to her by then. He'll be capable of doing just about anything."

"He already is," a man's voice said.

The wraith came forward and pulled back his hood.

It was Mr. Brownstone, Maxine's father. Beside him, Mrs. Brownstone removed her hood too. Her eyes were soft with a deep, black sadness.

"Oh my god," Kayla said, feeling guilty. "Now you're in danger too?"

"No," he said, blood appearing at his neck as he began to fade to black, becoming one of the shadows. "Not anymore."

CHAPTER TWENTY-FIVE

WHILE KAYLA HAD BEEN DRIVING to the trails, Jeff Brownstone was driving to Snowden manor. He knew where the place was. Back when Arthur Snowden had disappeared and the daughter committed suicide, the manse had become somewhat of a spookhouse, and when he was a teenager he and his buddies would dare each other to climb the fence on Halloween night and toss toilet paper, soap windows, or smash a pumpkin on the porch. As he'd gotten older he felt bad about that, realizing Mrs. Snowden had had enough heartache in her life without a bunch of punk kids wrecking her house just because there was a local legend about her being a witch.

Of course, those days were long over. People didn't consider the manor a spookhouse anymore. The stories had become old and stale, and teens these days weren't into Halloween pranks. The kids who went out on Halloween were younger now, all of them growing up too fast, just like his little girl.

Maxine was he and Fiona's only child, and she was rapidly becoming an adult. It depressed him. But Jeff was a hard man who kept his feelings locked up. His sorrow over seeing his little princess dating boys, driving and preparing for college was a private sadness he couldn't even share with his wife. He missed his daughter's innocence, how once he'd been the only man she loved, but while there was a barrier between them (now that she was old enough to rebel against her parents and find them totally lame) he still loved his little girl, and in his eyes she would always be the sweetheart in a pink ballerina costume, the one she'd worn for her first daddy-daughter dance.

The chance she was in danger sent him into protective over-drive. His hands sweated, his teeth were grinding in his head like sandpaper on jagged rocks. In the passenger seat, Fiona was balling up another tissue to wipe her runny nose. She'd been crying since she'd called the school and they told her Maxine hadn't come in today. Jeff had been against the idea of calling because it made them look like bad parents to not know where their child was (and maybe they were), but his wife had insisted after not being able to reach Maxine on her phone.

What exactly was going on? Kayla had been a little too vague for his liking and he got the sense that she knew more than she let on. She was probably trying to keep herself out of trouble. He'd devel-oped a quality bullshit detector over the years. But while he could tell Kayla was holding back, he also sensed her fear was genuine, and he knew how much Maxine meant to her. Besides, he liked Kayla and trusted her. So did his wife. They knew the girl wouldn't have called if something weren't really wrong.

He'd called out of work after talking with her. He was the boss and could work whatever schedule he liked. He was in his late for-ties now and sleeping in was something he treasured. But he wouldn't be getting any sleep tonight, not unless his daughter was safe at home again.

The day was gray, but as they drew closer to the manor house it grew grayer, washing out all the color of the world, the town re-sembling an old black and white photo. He'd left the house in just a t-shirt and was beginning to regret it. The cold had a vicious cut to it. He finished his cigarette and flicked it out the window. Beside him, Fiona sniffled.

"It's gonna be all right," he told her, patting her knee.

His wife didn't say anything. She just kept wiping her tears. She'd always been an emotional woman. It didn't take much to turn on her waterworks. Sad movies as well as happy ones brought tears from his wife, as did strangers' weddings, and anything pertaining to their daughter always overwhelmed her.

Jeff didn't slow down as they reached the turn. The tires screeched as he burned five bucks worth of rubber, the car jumping up the manse's driveway, sending pebbles spraying like hail. He recognized Danny Knox's shitbox parked out front.

Why the hell isn't he at school? Must be they're playing hooky together. She'd better be there by her own will. She better not have a needle in her arm or powder up her nose. Not my baby. No way.

He spat bitterly as he got out of the car and Fiona followed close behind him, her hands around his arm. They walked to the door and only had to wait a few seconds before it came open. Danny stood there in stained jeans and no shirt. His hair was as messy as the leaf piles beside the porch and red rings clung around his eyes. They widened when he saw them. He looked stoned, and that just got Jeff's blood boiling all the more.

"Is my daughter in there?"

Danny had a look on his face like a child who had just been caught drawing on the walls. "Uh . . . um . . ."

That was all Jeff needed to hear. Maxine was there, but for some reason Danny was trying to think of a way to deny it. He was stalling until his big, dumb head could come up with something.

Jeff didn't give him time. He pushed the door in, forcing Danny to step back, and led his wife inside the manor. The door closed behind them, shutting them in.

Joe heard the man ranting and raving downstairs, demanding Danny tell him where Maxine was.

She's with them now, Joe thought, *with the others.*

He didn't fully understand what the goddess did with them all but knew she had great power and was to be obeyed always. He didn't understand what had happened in the cellar either but would not ask questions. The goddess would show him the way.

She could easily transform into Maxine, but if she did the Brownstone's would want to take her home, and Joe couldn't have that. He refused to let them take her. She belonged here, in her true home, in the great manse, with him. More than jealous now, he was possessive, obsessed, addicted.

When he reached the landing he heard Danny mumbling in the kitchen. The other man hollered, raving and threatening. Joe went to join them. Danny stood there, his eyes doing a bad job of hiding panic. But Joe was calm and cool, his love for Hazel giving him the strength to handle any situation without fumbling the way his goony friend was. He'd never met the Brownstones, but could see how intense the man was, how distraught the woman. Joe wasn't happy about what happened to their daughter, but he wasn't particularly sad about it either.

The goddess does what she has to do, he thought. *What she wants is what matters. Maxine was expendable. So are her parents.*

All eyes fell upon him.

"Where the hell's my daughter, boy?" Mr. Brownstone asked.

"Well," Joe said, smiling. "She *was* here."

"That's not what I asked, shitbird. Now quit fuckin' around. I want to know where my daughter is right now!"

"Sir, Maxine came by last night with Kayla, but they left together. I suggest you get in touch with her."

Mr. Brownstone stepped closer, but Joe held his ground. "Bullshit! Kayla told me she was here, and Danny over there couldn't give me a straight answer when I asked! Now I want to know if she's here, and I'll tear this whole place apart to find her if I have to."

He charged out of the kitchen and into the next room, going for the stairs. His wife tagged behind him like a puppy, sniffling and not making eye contact with anyone.

Joe seethed, his mind fluttering like a murder of pissed-off crows. He couldn't allow this. If the Brownstones were convinced Maxine was missing, that he and Danny were hiding something, Lieutenant Buchinsky would be back, and this time it wouldn't be as easy to get him to go away. He would want to take Joe out of the house, away from Hazel.

A surge of flame bloomed in his heart like a thorny rose. He was imbued with Hazel's passion, and yet he felt it slipping away at the threat of them being exposed. He clenched his fists, knuckles white. He turned to the wooden block and slid the butcher knife from its slot. It glistened in the pale light like an unearthed jewel, and Joe heard a soft whisper of approval from within the walls.

Danny looked at him with wide, staring eyes.

"Shut up and do what I say," Joe told him. "Call him back."

"What?"

"Call him back, fat shit. Tell him you know where she is."

Danny paled, looking at him like a cornered animal.

"Do it!" Joe snapped.

Danny swallowed hard. "Mr. Brownstone, Mrs. Brownstone! Come back. I know where she is."

Joe listened to the footsteps on the hard wood and tucked himself behind the corner, using the closet door as a barricade to hide his intentions. He waited for the man's shadow to appear.

"You better not be fuckin' around, kid—"

Joe lunged, and Mr. Brownstone didn't notice the attack until it was too late. The knife entered his neck with a slick pop and Joe put his other hand on the end of it, pushing the blade deeper and widening the wound. He must have hit a vein; blood didn't just flow, it spurted, ropes of crimson zipping through the air like lava from an erupting volcano. A wet scream filled the man's throat and Joe pulled the blade out. This further cut the man's neck, shredding the exposed tissue, and he stumbled backward, blood raining onto the floor as his wife shrieked and flapped about.

Joe didn't waste any time.

He jabbed forward to stab the man in the stomach, but Mr. Brownstone was on the defense now and he swung at Joe, knocking him upside the head. Joe crashed into the closet door and struggled to hold onto the knife while regaining his balance. He looked to Danny for help, but he was frozen.

Mr. Brownstone came at him again, blood sluicing through snarling teeth and gushing from his opened throat. But Joe was younger, faster, and rich with the power of his love for Hazel. His desire for her was like electricity in his veins, a white-hot bloodlust that fueled his violence. He moved in a flash, ducking the man's flailing limbs, and sent the blade into the fat roll at his side, piercing through to pop an organ. Brownstone crumpled, blood flowing over his chest and belly, splashing over Joe's feet. The knife slid out, and just as Joe was about to finish him off, the wife became a hurricane of spinning arms. A whirlwind of nails cut into Joe's face, digging for his eyes, tumbling him into the chairs at the table.

"Leave my husband alone, you monster!"

As Mr. Brownstone struggled to get up, Danny suddenly seemed to grasp the danger they were in and made a move. Grabbing Mrs. Brownstone around the waist, he picked her up and pinned her arms back. She screamed and kicked at his shins, her hands trying to reach for his balls to twist them like a tomato from a vine. Her husband was growing weaker and failed to get up. Instead he slid down the wall, smearing it with blood so thick it was purple. Joe snarled at the woman who had cut open his cheek in three places. She was hysterical, spitting and crying, writhing like an alligator. Joe lunged, sinking the knife into her soft stomach. It twisted, and Joe pushed deeper still, sliding into her like a lover. He moved the blade back and forth, sawing. Blood flowed from her new hole, the excess coming up her gullet and trickling from her mouth. Another wet scream came from her husband, and then Joe stabbed her repeatedly, the blade a furious blur as he pummeled her with it, making sure she wouldn't scratch anyone ever again. Danny's face went green and he let the woman go. She fell to the floor with a thud, her head cracking on the hardwood.

"Noooo!" Mr. Brownstone gurgled.

Joe saw the tears in the man's eyes and felt neither joy nor remorse. The knife felt good in his hand though, all warm and dripping. It was helping him please the goddess. There would be sweet, wonderful rewards tonight. Treats and treasures for this ritual sacrifice.

For these murders, she was going make love to him in ways he'd never imagined.

CHAPTER TWENTY-SIX

DANNY HAD JUST BEEN TRYING to break up the fight.

When Joe first stabbed Maxine's father, Danny was in such a state of shock that he didn't know how to react. The sudden, intense violence had stopped him from breathing, his hairs on end and his balls drawing closer to his body. He'd been feeling out of his head for a while now as it was, like he was lost in a fog that kept changing density, but Joe's murderous actions made him even more frazzled and delirious. When Mrs. Brownstone started clawing at Joe's face, Danny snapped into action, hoping to keep she and Joe from killing each other. Despite what he'd done to Mr. Brownstone, Danny hadn't expected Joe to stab her three times without hesitation. He didn't know what he'd expected, but it hadn't been that.

Something was clouding his judgment and slowing his reaction time. There was a mind-mist swarming inside of him, a spellbinding murk that changed his thoughts for him and guided him into bizarre, unfamiliar territory. Life didn't seem real anymore. This somewhat calmed him as he watched the Brownstones die in gore.

Hazel could worm into his head. She could nestle there like a burrowed tick and suck out all of his self-control. He knew that, just as he knew he couldn't resist her even if he wanted to. And sometimes he did, especially after what had happened to Maxine.

Now her parents were gone too, and this time it wasn't Hazel who'd done the dirty work. She'd convinced Joe to do it for her, clouding Danny just enough to keep him from stopping it.

"Jesus," he said, looking at the still-warm bodies.

Blood was everywhere. Joe was eerily calm. He wasn't even breathing heavy. He took the knife to the sink and began washing his hands.

"Jesus," Danny repeated. "You fucking *killed* them."

He'd never seen anything so brutal.

"What's done is done," Joe said, so calmly it grated on Danny's nerves. "We had to do it."

"*We?*"

Joe turned around. "You held her for me, didn't you?"

"Yeah, but—"

"So we're in this together. They would've gone to the cops, dude. That detective would've come back and taken us outta here, away from Hazel. You want that?"

"No," Danny said, without having to think about it. "But did you really have to stab them to death?"

Joe smiled and looked to the ceiling. "The goddess is pleased. Can't you feel it?"

CHAPTER TWENTY-SEVEN

IT HAD BEGUN.

Joe had spilt the blood, the ultimate act of devotion. Danny had helped without trying, but he was dedicated enough to have assisted Joe in driving the Brownstone's car out to the woods where they buried the bodies in shallow graves as night fell upon the mountain. The boys walked all the way back and spent the night cleaning the kitchen with sprays, powders, wall erasers and bleach.

Hazel watched it all through their eyes, turned on and flushed with magic.

Joe would reap the rewards tonight. Danny would be allowed to watch, but would not taste of her again until he understood that he needed to be one hundred percent devoted, just as Joe was.

Her pussy grew wet and her eyes sparkled.

She had her boys now, and the moon was coming, growing bigger every night as it drew closer to the earth. Samhain was almost nigh, the ancient Celtic ritual that celebrated the harvest and the dead. Modern times knew it as Halloween, but Hazel was a sorceress and understood the day's true power. Soon she would be at the zenith of her capabilities, and everything was falling into place just so. Soon she would be able to move outside the manor, through the shadows, and walk among the living. Her pleasures would be endless.

The youngest boy was still locked in the black prism behind the walls, but despite her seductive efforts he still begged for release. His fear outweighed his desire. Perhaps he was too young. But she'd still taken his virginity, and she kept it within her core, waiting for the right moment to manipulate its innocent power, making it her own as she offered him up to the black art within the mountain. She wanted the girl too, and she may still be able to get her, but she already had all she needed. The night would soon belong to her entirely, and the world would be her canvas, upon which she would paint a masterpiece of blood.

Her daughter was getting stronger. Gladys could feel it in her old bones and was as enticed as she was terrified. She knew what Hazel was capable of. Gladys herself had mastered some witchery, but her daughter had become a black princess of the art, and now she was unstable, perhaps even psychotic. And with the harvest moon coming—a super moon at that—the black mountain would endow her further, the witchery full and bright. By now the boys would be seduced or imprisoned, and soon Hazel would have an army of adoring souls drifting through the great manse, slithering through the walls like leeches, hiding in every crevice like cockroaches, their black eyes rolling in their ghostly, skeletal faces and their smoke bodies dousing the halls in a froth of blackness.

Gladys lit another cigarette off the one she'd just finished and snuffed out the butt in the overflowing ashtray. She sipped her glass of vodka and looked out at the night sky. The trees sighed in the October wind, a crackling like a low tide. The air was rich with the smell of firewood. It was cold out, but she'd been cooped up in the hotel, and she had the balcony to herself. The world had hushed now that it had grown late. Only the occasional lone car moved through the streets. She felt wonderfully alone and it gave her a false sense of hope and peace. She knew there was nothing to be happy about. No reason to be calm. But she was doing her best to deny it all. She couldn't take knowing what was about to happen. All she could do was hope Hazel wouldn't take things too far, and that maybe, somehow, they could be mother and daughter again.

The vodka hit the back of her throat like rusty nails. Her body tingled as if someone was touching her in her private places. Gladys enjoyed the caress of both sexes—always had, even back when being a lesbian was considered taboo, a mental illness treated with electroshock. She was attracted to power, and women had *all* the power. Though it seemed like a man's world to the unknowing eye, women had all the true power: the power of birth, life, the creation of *souls*. Nature itself was a mother, and mankind was nothing but an extension of her. Women were related to the dirt, the trees, the oceans and the wind. Even if they were not conscious of it, all women held that in their hearts. They were the birth givers—the *creators*—the keepers of the magic, white and black. Masters of the land beyond what the eyes can see. And now her daughter was poised to be the next great one. The sorceress. The witch. The goddess. Blackest of the black. The one that moves among the living, to shape-shift and enchant to have her way. And she *would* have her way. She would seduce them all, of that Gladys had no doubt.

What would Arthur think of his little angel now?

Gladys smiled, knowing the fucker was down there in the cellar, forced to watch it all.

Good.

Over the next two days, Hazel groomed her boys and riled up the souls in the walls. She amped up her seduction, filling the restless spirits with confused excitement. Danny stopped caring about school and football. He stayed in the manor, as did Joe. They spent a chunk of their up-front money on Halloween decorations. Scarecrows on stakes; Styrofoam tombstones; orange string lights; witch cut-outs; plastic skeletons and plenty of pumpkins. Friday was creeping up on them, and Hazel was aroused by the idea of so many horny youths inside the manor, on the night of the great moon. She would feed off their youthful exuberance, enjoying a real party, something she'd never been able to do when she was their age. Then she would use her newfound abilities to coax more boys into her bedroom, and one by one she would lick and suck and fuck them. She would possess them wholly and stack their souls in the catacombs of the house, and her offering to the mountain would be bountiful.

The darkness would be pleased.

CHAPTER TWENTY-EIGHT

KAYLA WENT BACK TO SCHOOL on Wednesday.

It took some convincing. Her mother was against it, but Kayla assured her she was already feeling much better and didn't want to jeopardize her potential scholarship. She'd been bringing home all A's; no sense in breaking her streak. He father (over the phone) backed up her decision, and the next morning she was roaming the halls again, only this time with an extra swagger to her hips and redder lipstick than usual. She'd bought a schoolgirl skirt and white stockings and went without a bra, letting her breasts bounce and her nipples grow erect in the chilly October air.

It was time to lure the boys in.

She flirted her way through lunch, P.E., and drama class. She batted eyes at jocks, metalheads, hipsters, and nerds. She warmed up to the football team, cooed at the boys in Odyssey of the Mind, and shamelessly flaunted her beauty, bending over, crossing and uncrossing her legs, pushing her breasts together with her upper arms and licking her lips. She hoped she wasn't overdoing it. But from the looks guys were giving her, it was working. The other girls may have snubbed their noses at her, but their opinions didn't matter much now, did they? If Kayla didn't get these boys wild for her, there would be blood. Souls would be lost forever and that goddamned witch would grow powerful enough to escape the confines of the manor. Then the whole town would be at risk. No one would be safe. It was all riding on Kayla, so she let her hips sway and giggled when the breeze blew her skirt about, teasing the boys, almost giving them a glimpse of the goods, but not quite.

For the first day of her life, everyone noticed her.

By Thursday seven different guys had asked her out.

Kayla held off on dating them but asked if they would be going to the Halloween party at Snowden Manor. Everyone was talking about it. Joe and Danny had called everyone up, and the invite was open, so anyone and everyone were welcome. Her admirers told her they'd be there, and she promised them all she'd save a dance for them. The fact that so many boys had tried to court her overwhelmed Kayla. She kept having to remind herself she was doing this to stop Hazel because she was getting wrapped up in being so flattered by all this attention after feeling like a wallflower for so long. She had a newfound confidence that squashed the festering feelings of never being good enough, those dark, self-hating vibes that had been stalking her since she was twelve. She believed in herself now; not just as a bookworm honor-roller, but also as a budding young woman. At last she felt like she had mastered her essence. She was a sexual being now, not just some awkward little virgin.

But she made sure to let the boys know she was one.

Whenever anyone mentioned sex or she caught one of the guys checking her out, she always found a subtle way to insert it into the conversation.

I'm so nervous, she'd say. *I want my first time to be really special, but I think it's time I lost it.*

I really want somebody to teach me how to pleasure a man.

Lines like these got guys salivating, and Kayla realized just how simple men really were. They ran on a biological need, and girls had power over them because of it. All those years she'd spent so nervous around them, so self-conscious, and now she had them all in the palm of her hand.

It was exhilarating.

Kayla stopped taking the pills.

There was no way this was all in her imagination.

Her new confidence assured her she'd been right all along. She wasn't crazy. As outrageous as it sounded, there was a witch in Snowden manor, and she was reaping souls.

Maxine and her parents were all missing now.

Buchinsky sat across from her. They were in her living room and Kayla's mother was sitting next to her on the couch. The lieutenant looked tired. He needed a shave.

"You haven't heard from her at all?"

"No."

She needn't tell him about how she'd called the Brownstones, or how she knew they must also be victims of Hazel Snowden. That would only get her another trip to the shrink and a fistful of pills she didn't need.

"It just doesn't make sense," her mother said. "No one knows where they are?"

Buchinsky leaned in. "Well, their car is gone. It's possible they took a trip. But none of them reported to work and their cell phones are turned off. Mrs. Brownstone called the school on Tuesday, looking for her daughter, but Maxine hasn't been back there."

Kayla almost asked about Linda, just to drive a point home, but she quickly thought better of the idea and kept her mouth shut. She'd tried steering the police in the right direction but they dismissed and mocked her. If all this madness were going to end, she would have to do things herself. She knew that now. She only regretted involving the Brownstones. It had seemed like the right thing to do at the time, but she cursed herself for not realizing what would happen to them.

It wasn't just about saving the boys now. She wasn't even sure if they *could* be saved. It was about stopping Hazel, and putting an end to her sorcery, severing the umbilical cord that let her feed upon the mountain.

Patricia came into the room, holding the Barbie she'd cut all the hair off of, and Buchinsky smiled at her.

"Hello, sweetheart," he said. "What's your name?"

She was too bashful to reply. She went to her mother and buried her face in her lap. Buchinsky smiled at her anyway.

Her mother smiled. "Honey, the grown ups need to talk. Why don't you go play in your room."

It took some coaxing but Kayla's sister went back to her room full of dolls to continue watching *The Little Mermaid* for the thousandth time. Kayla began to feel restless sitting there. She hoped the lieutenant would be leaving soon. It was now Thursday night and she had enough on her mind without having to go through this rigmarole. In twenty-four hours she would be preparing to duke it out with a deadly foe. She had to concentrate and continue to throw lines out to reel in the boys. She wanted a big following for the Halloween party, so she could show Hazel she was in for a contest. It was more than a fight now; it was destiny.

"Well," Buchinksy said, standing. "I've taken up enough of your time." He turned to Kayla. "Your mother tells me you've been feeling better."

She nodded. "Yeah. I'm on medication now. It's helping."

"That's good. There's no shame in psychiatric help."

There was a silent moment and then he started walking toward the door. Her mother saw him out.

"You have my number," he said.

But Kayla had no use for it.

CHAPTER TWENTY-NINE

ROBBIE WAS LYING IN THE darkness.

Or at least he felt like he was. It was hard to tell now that he was formless. He could sense his body was *somewhere*, not fully detached from him yet, and he clung to the hope he would be reunited with it. To be normal again, human. Not like *her*, whatever she was.

He wasn't sure how long he'd been on the other side. It could have been hours or years. It felt like a dream state sometimes, but he had trouble separating it from consciousness, particularly because of the nightmare his existence had become. He wanted his mother, for all her flaws. He wanted to take Joe, Danny, and Horace and run from the house and never look back. But he was beginning to lose hope. Hazel was a madwoman. She had all the control and wasn't about to just let him go, no matter how much he begged or retracted what he'd said about giving himself to her. She wanted him. More than that, she seemed to need him for something, and that frightened him more than anything else.

Once again he heard the scratching.

It seemed to come from everywhere—left, right, above and below. It was a frantic tearing, followed by a series of mewing.

Horace.

The dog was still trying to get to him.

"Here, boy!" he said.

He wasn't sure how the dog would be able to rescue him, but if Horace could rip through the wall, maybe he could escape. He would worry about fully reconnecting with his body afterward. *First things first*, he thought.

"Come on, Horace! Get me the hell out of here!"

The scratching grew louder. It sounded like his paws were breaking through and ripping deeper. The sound of tumbling rattled the darkness, a welcomed avalanche. Something crumbled and fell. The dog barked excitedly.

"All right, boy!"

Robbie hushed himself. Hazel could be anywhere, and sometimes it seemed like she was *everywhere*. They would have to be stealthy if they were going to sneak by her.

A bullet hole of light appeared in the darkness, beaming like a lighthouse on a rocky shore.

Robbie laughed with relief.

The hole grew bigger, the size of a basketball, and a moment later Horace's head peeked through, slobber dripping from his jowls. Robbie drifted toward the light. Not walked, but *drifted*. He realized he could see his own hands, or at least the faded reflections of them. They were coming into focus, like a movie dissolve, the light returning his flesh.

"Oh my god."

Maybe he wasn't far from his human form after all. If he could just escape from her spell, and from this house, he might be all right. Sure, she'd seduced him once, but she didn't have the hold on him she desired. He knew that by the disappointment and rage she displayed whenever her seduction techniques failed. He did not lust for her anymore. He feared her, *hated* her, and maybe that was enough to break the spell; that and the light of day that spilled over him as he pushed his way out of the wall.

Horace spun in circles, too excited to contain himself as Robbie entered the living room. He could see his entire body now. It flickered for a few moments, twinkling like the cosmos, before the image stuck. At first his hands went through him when he tried to touch himself, and that gave him a start, but then his body started to take on a tacky form, solidifying, and Robbie could actually *feel* his intestines and inner organs forming inside him in a gassy swish. He felt bones snapping into place like Legos and every hair on his body pushing its way through his spongy flesh. His heart began to beat. Suddenly he was whole again, human, and he had never felt so

TheLONGSHADOWSofOCTOBER

happy to be alive. He didn't fully understand what had happened, but he wasn't about to stick around to figure it out.

"Good boy, buddy," he whispered, petting the dog all over. "Now come on. We've gotta get the guys and get outta here."

Horace followed behind him, his nub of a tail wagging, his paws doing a happy tap-dance. Robbie looked around the living room, listening. The house was still and silent. He tried to keep from shaking, but it was a losing battle. He'd just been a specter inside of a wall, buried in the core of the manor's pitch-black heart. It was almost too much for him to comprehend, and fear throttled him like a hangman's noose.

Walking through the room, he rounded the corner and peered into the kitchen. Empty. The afternoon sunlight illuminated the dust in the air. He stepped gingerly, still listening. Horace trotted away from him, and when Robbie turned to look he saw the dog sitting by the front door, whimpering.

Let's get out of here, he seemed to say.

"Just a minute, boy."

Robbie didn't want to go upstairs. That was where she'd first taken him. Would he be vulnerable up there again? But he couldn't leave without the guys.

On the other hand, he thought, *maybe I should get out of here before it's too late and get some help. Maybe Horace is right. Maybe he senses something I'm not.*

He hated the idea of leaving them there, but . . .

A terrifying thought hit him.

What if Joe and Danny are in the walls now?

He would need more than the police. He would need a priest, an exorcist. Ghost hunters or psychics or something. The best place to start was his mother. If he could get her help, maybe they could get Joe out of there. They were latchkey kids, but as neglectful as their mother could be at times, she loved her sons. If Robbie could convince her Joe was in trouble, something would be done about it.

Horace whimpered in the hall.

"Okay, boy," he said.

He turned around, coming face to face with Danny.

Robbie jolted and put a hand to his mouth to cover his startled scream. Danny stood before him, his face thinner, eyes bloodshot.

"Jesus, Danny. You scared me, man."

Danny's eyes began to mist over. A look of grief came upon his face and rested there.

"Get out," Danny said. "Get out of here before it's too late."

195

Robbie took a deep breath. "Where's Joe? We can all leave together."

"It's too late for us. Too much has happened."

"No, man, come on . . . "

"*Go now.*"

Robbie stood firm, surprised by his own courage. "Where's my brother."

"You don't want to see him."

"Yes, I do."

"If he sees you, he won't let you out." Danny lowered his voice. "*She* doesn't want you to leave . . ."

"Dude, what the hell is going on?"

"There's no time! Run, now, before they catch you. They're upstairs together. But if they hear you they'll—"

They hushed as footfalls came from the stairwell.

"Shit," Danny whispered.

Robbie heard the walls grind and Horace cried softly. Danny pushed him toward the door, his eyes crazed and desperate. Robbie ran. But he should have run sooner.

As he charged into the hall his feet slid. The floor was turning to mud. The tiles became white liquid and he instantly sank up to his knees. He grabbed onto the doorknob to the closet and hung on. In front of him, Horace was jumping on the door, clawing at it as he mewled and splashed in the cold liquid. All around them the walls churned like glue in a drain, morphing into powdery hurricanes. Arms of drywall grabbed at him, tugging his clothes and taking fistfuls of his hair. He writhed against them, and as he pulled himself out of the goo he heaved forward and cleared the watery floor. The space between him and the front door was a lagoon now, and Horace was paddling through it. Robbie went to the edge and helped the dog out. Around them a galaxy of hands blindly groped the air.

The back door!

He zipped through the kitchen, ducking the knives and other utensils that began whipping through the air like arrows, flung by an invisible force. The chairs spun toward his feet and he stumbled but didn't fall. Horace jumped and dodged. They reached the double doors of the patio and when he grabbed for the handle it was so frozen it burned his skin like dry ice. He hissed and withdrew, then began kicking the frame. The doors shook, and he punted the glass. It wobbled at first and then it cracked in a large, circular pattern. One more kick and he would be free.

Beyond the glass he saw the pool. It was overflowing, waves

breaking upon the base of the door like a hungry, raging ocean. Light made of impossible colors filled the center of the pool like a kaleidoscope, twirling and mixing, a horrifying phantasmagoria. It dizzied him and he had to turn his head away to avoid vertigo. He missed a kick and squinted against the light. He aimed for the crack again, but through the splintering glass he saw a black shape emerging from the water, an outline of a woman as voluptuous as a pinup. There were bizarre antennae coming out of her back. These spindly things twitched in the light that overpowered the setting sun.

Giant spider legs.

Where her feet should have been, a dozen tentacles writhed, an aroused squid, slapping and slithering, pulsing with incandescence. Their feelers snapped with piranha teeth and glistened with staring, primal eyes. Black ooze spilled out of the she-beast like a river of tar.

Hazel was coming for him.

There had to be another way out. The house was big. There were multiple exits. He would just have to find another one. Robbie spun around to head toward the den, and as he did so a fist came at him in a sudden blur. He fell backward.

Joe was standing over him, naked, hands balled like sledgehammers.

His eyes were glowing.

CHAPTER THIRTY

HAZEL WAS VERY DISAPPOINTED.

More than that, she was baffled by her familiar's behavior. The dog had been her spirit animal for as long as she'd been practicing the dark arts and had never let her down before. He certainly had never turned on her like this. Had it not been for him, Robbie would not have escaped the walls. Being not of this world, the dog was able to break through to the other side. He too was between life and death, capable of passing through the boundaries. Had a normal dog clawed into the wall it would have torn up the house but wouldn't have found and freed Robbie. Only her familiar was able to do that, and for some reason it had. It *chose* to disobey. Even now he was whimpering, wishing he could get to the boy who was tied to a bed in the next room. Hazel couldn't drag Robbie back into the blackness again. He had escaped it, renouncing her, and in doing so he'd regained his flesh. Had he made it all the way out of the house it would have been hopeless. Her great sacrifice would be gone. But she'd caught him just in time and, better still, Joe had stopped him, turning on his own brother for her. This gave her a rush of power. She wished as much could be said for Danny. While the big boy was enchanted, at the same time he had a conscience to him that troubled her. Instead of celebrating in the glory of her, he was often withdrawn, harping on the murders he'd been a part of. He missed his precious fucking Maxine and his pathetic former life. But he was hooked on Hazel now, and like every junkie he couldn't turn away from his poison even when he knew it was killing him.

But Joe was a good boy.

Not like her familiar.

The dog mewled at her feet, lying as close to the floor as he could. He was afraid now, as well he should be. Hazel was furious with him. She'd never thought a familiar could turn on its master. It had happened when she had needed him most of all. It was time for him to be put in his place within the walls. Let him sit in there, alone in the blackness, to think about what he'd done.

She cupped her hand. The pink light swirled and the dog whimpered, knowing what was coming. The light blossomed into a large bubble and began to dome over the dog. Normally when she did this, he stayed still, as he'd been trained to do. But once again his training was failing her. He was turning from side to side, jumping. He started to bark at her.

She tried to speed up the process but as the bubble grew larger her familiar charged forward, knocking into her legs as he fled. She stumbled and when she turned around he was standing there, his haunches raised, his wet teeth bared, growling.

He couldn't be this stupid. He knew she was far more powerful than he was. He was merely a peon, a pawn in her wicked games. The laws of the material world did not apply to them. A normal Rottweiler could pounce on a woman and cause serious damage or even kill her. But this dog was not just her spiritual inferior, he was also her familiar, like it or not. He may want to hurt her, but he was incapable of doing so, no matter how he tried.

"You lousy mutt. You've disobeyed me for the last time."

Pink flames rose from her fingertips like birthday candles, her hair becoming a nest of worms as her shoulder blades parted. Her back split and the arachnid legs pushed out, their hairy forms reaching for the dog. He ran toward the door, using all his strength to break through the wood like a battering ram. She yelled after him but he was too fast.

Fine, she thought, *let him go.*

She didn't need him for what she was about to do.

The yard was pitch black, but he could smell traces of the boy where they had played. Horace saddened. He'd tried so hard to save him and now the master had trapped him again. Horace had to go against everything he knew to rescue the boy, rebelling from his master.

He whimpered.

At first he'd felt ashamed as the master scolded him, but when he thought about what she was doing to the boy he felt angry, angrier than he had ever felt, even more than he'd been at the ones who'd tried to defy the master in the past. When she wanted someone gone he had always taken it as a must, but he just couldn't bring himself to help her trap the boy. The boy gave Horace something he'd never had before, something all dogs wanted and needed. He was not about to give that up.

The lights were off, the only illumination in the manor coming from the moon. Its azure flooded the house through the open curtains and blinds, and Joe felt a strange quiver as he moved within it.

Something was happening to him. Something beautiful.

He looked at his brother who was still wide-eyed and staring upon the bed. Sweat had beaded on his brow and occasional tears rolled down his pale cheeks. Joe didn't understand. Robbie was set to serve the goddess in the most glorious way. If Joe were in his brother's shoes, he would be euphoric.

"Get some rest," he said. "Tomorrow is a big day, and an even bigger night."

Robbie groaned. "Joe, man, you have to untie me. We have to get out of here before it's too late."

"Don't talk like that, little brother."

"But Joe—"

"Disrespecting *her* wishes is blasphemy. I won't have it."

His brother was shaking now. *Once a pussy, always a pussy*, Joe thought bitterly.

"I'm scared," Robbie said. "What is she gonna do with me?"

"You don't understand. Serving her is the highest honor you can receive. It will give you more pleasure than you've ever dreamed."

"But what does she want from me?"

A great sacrifice was going to be made, and the goddess would become even more splendiferous, divine. If that meant he had to lose his little brother, so be it. He had long ago accepted that these things were not up to him.

"Joe, talk to me, man!"

"We've talked enough."

He turned to leave.

"Have you looked at yourself?" Robbie asked. "Have you seen a mirror lately? You're as white as a sheet and your face is all sunken in. And dude, *your eyes are glowing in the dark*. They're a creepy blue, just like the light from the pool."

Joe grimaced. "That's all right. It's fine."

"Fine? How is that *fine*?"

"She's improving me, so that I may better serve her."

"She's fucking killing you!"

Joe trembled unexpectedly, as if a winter wind had blasted him. His brother's words stung like wasps. There was something to them he didn't like, a bitter truth finally said aloud. He knew he shouldn't listen. He didn't want to get in trouble and end up cut off like Danny.

"Go to sleep, Robbie."

He walked out the door, even as his little brother begged for his help.

The nylon rope dug into his wrists, turning them pink. If he could get one hand free he might be able to undo the knots. His brother had made the loops extremely tight. If Robbie was going to slip out of one, he would have to break his thumb to get through, and he didn't think he could do something like that. That sort of thing was better left to Stallone movies than the real world.

Robbie cursed the restraints. He cursed the blue-black room and the wicked witch who ruled the house. He would curse his brother, but Joe wasn't in his right mind anymore. Hazel had poisoned his thoughts and had some kind of stranglehold on him. Joe's head was full of delusions and nonsense, scrambled by her devious, hypnotic spell.

Tears of frustration burned in Robbie's eyes and a sick pain hollowed his chest. He was trapped. They all were. And something big was happening tomorrow night. Robbie did not want to be here when it came. It could mean the end for all of them, or maybe worse.

CHAPTER THIRTY-ONE

THE DAY BROUGHT MORE GLOOM, heavier and darker than before, the gray clouds drifting like wolves. The leaves had turned from yellow and red to a muddy brown, looking dried out and death-choked as they clung to skeletal trees. There was no wind, only a dead calm that let the cold air sneak beneath flesh and settle into bones.

Kayla zipped up her hoodie as she got out of the car. On the sidewalk, leaves spun at her boots. When she reached the store the heat hit her in a nauseating wave and she had to remove the sweater altogether. The fluorescent lights were cruel, especially after the gloom of outside, and she squinted as she made her way toward the back.

The pop-up store was full of costumes, props, and customers now that the holiday was rapidly approaching. School had let out and children were running through the place, stepping on the activation pads for the animatronics and decorations. Mummies groaned; black cats spun their heads in 360-degree turns; a bloody body twitched in an electric chair; giant bats fluttered their wings above a scarecrow with a lit-up jack-o-lantern head. There were bags upon bags of cobwebs, fake spiders, and cheap fangs, and the far wall was completely covered by rows of latex masks. Minions,

Spider-Man, Leatherface, Chucky, and Yoda looked down at her, as did cartoonish mockups of political figures.

She walked toward the other side of the store where clothing racks held bagged costumes, bypassing the practical ones and going for the slutty stuff she'd always thought were more like lingerie than anything else. She would need something really good for tonight, to get the boys foaming. If she were going to outdo Hazel, in her own house, she would have to bring the thunder.

She sifted through the normal devil and nurse costumes and smiled at the angel with a dark sense of irony, given what she'd be going up against. There were sexy costumes of *everything* nowadays. She found Little Red Riding Hood, a bumblebee, a prisoner, and even a sexy Freddy Krueger costume (sans the creepy face, of course). There were the obvious Elvira and Catwoman suits, but Kayla wanted something more original, something that made her look movie-star-hot but still highlighted her innocence, to tease the boys while suggesting the virginity one of them might be lucky enough to take.

As she ran through the tail end of the first row, pushing past more variations on sexy vampires than anyone could possibly need, she found it. It was white, tight, and perfect. It not only suggested innocence, it outright *screamed* it. She went to the dressing rooms, already sure it would fit like a glove.

CHAPTER THIRTY-TWO

THE MANOR GLOWED PUMPKIN ORANGE, the strung lights dangling from the roof. The steps were lined with flickering jack-o-lanterns, windows decorated with back-lit images of werewolves, zombies, and Jason from *Friday the 13th*. Phony cobwebs stretched across the porch's railing and latex body parts hung from the gutters by plastic chains.

But inside the house was even better.

Joe and Danny had spent all their money at the Halloween store, splurging on latex ghoul babies, black lights, glow-in-the-dark faces to mount on the walls, even more jack-o-lanterns, and liters of fake blood, which they splattered in the bathtubs. A life-sized mummy was in the corner of the kitchen, and it had a motion sensor that made it move and groan whenever someone walked past. Huge spiders hung from the ceiling fans, scary clown stickers were put on every solid surface, and severed heads were scattered across tables and counters.

Joe looked in the mirror and sized-up his demon costume. His black cloak was long and flowing, his hands covered in red gloves with jagged yellow nails. Over his head he wore a latex mask of a devil, with snarling fangs, a pointed nose, and long, curling ram horns. He thought he looked pretty damned scary.

Danny had chosen a Frankenstein costume, getting a cheap suit at the thrift store that was one size too small for him to make him look bigger. He also bought an old pair of platform shoes and painted them black, giving him monstrous height, and used some of his football padding to give himself big, squared shoulders. He had a headpiece with stitched and shaggy hair and painted his face green with seeping stitches. Rubber bolts stuck out of his neck like tumors.

Joe's breath blew back on him from inside the mask, making him sweat. He felt the costume suited him, now that he'd crossed certain lines. He'd given in to evil impulses, imprisoning his brother, submitting to a witch, and stabbing two people to death before burying them in shallow graves. The costume was a more appropriate look for him than his own skin was anymore. He had become something new over the past week, something sinister, black as soot. By dressing as a demon, he hoped Hazel would understand his subtle message.

I would sell my soul to be with you, forever and always.

Tonight was going to be a very special Halloween.

Hazel knew the druid practices inside and out. She'd mastered the art of the ceremonies of Samhain. And with her souls, followers, and adoring servants of the natural world, she was ready for the super moon, the *blood* moon. The boy whose virginity she'd harvested was a splendid bonus, one she was looking forward to redeeming in a wet, warm crimson. At first she'd been enraged that he'd escaped from the blackness, but now she had a new plan, one even more diabolical. It would prove to the mountain just how powerful she truly was, that she was the greatest seductress in the history of the druids and was therefore deserving of being the vessel of the timeless magic, the eternal black.

She would make Joe kill Robbie.

This would be the ultimate act of devotion, brother killing brother at her request before submitting to have his own soul taken. The very idea of it aroused her, stirring and moistening her hungry loins.

She would walk in flesh once again.

Tonight the house would be filled with young bodies. Soft skin, supple forms, fresh genitalia. There would be a plethora of innocent hearts. Life had not had time to tarnish these teenagers. Their souls would be naked and open to suggestion, waiting to be harvested like little cornhusks.

The festival would be a gala, a variable orgy of innocent souls, and she would be the bell of the ball. This was the prom she'd never had. This would make up for the youth her abusive father had robbed her of, and he would have to witness it all from the prison of the cellar where she had damned his dog-shit soul for all of eternity. This night of black art was a spit in the eye of his pathetic little god, and the old man would witness true devotion tonight.

The door would remain locked. Robbie would be gagged. The house was huge and nobody would care about one closed-off room. There was nothing Danny could do about it right now. He'd tried to get him out of the house, but now Joe was keeping a watchful eye on the room. It was as if Joe could sense his desire to help Robbie escape. He often looked at Danny out of the corner of his eye, a hint of malice winking.

Danny could hardly recognize his friend anymore.

Something terrible was going to happen tonight. It was throbbing in the house and tainting the air that swirled the leaves outside. There was a wickedness he could not put his finger on but was there nonetheless, pulsing and churning, building to something he doubted he wanted to see. The macabre mood that had been cast over the manse outweighed his desire for Hazel, and her spell was weakened by the sick fear in his stomach. She was evil incarnate. They were all in mortal danger, as was anyone else who stepped across the threshold of this house. And now they were having a fucking party. Half the school was on the way.

He shook within his bulky costume.

His only hope was to wait until the commotion of the party began. Perhaps then he could free Robbie and they could sneak out undetected. He'd purchased two additional costumes, a gorilla and a space man. Both had masks that would completely cover their faces. If they could change into them, they could blend into the crowd and get out to the yard where people would be rocking around the bonfire. Then it would just be a matter of slipping into the shadows and climbing into his car.

This was all he had. When the time came he could only hope he would have enough courage to go through with it because the thought of defying Hazel made him want to vomit. Even just plotting this out made him paranoid. Maybe she could read minds. And seeing what Joe had done to the Brownstones, Danny didn't want to go toe-to-toe with him. He would have to carry a weapon to protect himself, and the thought of potentially killing his best friend in order to escape filled him with a crushing feeling that made it hard for him to breathe.

That was what had become of their relationship, after Hazel. What had started as a fling had become an obsession that led them down this dark and blood-slicked road. The bitch had ensnared them in her necromancy, scooping them out of the doldrums of their lives by enticing them with otherworldly euphoria, only to wash their minds and twist their souls into tools of her bidding. Had it not been for his fear and Hazel's withdrawing of affection, Danny knew he'd be just as lost to her as Joe was, a subservient mongrel, and that was the most terrifying aspect of all.

CHAPTER THIRTY-THREE

JOE LOOKED IN THE MIRROR, seeing himself for what he was even though he was behind the mask.

In the master bedroom, Danny sat on the edge of the bed, his head in his hands, waiting.

On the bottom floor, Robbie writhed against the ropes, bouncing between determination and exhaustion.

Outside the room's window, Horace lay in the dead grass, hoping.

Inside the walls, Hazel swam amongst her adoring souls, charging up on their thunderous passions.

And the manor thrummed with anticipation. The windows shuddered like hatchlings and the ceiling and walls creaked, little cracks appearing in their corners. The front of the manse was glowing and not because of the decorative lights. A different illumination was forming, surrounding the house, a haunted aura imbued with alchemy.

Black Rock Mountain shifted slightly, and the moon hung sallow, a frozen tangerine, slowly turning to blood as it stalked the horizon like a gory skull, night falling all around it in an enveloping black squall.

CHAPTER THIRTY-FOUR

WHEN SHE ARRIVED, THE MANOR was already hopping.

There were at least two dozen cars in the driveway and parked alongside it, and the front door to the house was wide open as costumed guests went in and out, some smoking and drinking on the porch. A bonfire glowed in the backyard. Kayla smelled the burning embers. The night was the coldest one of the season and she shivered in her skimpy outfit, wishing her cape were a little longer. But it only came down to her waist, so as to show off her ass. She held her hat as a breeze came and walked carefully in her white pumps.

On the porch, she noticed three boys she knew from school sharing a joint. The tall redhead was Bob (he was dressed like a hobo tonight), the short guy was Ryan (a Wolverine with his mask off so he could take hits) and the other one she recognized but couldn't put a name to (he'd gone as a hamburger). When they saw her they stopped talking, their mouths hanging open like cartoon characters. Bob couldn't help himself. He whistled.

"Damn, girl," he said. "You look good enough to eat."

The other guys laughed. Normally she would have been offended by such a crass comment, but tonight was different. Even lewd attention was good.

"Thanks, boys."

She winked and wiggled her hips for emphasis, the boys hooting like jackals. Kayla snickered to herself.

No wonder they don't have dates.

She walked up the steps gingerly. There was static in the air the closer she came to the front door. There was danger here, and she could almost smell the blood that would be shed tonight, the rich coppery taste hitting her lips in premonition. She took a deep breath and crossed the threshold, every hair on her body at attention, eyes wild in their sockets, nails digging into her palms so hard they nearly cut into her.

As she went inside she heard the boys still catcalling and whistling after her.

"Holy shit," Ryan said, adjusting his nuts. "That is the sexiest witch costume I've ever seen!"

Initially Kayla had wanted to wear a little mask, the kind that goes around the eyes, in the hope it would keep Joe and Danny (and maybe even Hazel) from recognizing her straight off. But she decided against it. She had to show she was confident, right from the start.

She'd chosen to dress as a white witch. A *good* witch.

She wore a pointed hat. Cartoonish in a way, but effective. It matched the white lace of her corset with the little bows that made a straight line down past her navel, where a skimpy, panties-style bottom was all that covered her. A cream-colored garter belt held up her stockings, lacey and transparent as her gloves. The outfit was very sexy, but the color was symbolic for virginity, like a bride, and she'd blushed her cheeks and put on fake eyelashes to give her the look of a cherub. She had curled her blond hair and the shimmering coils fell around her shoulders like birthday streamers, occasionally sweeping the tops of milky breasts that pushed out of the corset like white plush.

Heads turned. Mouths fell open.

In the glow of the black lights, her white outfit shone, making her look like she was from another world. In the crowd, eyes gleamed within the purple glow, the men longing, the women envious. From their glances alone Kayla could feel a warm surge ripple through her. It was more than just the thrill of being desired. There was a new titillation involved now, one that flushed her the moment she stepped into the house.

The manor was a source of great vitality, swarming with the energy of lost souls. The blood moon and abundance of living bodies no doubt intensified this energy, and Kayla was able to draw some of it in when she awed the partygoers.

With this many people around, she was confident Hazel would not attack her. Not yet. Joe and Danny would recognize her, of course, but no matter how lost to the succubus they were, or how possessed, Kayla felt safe in the crowd. Once she started to harness power, Hazel was bound to get pissed off, but for now Kayla was confident.

Before anything else, she wanted to find out where Robbie was. She sensed he was somewhere in the house against his will, but she didn't know where or if he was even in the world of the living. Hazel might have taken him over a line.

As she moved through the kitchen she felt the stares of the boys filling her up with a new energy. Her heart pulsed harder, her blood a freight train. The floor trembled slightly and Kayla thought of the souls trapped within the house. There were other girls at the party dressed in skimpy outfits, and most of them looked really good; long legs, fishnets, perky breasts, vinyl, glitter, lace, and heavy makeup. But Kayla was a known virgin. It was known by the boys and sensed by the trapped souls. She'd been universally singled out as the bell of the ball, and the heat within her burned like the flames of the jack-o-lanterns. And with that heat came a rising power she could feel.

She was appeasing the magic.

It was coming to her, lured just like the boys.

When Joe saw her, a shudder of lust coursed through his veins. Kayla looked positively angelic. The black lights made her ethereal, a specter floating through a purpled heaven. He pulled up his mask to get a better look. He had an urge to run to her and scoop her into his arms like in some soap opera. The memory of her bare breasts in his hands gave him a pang of jealousy of his previous self. He knew he'd blown it with her, and seeing her like this tore at him like a serrated blade. Joe began to sweat. His fists balled and his penis stirred. For the first time since he'd been with Hazel, she abruptly left his mind, replaced by sweet, innocent Kayla, the little blond beauty who was *begging* to be sexually crushed.

Behind him, Danny was staring at her too. Joe seethed. He'd

been forced to share Hazel, but he wasn't about to let him near Kayla. Even if Joe couldn't patch things up with her, he still wouldn't allow Danny to have a taste. No fucking way.

Kayla looked at Joe and his breath stopped. She smiled. His feet froze but she moved forward. The sound of Alice Cooper's "Feed My Frankenstein" blared from the stereo, so she had to get close to him to talk. There was a subtle, perfumed smell coming off her that reminded him of autumn rain. He felt like if he licked her she would taste like heavy cream and strawberries, and if he were to touch her she would be soft like baby blankets and kittens.

"Hi," he said.

"Hi yourself. Surprised to see me?"

"Um, yeah."

She tilted her head to get a better look at him. "I like your eyes. Pretty cool contacts."

There were none, and he'd forgotten about his eyes' new glow. "Yeah. I'm a demon."

"I can tell." There was an edge to what she'd just said, but he let it slide rather than try and analyze what she meant. "Where's your brother?"

Joe tensed. *Is this some kind of trick?*

"Haven't seen him in a while," Kayla said. "Isn't he coming to the party?"

"Yeah. He'll be here. He's playing a big part in all of this."

"Oh?"

"Yup," he said with a small laugh. "You'll see."

"So is he around?"

"Why?"

She crossed her arms beneath her breasts, hoisting them a little. "I wanted to ask him about the dog. I was wondering what he plans to do with him."

"Shit, I dunno." He looked her up and down again. "Baby, I'm sorry things got all screwed up between us." Her eyes seemed to sparkle at that. Maybe he still had a chance. "You think we could patch things up?"

Kayla shrugged. "Anything's possible."

"You look amazing."

She let that linger for a moment. "I know."

The house was crawling with teens, an anthill that had just been struck by a lawnmower. Strobe lights flashed like heart attacks, glow sticks spinning, people grinding to the electronic music in an animal frenzy. Drinking games were going on and some people had jumped into the pool. The house was secluded. The police would not be called to break it up.

Kayla went upstairs, pretending to use the bathroom. The new warmth in her body was telling her Robbie was in one of the rooms on this floor. She opened the doors one by one, trying not to think of the last time she'd been up here with Maxine, as they had run for their lives from Linda (or her image, anyway) and the gathering of hungry hands. She searched Robbie's room thoroughly but found no trace of him. The bed was made and everything was in perfect order. She kept expecting Hazel to appear, but luckily there was no sign of her. Despite the otherworldly warmth spreading inside her chest, she still didn't feel ready to face the black witch.

But what is Hazel waiting for?

Surely she knew by now Kayla was there. Maybe she didn't understand Kayla's intentions, but she must be aware of her presence, and didn't it make sense that she would feel some of the power being diverted?

She's preparing, she thought. *That must be it. Tonight is a very special night. She wants everything to be just so. Maybe it has to be perfect for her to get what she wants.*

Kayla was on guard anyway. She knew what the bitch was capable of. She wasn't worried about Joe now, despite his strange eyes, which she wasn't exactly sure were just part of his costume. She'd seen the way he melted for her at first sight. She had him, and taking one of Hazel's adoring young men away from her was a victory all its own, one that would give her a competitive edge.

She started back down the stairs and moved through the reeling crowd, wondering if she should try the library or the playroom. *No, the playroom will be packed*, she thought. All those games were bound to draw her classmates in. She moved around the den and the back doors came open, people going in and out. The party was growing. There must have been close to seventy kids there. She looked to the yard at the spinning stoners, giggling girls, and beer-guzzling dudes, all decked out like vampires, rock stars and Disney princesses. They partied by the light of the bonfire, their black silhouettes covered by the overhang of tree branches that wrestled in the night wind. In the deep, orange glow, she glanced something short and stocky scurrying about.

Horace!

She went outside and approached the dog. When he saw her he began to whimper and ran to her, doing circles in the grass. He kept mewling. Not from excitement, but stress.

"What is it, boy?"

The dog ran past her and entered the house. Then he looked back at her and barked, telling her to follow. She did, and Horace led her through the maze of people and into the den. He moved fast, making people stumble as he pushed through them like a cow-catcher. They went through the hall and around the corner and then came to a small door. Horace jumped at it.

"He's in there, isn't he?"

Horace barked.

She tried the doorknob. Locked. She put her ear to the wood but heard nothing. But she was sure Robbie was inside and looking at the small, circular hole in the knob, she could see it was one of those easy locks that could be flipped by a simple flathead screwdriver. She just needed to find one.

"I'll be right back," she told Horace.

The dog didn't follow her as she walked off. He just curled by the foot of the door and whined softly. She made her way through the house and went to the cellar. Slipping inside, she was shocked by the deafening silence. With the door closed behind her she couldn't hear the raging party at all.

She stepped down, the cold, damp air rising up to greet her like a bog. Even the warmth that had been growing inside her turned cold. She could still feel it churning, strengthening, but it was an arctic force now, icy and mean. When she reached the floor she went to the workbench, which had an old, rusty toolbox resting on it. She brushed away the cobwebs and popped the top, and when she found what she needed she slipped the thin screwdriver into the side of her corset.

The air turned suddenly colder. It was *freezing* now. A stench came up, the reek of copper and rotted meat, almost fecal. There was a vibration in the cellar now, something hidden but unmistakably alive.

She heard the hissing breath again. This time it sounded like words.

Jez ... bells ... hoard ...

Kayla tensed and crossed her arms, her skin rippling. At first she was worried Hazel was coming for her, now that she was alone, but somehow she knew this wasn't the witch. There was someone else down here—*something else*—and it was as dark as the black witch herself.

Hoard ... Jeza ... bells ...

Kayla walked backward, toward the stairs. The soles of her shoes began to stick to the floor, and when she looked down she saw blood seeping through the cracks in the floor. The voice became clearer.

Whore! Jezebel!

She ran, reaching the stairway in a mad dash, climbing up so frantically the railing shook. She fumbled at the door, pushing before pulling, and spilled out into the hall. Slamming the door behind her, she heard the ghostly voice's request.

Bring her to me! Bring me my daughter, the whore!

CHAPTER THIRTY-FIVE

THE LITTLE VIRGIN GIRL WAS here, and she was getting way too much attention. She was dressed immaculately and had a tender aura about her—equal parts innocent and mischievous, a blond Lolita in lace. Hazel saw the way the boys' eyes turned, and she hissed when Joe talked to the little bitch. It was as if she no longer existed. He would have to be reprimanded, but first he would have to be seduced. All the boys would. And now that the true witching hour was drawing near, it was time for her to join the festivities.

She nearly grinded the party to a halt. Jaws dropped. Cups slipped from hands.

A nation of eyes burned into her with the force of their lust, fueling and intoxicating her. She'd chosen her voluptuous adult form and the skin-tight, black outfit. She was wrapped in fishnet and vinyl, with ash-black eyes and lips, little black devil horns atop her billowy hair. Her knee-high boots clacked the hardwood like bullwhips, turning more heads as she parted the sea of people like a sexy Moses.

Without touching the stereo, she changed the song and climbed onto the living room coffee table. It was the largest room with the most people in it and was adjacent to the kitchen, stairwell, and den, so guests in those areas would have a view. The new song began to pulse like a massive heartbeat, the electronica making the walls throb. The drum machine kicked in as the synthesizers raged and Hazel began to sway her hips, her body flowing as if lost to tornadic winds. She ran her hands up and down her, letting them slide over her breasts and between her legs. The crowd drew closer, the boys pushing past one another to get a front-row view. She took the zipper at the front of her top and slid it down just enough to reveal her ample cleavage. Her hands went into her hair and she licked her lips. She was a queen of erotica, and she used her decades' worth of practice to pull the youths toward her, feasting on their young desire like a lioness with a hot, wet kill.

The power began to fill her up like a great lover.

The mountain was watching.

Kayla hushed him as they crept down the hall. She had found Robbie alive and was able to free him. He was pale and looked malnourished, but he was going to be all right, provided they could get out of this alive.

But if she left now, more lives would be lost, more souls captured. Then there would be no end to the bitch's power.

"Take Horace and leave," she said.

Robbie shook his head. "No way. I'm not leaving you. And I'm not leaving my brother."

She didn't have the heart to tell him Joe might be beyond saving.

The crowd was thicker in the living room now. The music was loud, lights swirling in a psychedelic whirlwind. Everyone was pushing toward the center of the room, cheering.

"What's going on?" Robbie asked.

They inched through, and as they got closer to the center Kayla saw.

Hazel was writhing to the infectious music, her body nude from the waist up, leaving her in a thong, tights, and boots. Her flesh glistened and pink light emanated from her as if she was a comet raking the night sky. Her hair lashed the air like lariats, eyes blazing in the shadow of her face, two emeralds on fire. The music grew vicious, gaining speed and volume, and Hazel kept time with it, not missing a single throb or scream.

The crowd seemed to howl, a single creature.

Kayla trembled. "Oh my god . . ."

She was seducing them all at once. What Kayla had thought

would take time and spellbind far less people was now an all-encompassing incantation. The witch was more than an exotic dancer up there; she was a mad demon of sex, a succubus prepping her prey. How could Kayla compete with that? While the thought of trying filled her with self-doubt, she knew she had to make an effort. She'd had everyone's attention while making her entrance. Maybe she could get some of it back.

When she turned to Robbie, he too was looking up at Hazel with adoring eyes, despite all she'd done to him. She grabbed him by his collar, shook him back to his senses, and did the first thing that came to mind.

She kissed him.

It was a passionate kiss, filled with warmth and tenderness and longing. She ran her fingers through his hair and over his chest, drawing her leg up to his hip. She pressed against him, feeling her inner warmth returning. When they unlocked lips she turned to the next guy, one she didn't even know, and gave him the same treatment. The warmth grew heavier. She went into the crowd, running her palm under guys' chins, strutting her stuff, winking, blowing kisses, patting butts. Heads began to turn away from Hazel as Kayla kissed boy after boy, and when a girl came up to her for one, Kayla didn't hesitate. She clutched the girl in her arms and kissed her with a rolling tongue, making the crowd go wild. Some of them still watched Hazel while others seemed torn between the two of them, but more people were starting to gather around Kayla, wanting their turn.

She hadn't planned on this being a standoff of the sluts, but she had to do something to take attention off the sorceress. She went to the stereo and switched it off. She climbed on top of it and sat with her legs crossed. The crowd all turned to her now, including Hazel, whose face had turned a snarling red.

"I am a virgin," she announced to the crowd. "But that changes tonight. I just want to know who's man enough to make me into a woman."

The crowd roared.

Now she had them all, boys and girls alike. She saw Joe in the middle of the mob, looking awestruck. Kayla felt the warmth become full-fledged heat. The power was a furnace inside her now, erupting in a smoldering volcano of pure magic. When she looked down at her hands there was a pink glow coming off them. She was radiating. Energy rushed into her so suddenly it began to push out of her pores. She stood on top of the stereo cabinet, letting the light mist over the crowd, ensnaring them in her net.

Hazel went into a rage.

A bat-shriek left her throat and the windows behind her cracked. Now she was going for any kind of attention she could get. Some people turned back to her, but not many. The pink light coming from Kayla was washing over them. It had a gentle caress and gave them a sense of euphoria that grew stronger the more they submitted to it. She could feel their bliss intensifying. She was on the brink of divinity. Her body tingled, her mind adrift in the pale orb of her ecstasy.

A blast of violet flame burst from around the coffee table where Hazel stood and those around her stepped back, gasping. Their clothes were singed. Some had smoking hair. Hazel's own hair spun in the updraft and transformed into an orgy of black snakes. In response to her rage, shadow hands rose from the carpet and began clutching at the partygoers' ankles. People began to scream. Some fell and others trampled them in an effort to escape the madness. Limbs thrashed. Panic reigned.

Kayla looked to the ceiling, thinking it was on fire from the blast, but it was not a river of smoke she was seeing. It was dozens of hands and hollow faces, all of them rushing without direction. Their mouths were open in silent screams and their eyes were wide and empty, skull-like. They slithered down the walls, clutching at the teens, thirsty for their life force. A quivering, windy sound filled the house as the windows imploded, spraying glass and vacuuming in blowing leaves to create a hellish mélange. The night filled with cries of horror.

Despite the chaotic fear, Kayla's pink light kept her followers at her side, whereas Hazel, in her rage, was pushing people away. They weren't watching her because they wanted her. They wanted to get as far away from her as possible. Her own temper had sabotaged her.

She outstretched her arms, pointing her nails at Kayla like rifles. Beams of light shot out of her fingertips like bolts of lightning, carrying on them spiders, scorpions, and cockroaches. The insects flew and scattered in a brown fog. But Kayla's pink warmth protected her. The giant insects fell onto the panicking crowd, but Kayla's fan base stayed with her, shielded by her light. The others ran out of the house, which is just what Kayla wanted them to do. If she could get most of them to flee to safety, but retain enough of them to keep the power of the mountain filling her—siphoning it from Hazel—she could weaken the black witch and possibly destroy her for good.

But the sea of shadow hands was dragging many teens through the floor. They cried out as they were drawn into that dark abyss, arms reaching for help that wasn't there. Hazel cackled at their anguish, and the dozens of jack-o-lanterns in the house popped their tops as jets of flame burst from within them like landmines. From out of their mouths maggots and eels spilt forth and then slithered up the throbbing, bleeding walls.

"Joseph!" Hazel screamed. "Come to me! *Come to your goddess!*"

Joe spun around. He removed his mask and looked at Kayla. The whites of his eyes were gone, replaced by a sinister glow that filled them entirely. He gave her one last look, then started walking toward Hazel.

"No!" Kayla cried out.

But Joe didn't turn back. He went to his master, offering himself. He unzipped the front of his costume, retrieving a butcher knife that glistened in the strange light.

Danny screamed as Joe began hacking and slashing everyone around him. Blood burst, small pieces of flesh jetting in gory tufts—pieces of ear, fingertips, strips of cheek and arm. Joe hissed as he diced the partygoers, their spurts of blood sprinkling his pale face.

Danny had been hypnotized by Kayla's beauty and warmth. Now he could not take his eyes off his friend. Or what *used to be* his friend.

Tears burned in the corners of Danny's eyes as he watched Joe stab a girl in the throat while the shadows held her legs. He sent the knife into a guy's stomach, and when he withdrew the blade he widened the hole, sending a tendril of yellowish intestine tumbling out. It splattered on the floor and shadow hands ran their fingers through them, twirling the steaming guts like ribbons. The air filled with the stench of death—vomit, blood, piss, feces, and gore. As Joe hacked at another flailing young man, Danny heard a piercing cry and saw Robbie. The sight of his brother's violence brought tears that rolled down his pale cheeks. Danny looked to Joe again, seeing the slick blade rise, recalling how he'd plunged the same knife into Mrs. Brownstone while Danny had held her.

No more.

He charged into the crowd the same way he always did on the field. He shouldered away everyone who stood between himself and Joe, dodging the shadow claws that reached for his heels, and just as Joe was about to stab someone under their ribs, Danny tackled him. They fell to the ground and the knife spun from Joe's hand in a splash of red. When Danny saw his eyes, horror invaded his soul. Above them, Hazel's fury lifted her off the table she'd been dancing upon. She hovered in the air, her mouth unhinging, releasing a tunnel of psychedelic light. But Kayla was challenging the witch, and their forces were colliding in the air between them, clattering like swords on shields.

Joe looked up at Danny. His eyes were mirrors. In them, Danny could see himself starting to rot. His flesh fell away in greenish clumps, revealing gleaming bone beneath. A vile trash smell filled his nostrils, making him gag even as his nose fell from his face in a splatter of black decay. He looked away, screaming, and began to strangle his best friend.

Kayla laughed.

Hazel was in a tizzy. Her power was slipping away from her. Meanwhile, the power behind the mountain was flooding Kayla, telling her she was the more deserving sorceress.

Possessing this magic didn't just relieve Kayla; it excited her. She was smug, flaunting it before Hazel's eyes. All around her, her minions swayed under her glistening pink shroud, and when others noticed the safety she was providing they joined in adoring her. Pure force coursed through, a fire-hose blast. It was power like she had never dreamed. She felt like a celebrity, only better. She held not just their attention; she held their very being, their precious *souls*. They were hers entirely, and the more of them that fawned over her, the more that followed, dominoes tumbling into her welcoming abyss.

She was becoming more than a white witch. She was becoming a *goddess*.

Hazel was losing. The light that came out of her was growing fainter and the force behind it, which Kayla had struggled to push away, was now exhausted. Kayla swatted through it like so much cigarette smoke. Hazel frothed with fury, but now her eyes held a hint of panic she could not hide.

On the floor, Danny pounded Joe's head against the hardwood. Thick blood had begun to pool, and the shadow hands in the floor were grabbing at Joe, pulling on his cloak. He started to move *through* the wood and into the netherworld beyond. Kayla watched him sink, feeling little emotion. She knew he'd been gone long before the souls took him. Hazel didn't even notice her slave dying below her. She was focused only on her opponent.

As Hazel floated across the room, Kayla could feel her arctic aura cast a pall over her pink waves. It sent pinpoints of frost through the shield that surrounded her followers and they looked up at Hazel with wonder as she hovered, her near-nude body swarming with snakes, rats, and insects. Maggots spilled from her mouth and coiled out of her nose. Worms chewed through her withering skin as they emerged from her body.

"Love me!" she demanded of the crowd.

Kayla stretched her arms forward, guided to do so by a strange intuition. Her hair swirled and her body flushed as white light came from her palms. The light blinded Hazel, and her flesh began to sizzle and smoke. Patches of her skin burned away and she flew toward Kayla, knocking her backward. They fell to the floor, thrashing like a dogfight. Hazel straddled her. She held up her hand, her fingertips now household razorblades.

"You remember these, don't you?" Hazel asked. "The little friends you turn to when you cry like a fucking baby?"

The blades raked her exposed flesh. As they sliced into her, she flashed back on all the times she'd cut herself. The crippling self-doubt returned as all her feelings of abandonment, hopelessness, and despair came stinging back through her heart. She thought of her absent father, of her awkwardness and her fear, and as the terror tried to swallow her, the pink glow receded.

"Slice and dice, little cherry," Hazel said. "Gonna bleed again for daddy?"

Kayla whimpered, fighting the feelings Hazel had tapped into. The black witch was using them to her advantage, but Kayla knew she could get the power back if she tried. She'd overcome her nervousness around boys. Her confidence in everything she did had improved. She wasn't a scared little girl anymore. She was becoming a woman. More than that, she was becoming a sorceress . . . and she *fucking liked* it.

Hazel came down with her razor claws and Kayla grabbed her wrist. There was a struggle, but as the white heat came back she was able to flip Hazel off of her. Kayla rose, her anger forming a solid ball of fire inside her. The light of her body burned, her limbs lighter, hair blowing in the air though there was no breeze.

She began to levitate.

CHAPTER THIRTY-SIX

ROBBIE RAN TOWARD DANNY, AFRAID he was going to murder his brother. Despite how Joe had gone into a killing spree, Robbie couldn't stand to see him snuffed out. When he reached Danny he slammed into him with all he had, and to his surprise he managed to push the big football player off Joe. They tumbled to the floor. Joe was still breathing, half submerged in the floor, the shadow hands pawing but unable to pull him all the way through. He looked unconscious.

Danny got on his knees.

"We have to get out of here," he said. "Now."

A flash of light filled the room, making everyone shield their eyes. When the light receded to a warm glow, they saw Kayla hovering, a beautiful ascending angel. Hazel was beneath her, screaming and cowering. Robbie felt a prickle of hope.

"Come on," Danny said. He held out his hand. "Now's our chance!"

Robbie let him help him up but then hesitated to move. He and Horace were watching the bizarre battle of the two sorceresses. Danny couldn't help staring either, but he still tugged at Robbie's arm.

"We're gonna *die* if we don't *go!*"

Horace barked, then ran from them and parked himself right beneath Kayla, watching her. He remained in a sit, looking up.

What's he doing? Robbie thought.

He stepped forward but retreated when Hazel thundered across the floor, pieces dropping from her body in black sludge.

She scowled at Horace. "Traitor!"

Kayla's eyes were projecting beams like a pair of truck flood-lights in dark woods. She lifted her arms and the shadow hands rose from the floors. The walls throbbed. The souls of the manor prayed, worshipping her.

Hazel bent over, clutching at her exposed ribs and the blackish sinew beneath. She was trying to scream but only gasps came out. Her hair went from snakes back to normal hair, withered and gray, and what little glow surrounded her ebbed away completely now, fading into dust and dreams. She was shutting down and was unable to control the process.

Kayla was winning.

Robbie and Danny stood side-by-side, watching the phantasma-goria that swirled before them, a kaleidoscopic dimension unfurling in a blinding gate. The crowd in the room stared on, still in love with Kayla, and Robbie suddenly understood it was their adoration fueling her, so he allowed himself to get lost in her beauty, hoping it would give her more of what she needed. Hazel was on her knees, her hands at her temples as if trying to block a sound only she could hear. Kayla was now so rich with light she could hardly be seen, and Robbie felt drawn to the light like a moth, and he and Danny stepped closer until they were beside Horace.

Horace watched his new master with a profound sense of obedi-ence. He would do anything she wished. He was now *her* familiar and was glad to be freed of the old master. The new master liked the boy, and Horace liked that. And he felt safer now that she was in control. This gave him a sense of direction again, one that was positively reinforced rather than beaten into him by intimidation and punishment. He would submit to his new master, for he knew she would never even ask him to. It was a relationship that was not symbiotic the way the previous one had been. It was a bond that would stick and work, keeping them both happy.

He sat there watching her, hoping she would ask him to rip out the throat of his old master.

Kayla could feel the pull. Something was pointing her toward the right path like an internal compass. She had Hazel on the ground and the black witch was very weak, but it wasn't enough to banish her forever. There was another step she had to take, but she wasn't sure what it was.

Something was guiding her. She could feel the force coming off Black Rock Mountain. She had elevated senses. She could see beneath the walls where the lost souls writhed and hear the frantic conversations of the people who'd gathered outside, watching the light show through the shattered windows. She could taste the blood in the air and smell the fear-sweat. Moving things with her mind, she sent framed pictures off the walls to smash onto Hazel's head and back. And Kayla could feel things in a way she'd never imagined, just as she felt she had to drag Hazel out of this room. She had to take her down—possibly into the floor? She wasn't sure. She wasn't even certain she could pass through to the other side, but felt she could. The power within her seemed limitless, nothing she couldn't do, no soul she couldn't conquer. They could love her, or they could fear her, but they would be hers, and Kayla wanted them now.

Going with her newfound precognition, she lassoed Hazel with ropes of lightning and the witch flailed as her wrists and ankles were caught in the snares. Below Hazel the shadows rose to grab hold of her. At first Kayla thought they were trying to pull her into their underworld, but instead they pushed her toward the hall, passing her off to one another. Kayla floated along and above, keeping Hazel in her electric pinions as they entered the kitchen and wound around the counter. The crowd of admirers followed close behind, and some of the teenagers outside came back in, lured by the spectacular commotion, by Kayla's decadence.

Horace led the way, barking excitedly as the black hands followed him, carrying Hazel along as she writhed and bucked. The dog reached the door to the cellar. He jumped on it, scratching, and she felt a sudden bond with Horace beyond what could be had between a normal animal and human being.

She could hear his thoughts.

Take her down here.

Kayla remembered the haggard old man's voice she'd heard down in the cellar and tried to think of what it had said. It was something about his daughter being a whore and that he wanted her—

His daughter?

Hazel.

Of course.

The revelation hit her like a lucid dream. She could see the manse on that blood-soaked night and watched the violent images as they flickered through her mind. The angry father catching the young lovers—the blood and the bruises and the murder. Mr. Snowden was buried down there, killed by his own wife and daughter. His spirit was trapped down there. And all these years he'd festered over thoughts of vengeance. Hazel seemed rather fearless, but there was one thing Kayla felt certain would paralyze the witch.

Her horrible father.

No child ever truly gets over an overbearing, abusive parent—even after they're dead. The fear remains, even if it is hidden from the surface. It lies in wait, ready to strike when you least expect it, a stealthy, emotional predator. That was why Horace and the shadows were taking Hazel toward the cellar, Kayla realized. It was the place she would become her absolute weakest, the place where she could be pushed through to the other side, never to return again.

Horace stepped back and Kayla sent a gust that blew the cellar door right off of its hinges. It fell to the side and drifted away like a leaf in an updraft, smashing into the ceiling, sticking there. Red light blasted up from the cellar like the licking flames of hell and a piercing voice rose from the deep.

Bring her to me! Bring me my disobedient whore of a daughter!

Hazel's eyes went wide. Kayla flew past and started down the shaft, pulling her behind her. The earthen walls of the cellar rumbled and the shadowy souls pushed out to their waists, watching and cheering her on. They reminded Kayla of people who gathered around prisons, waiting for the lights to flicker as a serial killer was toasted in the electric chair. She knew that if the shadow souls could, they would be throwing rotten fruit at Hazel, or eggs or excrement. All the love they'd felt for her had now shifted over to the more powerful witch, and with Hazel's spell broken they wanted vengeance for being trapped inside the manor, enslaved for all these years.

Just like Mr. Snowden, who was roaring like a grizzly bear.

Jezebel!

Hazel's scream was deafening, and Kayla delighted in her foe's terror as she pinned her to the floor. Black blood pooled around her body, swallowing her. She was in thrall, blood splashing over her bare chest and the insides of her legs. It soaked her hair and bubbled at her lips and nostrils, the cheers of the lost souls sounding like a hundred trains barreling over a cliff. It was a great, steam whistle sound, filled with a noise like clanging chains in a boiler room. Kayla's pink light engulfed the cellar, making it pulse and shimmer brilliantly.

A man's head appeared in the floor where Hazel lay and pushed upward, revealing a black, tar body. The man grimaced as he towered over her, the white block of his preacher's collar stained with blood, his whole body slick with it. He had claw marks on his face and his punctured eyes seeped gore, the retinas and connective tissue shredded. From between his gritted teeth a dark smoke poured, cloaking Hazel who lay before him, shaking.

Mr. Snowden came into full form, lifted his daughter into his arms, and clutched her to his soaked chest. Blood poured off her saturated body like a thousand red tears, and she went limp with fear, a child broken. Her body began to shrink, and Kayla watched her metamorphosis back to her teenage self—smaller, frailer, more vulnerable. Her viciousness and confidence erased. She was hopelessly terrified, a weak little girl being taken into the darkness where she belonged.

Her father dragged her down, down, down, into the abyss below, and the shadow people pulled at her legs, helping her along. Kayla wanted to hear one last scream from the former sorceress, but the only sounds she made were pathetic whimpers.

But the room grew louder.

It sounded as if the world was caving in on itself right there in the cellar. Sounds like hurricane winds and shattering earthquakes, like tsunamis and nuclear detonations. They shook the earth beneath her, supernovas breaking across space. Every last drop of Hazel's power left her and coursed through Kayla's veins, making them stand out beneath her skin in a vascular display, pulsing and purple, her flesh flushing, tears welling in her eyes. Her veins had their own special glow, heavy blue like a winter sky. Her mouth was like lava, her insides a churning, boiling pot of oil.

She released her lightning ropes and drew the electricity back into her, watching as father and daughter sank beneath the pool of blood where dozens of angry fists awaited them, deep down in the blackness of the phantom world beyond.

CHAPTER THIRTY-SEVEN

THE BOYS RAN TO DANNY'S car.

The moon was bright red. It hovered in the sky like a massive heart. The wind ripped leaves from the trees and they clattered against the house as they swarmed around it in a raging vortex. All the guests were fleeing now. Cars fought on the driveway, grazing each other in sparks, racing to get to the street, to get away from the terrible manse.

Just before leaving, Robbie tried once more to rouse his brother, even though he was afraid of him. Joe stirred, his eyes still glowing, reflecting. A wicked smile twisted his face. He laughed sourly. Robbie stepped away as a dozen hands and arms swam through the floor and snaked around his brother's body. Joe did not resist. He put himself in a crucified pose, cackling with mad laughter, and the long shadows covered him with their wet blackness, welcoming him into their nightmare realm.

His brother was gone, lost to the world of shadows. And clearly that was where he chose to be. He was a killer, a madman. There was nothing Robbie could do about it, no matter how brutally it broke his heart.

He tried to get Horace to come with him, but the dog refused to leave. Horace watched the cellar intently, as if waiting for a command. It saddened Robbie to leave him behind, but something told him the dog truly belonged here, that he was a part this magic and was bound to it. Horace was more than a dog. He understood that now. Horace was a spiritual creature, an entity that could not be taken from its temple of sorcery and ghosts. As much as Robbie loved him, he could not take him away from this haunted manor.

The house was rumbling. Lights of unknown color had filled it up. Ice was forming in the rafters and Robbie saw his own breath as they escaped. The witches were in the cellar, and all hell was literally breaking loose.

Kayla had changed.

She wasn't just a sweet young girl anymore. She was powerful. More than that, she seemed to be thriving on her witchery. She had a look to her that he could only think of as power mad.

He wondered if she would leave, or if she was just like Horace now.

CHAPTER THIRTY-EIGHT

GLADYS SHOT UP IN BED.

In an instant she knew her daughter was forever lost, adrift in the world behind the walls of Snowden Manor. She could feel all the necromancy ripped away from her family like a toy from a brat's hands, which was exactly how she thought of the way her daughter had used the forces of the ancient druids. Tonight was the night to end all nights, but Hazel failed in her great sacrifice. Someone else had been victorious, taking all the power a witch would need to become the most magnificent sorceress this dimension had ever known. This great witch would take the magic of the lost worlds and the energy of the shadows and bring them into the living world. They would be a master of incantations and alchemy, unstoppable and omnipresent, a capricious god to the people of a new earth.

And it wouldn't be her daughter.

Gladys didn't know if she was heartbroken or relieved. She'd wanted the magic to stay within her bloodline but had always known her daughter was a hellion not to be trusted with it. The girl had never matured. She was a rebellious, unpredictable teenager in her heart. Always would be. This had made her a very dangerous witch indeed. Now there was another witch that had been blessed by Black Rock Mountain, beneath the aligned stars of late October, the hour of the darkest magic.

She lay down, waiting for her weary bones to settle. A numbing cold came over her, and she thought she could hear a faint, wolf-like cry in the corner of the room.

Gladys shuddered.

The smell of her dead husband's cologne hit her, and when she looked up at the ceiling she thought she saw a young face retreat into the plaster, the face of an innocent little girl, a face she had not seen in decades. She closed her eyes and the image of the manor flashed across her mind. It was not burning, but bursting with supernatural light. And all at once she felt the presence of the new witch and shook with horror as she realized she too was a rebellious, unpredictable teenage girl.

And she was calling to Gladys. The voice echoed through her mind.

The manor is mine now, the witch said.

Before Gladys could reply or even think, she felt her bones begin to twist. The pain of all her joints crackling made her convulse. A desperate cry escaped her throat. But she could not speak. The new witch did all the talking.

It's time for you to join your family, Mrs. Snowden. The one you destroyed and helped to destroy others.

Gladys croaked, words failing her.

Welcome to the abyss.

It wasn't possible. They had never been able to fully leave the house. Hazel had been able to throw apparitions at her mother from great distances and use her magic to get her way, even when her mother was out of town, but she was never able to truly appear the way she did now, standing at the foot of the bed with Arthur, both of them drenched in blood that looked purple in the moonlight.

They smiled at her with menace.

The new witch was making it possible, sending them to take her.

Gladys gasped in an attempt to scream and heard the sorceress laughing as her bones crumbled like dust within her, her muscle and flesh deflating. Her skull collapsed and turned to powder, and her face sagged in that hollow, eyes bulging out, tongue dangling from a toothless mouth. The hotel room filled with pink light, and as her family watched on her soul was ripped from her rotting flesh and pulled into the other world, snagged by the shadows that belonged, like her, in the abyss.

CHAPTER THIRTY-NINE

THE POLICE HAD COME AND gone again, but there was nothing for them to find. She had restored the manor, making the glass reconnect and fill the windows, reforming all that was broken as if she were rewinding time itself. The bodies were gone and the spilt blood was erased. Lieutenant Buchinsky had finally started to believe, thanks to the depositions of over fifty of her schoolmates, but there was nothing he could find within the walls of the manor, even though the walls themselves were alive with her devoted shadow minions.

Kayla whispered to them now.

Soon.

Beside her in the black abyss, Horace was panting with excitement, knowing what was coming. His breath misted in the emptiness and Kayla floated, recharging. The power was all hers now, and she felt no longing for the life she was leaving behind. There was no anxiety here, no self-doubt, no need denied. There were no distant, absentee parents. She felt no fear or stress—certainly no shame. The virginity she had once been so embarrassed by was now the hope chest of her admirers' love, and she was overwhelmed by her own incredible abilities.

She loved this new power.

She loved being a witch.

Now she could have all the boys she wanted. All the attention the men in her life had neglected to give her would be hers to savor; and they would just keep coming, one after another, adding to the energy of the souls she would keep within these walls, trapped forever and ever.

Refreshed, she moved out of the wall with Horace by her side. In the living room, Joe's spirit awaited her, her humble servant.

He smiled up at her. *How may I serve you, my goddess?*

Rest tonight, my pet, she told him. *Soon there will be much to do.*

He retreated into the wall in a smoking, black blur, and Kayla floated through the house and out into the yard. Horace followed, nubby tail wagging.

A new night was falling with a second crimson moon, and its pink light illuminated the backyard as she stepped out into the throat of the dark, listening to the scurrying in the woods and the tumbling leaves of early November. The bare branches swayed up and down, as if bowing to her, and the earth rolled and undulated beneath her feet, loving, worshipping.

Then she was off the ground.

Levitating, she spread her arms wide, taking in all the moon had to offer, for the power of the mountain was just the beginning.

Thanks to:

C.V. Hunt and Andersen Prunty for the hard work they put into publishing this book. Tangie Silvia, Tom Mumme, Josh Doherty and Gregg Kirby for their continued support and highly valued friendship. Fellow authors John Wayne Comunale, Brian Keene, Ryan Harding, Bryan Smith, Christine Morgan, Max Booth III and Chad Stroup for inspiring, supporting, collaborating and celebrating with me. Marc Ciccarone and Joe Spagnola for publishing and promoting me on a constant basis, and for convincing me to make a disgusting coloring book. Most of all, thanks to my readers, who make it all worthwhile.

Additional thanks to the following writers, filmmakers, actors and musicians whose work helped inspire this novel: Graham Masterton, John Carpenter, Richard Matheson, Dario Argento, Carpenter Brut, Dance with the Dead and Linda Blair.

Kristopher Triana is the author of *Full Brutal, Shepherd of the Black Sheep, Body Art, The Ruin Season, Toxic Love* and more.

His fiction has appeared in countless magazines and anthologies and has been translated into multiple languages, drawing praise from *Publisher's Weekly, Cemetery Dance, Rue Morgue Magazine, Scream Magazine, The Ginger Nuts of Horror* and others.

He lives in Connecticut.

Stalk him on Facebook, Instagram, Twitter and at: kristophertriana.com

Other Grindhouse Press Titles